Born in Internment

For Lyn & Jim

Enjoy the read

Anna Fiorina

Born in Internment

Anna Fiorina Hess

GRAPE and THISTLE PRESS

Grape and Thistle Press
10838 Skyview Drive
Kelseyville, CA 95451
(707) 289-4113
annafiorinahess.net

Born in Internment is a distillation of family lore and historical occurrences. Family names are accurate; all other names, places, and incidents may be fictionalized.

Cover by Sandra Ragan & Coco Franklin
Editor/Text Designer/Typesetter: Jean Laidig
Project Advisor: Vicki Werkley
Author Photograph: Christophe Genty
All interior photos are family-owned.

Printed in the United States of America

ISBN 978-0-9965516-6-3

Publisher's Cataloging-in-Publication
(Provided by Quality Books, Inc.)

Hess, Anna Fiorina.
    Born in internment / Anna Fiorina Hess.
    pages cm
    ISBN 978-0-9965516-6-3

    1. Hess, Anna Fiorina--Family--Fiction. 2. Italians --Great Britain--Evacuation and relocation, 1940-1945--Fiction. 3. World War, 1939-1945--Fiction. 4. Historical fiction. 5. Biographical fiction. 6. War stories. I. Title.

PS3608.E823B67 2015   813'.6
                          QBI15-600175

For my grandchildren:
Meg and Jack Franklin
and
Logan and Makenzie Hess

Preface

When I decided to write our family story—realizing that the world knew very little about the internment of Italians in Great Britain during World War II—I drew from the archives of my mind.

Historically: When dictator Benito Mussolini allied with Hitler in 1940, Prime Minister Churchill saw no alternative but to treat all Italians as enemy aliens. "Collar the lot," he said, and condemned thousands of resident Italians to incarceration or internment camps all over Great Britain.

Although loyal to Britain, the Bertellottis in Scotland suffered the frustration and hardships of internment, while those in Italy had to evacuate their home and abandon their businesses, hide in the hills, and watch their friends die.

Personally: I recalled loud, drunken Italian dinners; my parents' chats long into the *driech*, dark Scottish nights; my own childhood games, based on loss and fear, within the confining walls; and a trip to Italy in 1949, when I heard from Aunt Bruna about the man with his beard on fire, and from Uncle Tommy about his adventures up and down the western coast of Italy among anti-fascist resistance fighters and, later, the Buffalo Soldiers.

All the members of the Bertellotti family—each in his or her own way, in Scotland and in Italy—made extraordinary decisions during a time of war, a time of evacuation, and a time of senseless slaughter. *Born in Internment*, in showing how a family can survive grievous ordeals without losing their humanity, is a book about bravery and tenacity, forgiveness and hope, and—most of all—love.

Acknowledgments

Thank you to:

🌿 Ron Hess, for your patience, your help, and your abiding love.

🌿 The Edgy Writers, a superb critique group: Lee Meehan, Ann Cash, and Karen Baker. Thanks for the camaraderie and the caring.

🌿 Peggy Aaron, Laureen Lloyd, and Donna Kadel, for your encouragement along the way.

🌿 Linda Runyon and Paul Chutkow, for your creativity and mentorship.

As for my extraordinary book production team—
Many thanks to:

🌿 My editor and book designer Jean Laidig, for your incredible expertise and attention to detail.

🌿 My cover crew:

  ✷ my daughter Culzean "Coco" Franklin, for your original flags-and-flames concept.

  ✷ my project advisor Vicki Werkley, for an abundance of productive contributions.

  ✷ my graphic designer Sandra Ragan, for pulling it all together with your own ideas and insights.

And, always, there's Rabbie Burns
—the Bard of Scotland—
whose poems and songs sustain me.

Prologue

Andy Bertellotti, inhaling the wet-dog stink of his damp wool coat, wrapped his arms around his body to keep warm. But when the freight train shuddered out of the munitions factory, he had to grab onto some crates to steady himself. As the train picked up speed, he sat in the pitch black, craving a smoke, and heard the clacking rails accuse, "*Enemy alien, enemy alien, enemy alien.*"

The fifty-minute journey to Kilmarnock seemed to take hours—and after that he'd face the long bus ride to the hospital. Could he make it in time? He remembered his promise to his wife Kathy not to do anything daft. Again he pictured her wee self behind that huge belly. The pain in her eyes. The blood all over the sheets. Would their baby be all right?

"Dear God," he whispered, "please keep them both safe . . . please."

When—at long last—the brakes squealed, he knew the tunnel must be near. Moving to the door of the boxcar, he prepared himself to jump.

Andy

I

The Promise

O my Luve's like a red, red rose

Robert Burns, "A Red, Red Rose"

1936

"Will ye marry me, Kathy?" Andy reached across the linen tablecloth to hold both of her small hands in his, not at all sure that she would say yes. Breathing in her sweet perfume, he added, "Ye love me, don't ye?"

"Ye know I do," she answered. "More than is good for me." She leaned over and gently, ever so gently kissed his lips. "I like that ye take chances, and I don't like that ye take chances. I'm not sure I want to marry an Italian gambling man—" Her brow furrowed. "—and ye're asking me to spend the rest of my life here in this wee café in Kilmarnock."

"I'm praying ye will. Kathy, this corner fish and chip shop is all I have to offer ye. I'm not a rich man, as ye know, but I make a fair living. And . . . and I do quite well at the gambling." A wry smile played over his lips.

She glanced around the small wallpapered room that had once been a council flat before Andy remodeled it for his business. A smile played on her lips. "Some days ye do well at the horses, some days are a dead loss. Ye are a rogue, mister, but I do like it here in yer Ideal Café, and yer a fine cook." She put

the back of his hand to her cheek. "Ye know I love ye, but I am a tailor, not a shop keeper, and then, there's the other differences between us."

"What other differences?"

"For a start, ye are a Roman Catholic and I'm a Presbyterian."

"And?"

"Yer Italian, in case ye haven't noticed."

"Oh, Kathy, it's 1936; in Scotland it doesn't matter about nationality and religion."

"It matters to my very Presbyterian mother."

"Since when do we listen to our mothers? Mine hates all Scots lassies. She told me I would be better off with an Italian prostitute than a Scotswoman."

They laughed then, a long happy laugh that made their differences melt away. Kathy stood up and came around the table to sit on his knee. He moved slightly to hold her tight. "I can change my ways, tone down the gambling."

"I like that ye don't use too much Brylcreem." Kathy stroked his hair, breathing in his manhood, knowing full well that she was going to say yes. "If we marry, will I work here in the café?"

"Do ye want to?"

"I'm not sure, but it smells good and I like the flat behind the shop; it could be made into a nice wee home."

"I make the best chips in Kilmarnock." He pulled her head down and kissed her full on the lips. "Kathy, I love ye more than the world."

"Would we raise our children Catholic?"

"Well, I am a bit of a heathen and ye are a half-boiled Presbyterian. We can raise our children as Protestants."

"Ye'd do that for me?"

"Of course."

He eased a box out of his trouser pocket. "Would this complete the bet?"

"Oh, my God, Andy. It's beautiful. How did ye afford it?"

He smiled. "I won the daily double."

"I hope that's a joke."

"It is. I saved for it. Kathy, my darling, I love ye. I'm asking ye to be my wife. We are strong together. Please, please, marry me."

She looked at the ring sitting snugly in the black box on the white cloth. "Three diamonds, it is so perfect." She took his head in both hands, gazed into his eyes. "Oh, my gambling man, I have had more fun with you than I ever had before, yer never boring. I suppose I can take ye on. Help ye in yer shop. My mother will kill me, but God help me. Yes, I will marry ye, ye daft Italian."

He held on to her as if she would break if he let her go. "I love ye, lass, I love ye."

2

Happiness

I'm truly sorry man's dominion
Has broken nature's social union

Robert Burns, "To a Mouse"

Andy's family immigrated to Scotland in the early twenties, along with thousands of Italians who could find no work after World War I. His father, Arturo, joined many others who opened up the fish restaurants that became a common sight on every Scottish corner. Arturo and his wife Fiorina prospered in the fish and chip business and eventually owned not one but two shops.

The first was in Ayr, where their sons Guido, Armando, and Irmo attended school. There the children acquired broad Scots brogues and soon were nicknamed Rudy, Andy, and Tommy—names the Scots children could pronounce. Mamma Fiorina never used those Scots names.

In her forties, Mamma gave birth to a baby girl she named Bruna. This child was the boys' precious little sister. Bruna's cradle stood behind the counter all evening while the family moved around taking care of customers. The boys worked in the business every evening and Bruna, the toddler, amused the customers with her antics.

The family moved after the youths were out of high school,

to a small town named Hurlford. There, Bruna began kindergarten while the teenage boys became young men. Rudy and Andy chased girls, backed horses, and drank whisky; Tommy, however, was studious and conservative.

In a very few years, thanks to their hard-working father, all three young men owned their own fish and chip shops in Kilmarnock, an industrious, busy, growing town in Ayrshire. Andy's Ideal Café was a working man's chip shop on Gilmour Street, close to three factories. Rudy created an ice cream factory, located on Bank Street near the Kilmarnock Cross, and named his upper class café The Ritz. Tommy owned an ice cream and sweet shop, The Queen's Café, on Portland Street next to the bus station.

~   ~   ~

Surrounded by stacks of newly washed dishes on the counter in her tiny kitchen, Fiorina Bertellotti busily rolled ravioli dough, filling the squares with good-smelling sausage. Her face shone red with sweat. She looked up at her son and shook her rolling pin. "No, Armando. No, no, no. I-a no like Scottish girls." She added a lot more in Italian!

"Mamma!" His determined voice rose. "I am marrying Kathy whether ye like it or not. I love her; she is the woman for me."

"It no work!" Fiorina stormed away, flour flying from her talking hands.

On their next outing, Kathy ruefully suggested, "I think we best get married in the Registry Office."

"Perfect," Andy agreed.

Both mothers pouted anyway.

Andy's Mamma said, "The Holy Father will be angry."

"Mamma—" Andy shook his head. "The Pope will never know. Who's going to tell him?"

Kathy's mother Mary said, "The Registry Office! There goes yer white wedding. What on earth does a Presbyterian wear tae marry a Catholic in a Registry Office, of all places? There's nothin' Christian about that."

"Mother," replied Kathy in her sternest voice, "dinna fret. I'll make something special to wear."

Babbo reacted differently. He beamed and clapped Andy on the back. "*Bene, bene, Armando*," he said, and in English he added, "Kathy make-a nice clothes, she a hard worker. She will be a good-a cook for the fish and chips."

When Kathy told Tommy Brice, the fine old man who had married her mother when Kathy was ten, her stepfather lit his pipe and smiled wisely. "Oh, Kathy," he murmured. "Yer almost as old as yer mother was when we got married and she already had three weans. She became the light of my life, as ye will be to Andy."

"Thanks, Pop," said Kathy. "I needed yer blessing."

"Aye," he answered. "Ye will have quite the taming of a gambling Italian, if ye ken what I mean, but life has a way of working things out—if ye want it to."

Kathy shook her head but didn't ask him what he meant; she was glad to have an ally.

~ ~ ~

All in all, it was an intimate wedding ceremony in the courthouse. Rudy, Tommy, and Bruna stood beside Andy. Kathy had her sister and brother, Jean and Eddie, and her young stepsister, Violet. Mary and Fiorina stood aloof and unhappy.

Both Mary and Fiorina had given birth to late-in-life babies. Tall, willowy Violet was eleven and Bruna, a tiny, dark-eyed beauty, was only seven. Both girls wore pale pink party dresses Kathy had sewn for them, to match the bride. She herself wore a lovely dark pink suit and hat, which she had personally designed.

The high-ceilinged courthouse room was cramped and smelled antiseptically of Dettol. There was hardly enough space for the small group. A tall, bewigged judge gathered the group together in a courteous but very pronounced Scottish manner. Andy's face showed his emotions as he smiled down on his petite bride, who looked more scared than happy. He was beaming from ear to ear when he said his "I do"s. Kathy seemed to be in a fog when she repeated, "I do and I will."

"Can a man be this happy?" he whispered to her.

She replied, "I hope forever."

~   ~   ~

They had reserved a dining room at the well-known Ossington Hotel on John Finnie Street. Kathy's extended family was

seated on the striped Georgian chairs in the blue wallpapered parlor. Bill and John, Liz and Mary sat on the right, the Scottish side of the long table; the Italian family sat on the left. The seats in the middle remained empty, saved for the wedding party.

When she entered the fine room, Mamma Fiorina clucked her tongue and made sad motions with her head. Mary Brice stood tall and straight in a purple hat, smiling royally like a Queen Victoria. Kathy and Andy stood by the door while both families came over to greet them. The happy couple smiled and the two nationalities began to mingle. The Italians kissed the newlyweds on both cheeks, and the Scots hugged them. The dining room soon buzzed with broad Kilmarnock syllables and mellow fast-tongued Italian.

A warm smell of mashed potatoes and good Scotch whisky filled the atmosphere. No matter their other differences, Kathy's and Andy's brothers had one thing in common—they liked their whisky. After a few sips of Johnnie Walker, the voices warmed to each other and there was a smile on every face.

Rudy, handsome in his striped suit and spats, made the first toast. "Here's tae a long and happy life for the two o' ye. Peace and happiness." Rudy had been nicknamed after Rudolph Valentino because of his taste in clothes and girls. He stood beaming, glass held high.

Not to be outdone, Kathy's brother Eddie stood shakily and lifted his glass. "I am delighted that Kathy has married Andy, since I'm the one who introduced them. Andy and I have been pals for a long time and [hiccup] we have raised a few fine greyhounds thegether [hiccup]." His body weaved back and forth. "Andy and I, well, we love tae race dugs. So, Kathy, [hiccup] let yer man keep going tae the races wi' me and may a' yer troubles be wee ones." His swollen left hand waved around as he spoke.

"Sit doon, Eddie." Mary, his mother, was, as always, disgusted about the way the whisky was flowing. She turned to Violet and Bruna, who stood expectantly beside her.

"Can we go play, Mum?"

"Aye," decided Mary, "if it's all right with Mrs. Bertellotti." She gave Fiorina the ghost of a smile.

Fiorina nodded her head, and the two girls ran to the door. "No go far," she called after them.

Kathy and Andy glanced at each other as the girls scampered out. "Two children will be enough for me," she murmured.

"Aye, me too." He added, "I'm glad that so far no one has brought up the religious question."

"Shh," she answered.

Lunch became a party, thanks to the eating of good steak and kidney pie and the drinking of smooth Johnnie Walker whisky. Eddie wasn't the only one feeling euphoric.

"Andy, let's leave soon," urged Kathy.

"Sounds like a grand idea."

"Ye can't go yet," objected Tommy Brice. "I can't find Violet. She went off with the wee Italian girl a while back."

"Bruna will have taken her to explore the hotel," said Andy. "Bruna is forever getting lost, but we always find her."

"We won't leave till we find the wee girls, Pop," said Kathy.

The Italian brothers and the Scottish brothers banded together to find the missing duo. Since most of them were tipsy, the men managed to get in each other's way as they searched in different directions. Built in the eighteen hundreds, the red sandstone hotel had all sorts of hiding places in a maze of corridors that reeked of boiled cabbage and pipe tobacco.

The women's voices in the dining room climbed an octave as Mary chastised Fiorina. "My Violet is a quiet wean, she never runs off like this."

Tommy Brice tried to pacify her. "Don't worry, hen, they won't be far."

"Bruna likes to—how you say—explore," said Babbo, speaking over the women's shrills. "She is no a naughty girl."

Mary sniffed, "My Violet never does anything wrong."

It seemed like an hour, but really it wasn't very long, until Eddie ushered the young girls through the door. "Found them in the upstairs ballroom, dancing like two wee fairies."

"We were dancing like ye're supposed to at weddings," cried Bruna, the obvious ringleader. "No one was dancing in here."

"She made me go," said Violet, eyeing her mother's frown.

Amongst the laughter of relieved mothers, Andy and Kathy finally escaped from the room. Trailed by family members, they ran through the lobby and down three steps onto John Finnie Street, where a crowd of young urchins had assembled.

There were white streamers on the hood of Rudy's car, a Scottish wedding symbol to alert neighborhood children to gather for a *scramble*. A flurry of confetti followed the couple into the brisk afternoon air, and after Kathy blew kisses to the family, Andy opened the door to his brother's green Hillman Minx and tossed several handfuls of copper pennies and a few silver half-crowns out onto the street where the delighted youngsters dove for them. The children shrieked and yelled, pushed and shoved, trying for even one big lucky penny.

"Andy, look, Violet and Bruna are scooping up lots of coins from the scramble. We will have a long and happy life."

"We will indeed, Kathy. Indeed we will."

~   ~   ~

It took almost eight hours to reach Blackpool, a vibrant, happy-go-lucky resort town in the south of England. Andy and Kathy stayed a whole week, basking in the sun and enjoying the Palace Hotel. Little did they realize what lay ahead.

3

The Ideal Café

Warm-reekin', rich!

Robert Burns, "Address to a Haggis"

The Ideal Café stood on the corner of Gilmour and St. Andrew's Streets in Kilmarnock. For a wedding present, Babbo had presented Andy with the mahogany counter that had been central in both of his cafés. Andy had always loved the dark-red wood of the long counter and had polished it often. To move the huge piece into his shop took all three brothers, Rudy in charge as always, Andy and Tommy sweating as they pushed and shoved to get it in just the right place.

When Babbo had suggested to Andy that he take the massive counter to the Ideal Café, Andy realized that his father was planning to go back to Tuscany. By 1936, Arturo and Fiorina had been in Scotland for fifteen years—it was time for them to consider retiring to their homeland.

~ ~ ~

Kathy and Andy shopped for furniture for their small flat behind the shop, choosing two soft armchairs to sit in front of the coal fire in the living room and a three-piece suite for the bedroom. Kathy was proud of the tall ash wardrobe where she hung her clothes. The four-foot-ten woman, who always looked as if she had stepped right out of a band-box, owned very few

outfits, but her clothes were made of fine worsted material, and each blouse and skirt was interchangeable with the other. The bedroom had been wallpapered in a beige swirl pattern and still had gas lamps that were slowly being replaced in the council houses with electric lights. Each piece of furniture seemed just right, and there was room for Andy's bachelor bed in an alcove.

"Perfect for when we have children," said Kathy.

~   ~   ~

The Ideal Café opened at four p.m. every day. In the morning Andy prepared the fish and chips. Whiting was caught in the North Sea, crated and delivered in rock salt. Andy had a small room off the main shop where he filleted the fish every day. Next he would start on the tatties. They were stored in a tattie-bin out in the entry. He'd lift a great bag on his shoulder and tote them into the back shop where he had a washing machine to wash the dirt off. Next he chipped hundreds of slices into a huge stainless steel bin. When the bin was full of chips, he filled it the rest of the way with water. Meantime, Kathy would clean house and set whole dried peas to boiling with a slab of bacon on the small but adequate stove. The pot was huge and, when it had boiled all day, was filled with delicious tasty peas.

Andy and Kathy had a busy life; their shop was full of customers from four p.m. until eleven in the evening, and most nights the shop was sold out by ten-thirty. It was only then that the young couple had time to sit down and enjoy a wee dram, sitting comfortably in front of the small coal fire.

"Tell me about Italy, Andy, about your growing years there."

He removed the long white apron that covered his trousers and smiled warmly at her. "Back in 1916 when Babbo was fighting in Austria during the Great War, we boys lived with Mamma's parents in La Spezia, a charming fishing town on the coast of Liguria."

"Were ye born there?"

"*Sì*. Och, listen to me, I'm slipping into Italian."

"That's fine, Andy. Go on. It sounds so, so very European."

"Babbo was a *portantino*, a stretcher bearer, in the Italian Royal Army. The war was fierce. My father took care of men dying in battle while we three boys grew up without him."

"It was nice that yer grandmother took all of ye in," she murmured, moving him away from the sadness of his father's war memories.

"We called her Nonna. She was an angel. She taught me to play the mandolin. I was her favourite."

"Of course you were," Kathy said with a laugh, her dark curls glistening under the lamp. "What was your grandfather's name?"

"We called him Nonno. His name was Vincenzo Peri; he was Mamma's Papa. He was a tall, thin man with a deep voice and an artist's eye. Nonna Luigia was as round as a ball, but oh, her smile and her baking! Every day we had little cakes. We lived close to the Mediterranean Sea, and in the summer months we three brothers ran on the beach to play. Irmo was a toddler, but he came along too. Remember, I was not called Andy then. I was Armando, Rudy was Guido, and Tommy of course was Irmo. Every day in summer was an adventure for the three of us; Mamma only called us in to feed us."

"Was it difficult to leave?"

"Aye, lass, it was. I cried for weeks. I was homesick when we first moved to Scotland. I was only seven, and I felt as if I would die from the missing of Nonna and Nonno."

"Why did yer father take ye away from that lovely-sounding place?"

"He loved us, but when he came back from war, he was disillusioned with Italia. It was the beginning of the Mussolini years and life was brutal. Babbo did not agree with Mussolini's principles and his government. The country was in an uproar. Mamma had pined while Babbo was gone and she now expected him to make a home for us. Babbo was totally undone. All he wanted was to get his job back so he could take care of us, but there were strikes everywhere."

"Why did he choose Ayrshire?"

"Well it wasn't for the weather."

They laughed.

"Babbo did not know that the rain blows sideways here."

"Aye, Andy. My dad says that the wind that blows in from the Firth of Clyde has salt in its very breath."

"Yer dad is right. Anyway, Babbo's brother was already here working in the fish and chip business. His brother taught Babbo all he knew."

"Thank God for that."

"Ye can say that again. We brothers and even wee Bruna grew up in Babbo's shops; it's in our blood."

"Aye, it smells like it!" Another laugh.

"Babbo loves Scottish life, Kathy, but Mamma is unsettled. I think that soon they will go back."

~   ~   ~

Their conversations were many as they became a couple. Andy may have loved Kathy too much, because only nine months later she gave birth to a daughter, who was dark like Andy's mamma. The baby was born at home with a midwife in attendance. Kathy had a difficult time because of her small frame, but both grandmothers were there to help and both softened immediately. They sang lullabies to the child in their own languages and their girls, Bruna and Violet, played with the new baby as if she were a toy. Kathy and Andy named their child Aïda, after the opera they had seen on their honeymoon. Aïda was their princess. Andy said that his life had been blessed by a God he seldom thanked.

There were many large factories within walking distance of the Ideal Café, and each evening around five, Andy's shop was crammed full with workers from the Glenfield and the Saxone factories. Kilmarnock was a bustling industrial town in those days, and rows of work-soiled elbows leaned nightly on the long carved counter.

They'd comment, "How's yer nicht, Andy? It's bitterly ootside."

He'd nod, busy at the fry pan.

"Aye, it smells guid in here. Five pokes o' chips, please."

Their customers had become friends and Bruna, whose wee smile lit up the room, came often to play with Aïda. She would sit the baby high up on the counter and play patty-cake.

"Such bonnie weans ye huv' Andy," the customers would say—*weans* is the common Scots word for children.

"A fish supper, please, wi' salt and vinegar and mushy peas oan the side. Man, it smells good in here."

Kathy beamed with pleasure while she served the customers

in her high heels; she said she never missed the tailoring. Kathy was very conscious of her four foot ten height and even wore high-heeled slippers. She smiled and glowed with pride when the customers said "Ooh" and "Ah," cooing at her baby.

She was happy and content. She wanted her life to go on just as it was. . . .

4

World Turmoil

1937

Andy and Kathy got their news from the wireless and by going to the cinema where, along with a feature film, they watched, through a great cloud of cigarette smoke, a Mickey Mouse and a Donald Duck cartoon and a newsreel. The couple knew little about world problems, the Italian invasion of Ethiopia, the Spanish Civil War, and the recent invasion of China by Japan. The newspapers provided them with local news, and on that particular Tuesday, their only day off, they watched a lengthy newsreel of the Berlin Olympics showing Hitler charming crowds of Germans.

"Who in hell does that man think he is, Kathy?" Andy fumed. "It looks like the pipsqueak wants to own the world!" And as they walked briskly down St. Andrew's Street he went on, "His men march like puppets with their knees up so high. I'm thinking this country is in for trouble from that man."

A lone newspaper boy shouted, "Hitler wants war!"

"See, Kathy, I am right."

Kathy shivered and pulled her fur coat closer around her.

~ ~ ~

The next Sunday Babbo proclaimed in his broken English, "Andy, before any trouble starts in Europe I take Mamma and

Bruna home to Italia." Babbo, always a shrewd man, had purchased a large property in Pietrasanta in the province of Lucca.
"We go retire there."

"I don't want to go, Andy. Can I stay here?" Bruna asked her
brother in her tiny voice.

"You know better than that, Bruna. Mamma would never
allow it. I'm sorry, lass, but ye need to go with them."

"But Mamma and Babbo, they are so old. They're no fun."

Mamma and Babbo were only in their late fifties. Bruna was
Mamma's *bambina*, a middle-age *miracolo*.

"Then, ye must take care of them." Andy hugged his tiny
sister, trying to ignore her pain. "Kathy and I will visit and bring
Aïda."

In April, Babbo and Mamma took little Bruna, and left their
sons in Scotland. Bruna cried all the way. Bruna was the only
Bertellotti of her generation to be born in Scotland, but it was
her destiny to live in Italy.

5

War Breaks Out

August 1939

August in Kilmarnock was the traditional time for folks to take holidays. Most businesses closed, and during 1939 it was no different. Tommy took the opportunity to visit his parents and, wisely or unwisely, decided to go to Italy for a quick visit. He didn't return.

Later that month, a short telegram came from Babbo to say that Irmo (Tommy) had been detained in Italia and then there was nothing more. In early September, Poland was bombed by Hitler's Luftwaffe. France declared war on Germany and soon after, Great Britain allied with them.

Many of Andy's customers were called up or volunteered for the British Royal Army, and soon the Ideal Café filled with soldiers dressed in khaki uniforms. Hitler's war seemed distant still to Andy and Kathy; little did they know it would come to their very doorstep.

"Kathy, I'm going to volunteer for the army," said Andy.

"But, Andy, ye're an Italian citizen."

He talked to Rudy.

"We'd better try, Andy," answered Rudy. "In case Mussolini takes sides with the Nazis."

"Oh, Rudy, Mussolini would never choose Hitler. Italy has always been an ally of Great Britain."

"Yer wrong, Andy. Babbo never did trust Il Duce; he wants power just like Hitler."

~   ~   ~

The Ideal Café and the Ritz were packed every day feeding British troops as they deployed to the Ayrshire beaches before shipping out to Europe. Vida, Tommy's cousin, struggled to keep the Queen's Café open, but it was difficult for a woman all alone. Rudy and Andy registered for duty but were turned down because they did not have British citizenship.

War raged in Western Europe. Germany and the Soviet Union partitioned Poland, Finland, and the Baltic States. It still seemed to Kathy that the conflict was far away. She became a mother-hen to Aïda, who was walking and talking and pleasing the customers with her chatter. Andy cooked away on his big silver-coloured pans while Aïda sat on the counter amongst the bowls and pots the customers brought in for mushy peas. The tot would wear the bowls on her head and ask her mummy, "Whose wee poo poo is this, Mummy?"

When Kathy laughed, she forgot there was a war on.

6

The Holiday

10 August 1939

Tommy read Babbo's letter again and slammed it on his counter. "I'm coming, Babbo, whether ye think it's a good idea or not." He looked around his immaculate shop, realized no one was listening, and spoke aloud again. "Ye always think the worst, Babbo. There's not going to be a war. In any case, I'm coming to Italy, I miss ye all so much." The handsome young man could see himself in the long mirror that ran the length of the wall behind the counter. A tug on his tie and a smooth of his unruly hair made him smile. Not bad looking, he thought, for a twenty-one-year-old. *I wish I knew how to speak to girls*, he thought, polishing his clean manicured nails on his lapels.

This Bertellotti boy was proud of his accomplishments in the small café. It had once been a knitting shop, and Tommy had had it remodeled into a slick 1930s ice-creamery. He walked around the café touching the red leather seats of the aluminum chairs that surrounded four petite glass-topped tables. He sat in one, remembering the day before when customers filled the shop ordering ice-cream and chocolates; the shop still had the faint odor of their cigarettes. Tommy's location for the Queen's Café was next to the SMT Bus Station, and if there was something the Scots people liked more than fish and chips, it was vanilla ice-cream made by hand in the back shop of this bright sunny café.

Tommy and his older brothers had always tried to please their parents; the evidence was that all three had gone into the same type of business, aided of course by Arturo. Tommy looked forward to the time when he could expand to sell fish and chips as well as ice-cream but at this time he was tired. It was "The Fair," as it was called in Kilmarnock; many people would be on holiday and shops closed in the town. "I'm coming now, Babbo. If there's going to be war it won't be here or in Italy."

~   ~   ~

Tommy had been but three or four when his parents decided to immigrate to Scotland. His memories of Italy sprang from the tales Mamma and Babbo shared over the dinner table while his brother Rudy tickled him mercilessly.

"Tommy," laughed Rudy, letting his brother gasp for air. "Do ye remember when we played every day at the beach and never wore shoes? Ye were a fat wee boy who followed Andy and me everywhere. What a pest ye were. We'd play war. I'd be Babbo, the soldier—I always shot ye both dead. Ye were hilarious rolling in the sand, holding yer tummy and crying, 'Ye got me, Rudy.' Nonna and Nonno Peri were the best grandparents a wee boy could have."

"I can't remember them," answered Tommy.

"I used to play the mandolin while ye sat on Nonna's lap," intoned Andy in his soft voice.

Mamma chimed in, "Nonna played the mandolin like an angel, Irmo. How I miss her." Mamma always spoke in Italian, refusing to speak English except to take the money in the fish and chip shop; she disapproved of her boys' Scottish nicknames.

Babbo reached for the salt shaker, Mamma took it away, shaking a finger at him. He nodded back at her, used to her bossy ways. "I miss-a the sparkling blue-green Mediterranean with its seagulls and white sand." Babbo spoke in broken Scottish English. In the fish and chip shop the customers smiled when he spoke. Rudy, Andy, and Tommy spoke both languages with ease, but as they grew they lost some of the Italian words and their tongues had become broad and musical with Scots inflections.

~ ~ ~

Tommy was anxious to see his parents' new house; his older brothers had gone with Babbo to look at the property before he purchased it. Tommy would not say he was jealous, but he was. What he told himself, as he sat in his empty shop, was how much he missed Bruna, his little sister. He did not admit that missing from his life was a taste of Italy.

~ ~ ~

Bruna met him at the train station; she was a tiny girl with a smile that could break a heart. She was almost eleven and had walked to the station on her own. Pietrasanta was just a village in the nineteen thirties but the station was on the outskirts.

"Tommy," she cried, running towards him, "*mio fratello.*"

He dropped his valise and grabbed her tight. "Bruna, my Bruna."

They swung together, each of them smiling as if they'd never stop. "My, how ye've grown."

"Liar," she answered. "I'm still the shortest in my class."

"But I expect yer at the top of yer class."

"*Sì,* I am, now that my Italian is better. That reminds me. Mamma says I'm to call ye Irmo while yer in Italy."

"Whatever ye like, girl. I see ye still have yer Scots accent."

"That'll never go away!."

The two of them laughed and chatted all the way through the old *villaggio*. Tommy admired the old buildings, the scroll work in the square, and the tall spire of the Pietrasanta Cathedral. Bruna pointed out her newly built school, telling Tommy that it had been Mussolini who had built it.

"He can't be as bad as Babbo makes out, hah, Bruna?"

She shrugged and got really excited as they turned onto

Ospedale Street. "See, Tommy, I mean Irmo. The hospital is towards the town; our house is further up this hill towards the mountains. Ye can almost see the sea from our veranda."

They ran the last fifty yards to the gate, Bruna squeaked it open, and Tommy rushed in, ran up the seven or eight steps to his parent's veranda, and hollered, "I'm here, Mamma, *sono qui.*"

His little round mamma was waiting on the veranda, Babbo standing behind her.

"It is so good to see you," Tommy laughed between hugs and kisses.

Bruna danced around them all. "Come on, Irmo, let me show ye the house."

"Bruna, wait, let me just look around. Wow, Babbo, what a property ye have, *magnifico.* Ye're right, Bruna, I can almost see the sea." Below him was a plantation of grape arbors with pathways leading to an orchard of peaches and apricots. "I can smell the ripe fruit, Babbo."

"Okay, Tommy, now can I show ye my bedroom?"

"*Sì,* Bruna," he answered, leaning down to pet a large grey cat. "And who's this?"

"This is Mariah, she's mine; she sleeps on my bed."

Tommy laughed, his parents shook their heads, and together they turned to enter the house. There was a wide veranda with glass doors leading into a fine old kitchen where a pot boiled ready for the pasta. Old tools hung all over the white walls. "These were Nonno Peri's tools," explained Mamma.

The kitchen door opened into a large dining room almost filled with a long oak table and sideboard. A glass chandelier hung over the table, which was set for lunch in Mamma's best china.

"Oh, Mamma, so *magnifico.*"

"Come on, Irmo," Bruna tugged at his jacket.

They walked through the dining room past a well-fitted bath-room and her parents' finely furnished room with its blue walls and Venetian lamps, to Bruna's large, very pink bedroom. The cat immediately jumped onto the white duvet. "This is my *para-diso*, Tommy," she clapped. "Look, I have my own French doors; they look up into the olive orchards behind our house. I have magazines and my own books." She ran around the room showing off her stuffed animals. "This is my favourite, ye can hold him."

Tommy took the small bear with the glass eyes in his hand. He held it to his face. "It smells like you, Bruna."

She clapped with joy. "His name is Iggy."

"No wonder ye retired to Italia, Babbo. It feels like home."

"*Grazie, figlio mio. Benvenuto, Irmo.*"

"All this from fish and chips," said Tommy.

"*Sì,*" agreed Babbo.

~ ~ ~

For the next few days, life was very satisfying indeed. Babbo let his youngest son relax while he gardened—always with one ear tuned to the wireless. Tommy listened with half an ear, while he rested on a deck chair in the very welcome sun—the wire-less was background noise to him. The Italian radio announc-ers spoke so quickly that most of their talk went past his brain mindlessly. For several days, Babbo let him enjoy the deck chair; then, after dinner on the third night, he handed Tommy a cigar and poured himself a small cup of very strong coffee. The old man's face was stern and set, but Tommy listened to the constant buzz of insects, his fingers cupped around his demitasse, his nose inhaling the aroma of the thick espresso.

Babbo lit his cigar and blew the smoke skyward. He spoke slowly and clearly in Italian. "Son, it is not safe for you here in Italia."

Tommy sat up straight. "What?"

"Italy has been at war in Ethiopia and Libya. It has been bloody there."

"That's a long way from here, Babbo."

"That's what all the young ones say until it is their time."

"Their time to what, Babbo?"

"To serve. You know I have never been fond of Mussolini's politics. He has done a lot of good here in Italia, but he is like Hitler; he wants power, and then more power."

"What are you saying to me, Babbo?"

"You are too complacent, Irmo. You should have waited in Scotland until the world found out what Hitler is up to."

"Babbo, I had to come."

"Irmo, listen. I believe Mussolini will align with Hitler. They are both crazy dictators who believe they will rule the world. I hate both of those *bastardi*."

"Babbo, I am not interested in politics."

"I can see that, but believe me, son, war is imminent."

"Oh, Babbo, I had not realized that you were this worried."

"You are so young." Babbo's hand now covered his son's. "You should go back to Scotland, right away."

"But, Babbo," Tommy countered. "On the Scottish wireless they say that Chamberlain and Churchill believe Il Duce will ally with Great Britain. Why don't we wait and see?"

"You should go back home now, when you still can."

"But I just got here, Babbo. Besides which, I have an Italian passport. What will happen to the Italians in Scotland, if Mussolini chooses sides with Hitler?"

"Chamberlain will be good to the Italians in Britain. We have been excellent citizens. You must leave now, before Mussolini makes the wrong decision."

"Isn't King Vittorio Emanuele in charge of the Italian Royal Army?"

"Our king is a *burattino*, a puppet," Babbo snorted. "Il Duce tells Vittorio when he can go take a shit. I don't want you in the Italian army, son, I want you to go home."

"It's only ten more days till I leave, Babbo."

~   ~   ~

One week later, on September 1, Hitler's Luftwaffe bombed Warsaw. All transportation in Italy ground to a halt. Tommy packed his bags and Babbo took him to the train depot at dawn. There were masses of people trying to purchase tickets. Babbo and Tommy managed to finally push through to the counter where they found a uniformed soldier instead of the usual ticket taker. "*Prego*," said the *soldato*, "Civilian travel *é finito in Europa.* France has declared war on Germany."

Tommy blanched. "Babbo, I am stuck!"

"*Sì, figlio mio,* 'stuck' is the word."

7

The Holiday Continues

They hurried home, Babbo in a panic. "The Carabinieri will come for you soon, Irmo. They are drafting young Italian men for the army. If they do not comply, they are jailed. Even though you live in Scotland, you are an Italiano."

"What can I do, Babbo?"

"Here, people are either Fascisti, following Mussolini like mice follow cheese, or Partigiani like me—able to think for themselves. I have many *partigiano* friends," he answered. "They will hide you."

Tommy had come all the way to Italy, only to get caught in a vice. He would be expected to enter the Italian Royal Army.

"Babbo, I am no soldier, I am not like Rudy."

"I was no soldier either, that's why I was chosen to be a *medico* in the last war. I don't *know* what side Mussolini will choose, son, but I'm *sure* he will choose the Nazi because the two men think alike. They want more than just to rule their own countries. The Italian Royal Army will become a Fascist Brigade." Babbo spit out. "There is no way Fascisti will ally with Chamberlain or Churchill."

~ ~ ~

"Ye have to stay here with us now, Tommy," said Bruna in her small Scots voice. She had sat beside him to listen to the men talk. "We can hide ye." The child had tears in her eyes.

Sweat poured down Tommy's face, but not from the heat of the day.

Babbo put one hand on Tommy's shoulder and with the other he took Bruna's arm. "Don't worry about Tommy, I will keep him safe." He led them downstairs into the garden. As they walked, Babbo whispered in Tommy's ear, "I have a place where you can hide."

"Is it in the wine cellar, Babbo?"

"*Sì*, Bruna."

Her eyes grew large and black as she gazed up at her father and brother. "How could this happen, Babbo?"

Babbo led them to a trap door set in the ground by the east wall. It was well hidden by a layer of dirt on which rested four or five flower pots full of red geraniums. Babbo moved the pots aside. "This is my wine cellar. It's not too big, Irmo, but there is a small cot down there. When the summer sun is too hot, I often take a rest in here."

"I'm to hide in there? In the dark?" said Tommy with hesitation.

"I'll fetch ye some blankets, Irmo," said Bruna. "Can I sleep down there with him, Daddy?"

"No, Bruna. You may not," he replied in his best English.

Tommy squeezed through the trap door. He was a bit on the plump side and more than a little apprehensive.

"Here, Tommy, take Mariah; she will keep ye company."

"Thanks, Bruna."

~   ~   ~

Tommy had been in the cellar only a few hours when two Carabinieri entered the property through the side gate. He stood on a crate to look through a peep hole, the only place where light streamed in; he had been surprised by his father's preparations. Tommy had been prepared for nothing; he was twenty-one, a caring soul who did not gamble and drink like his brothers, simply happy in his shop and eager to meet someone to spend his life with. Now, he felt trapped like a rat. The odor of the barrels in which Babbo stomped grapes was overpowering, nauseatingly sweet. Mariah rubbed against Tommy's legs as he watched and listened.

Babbo left his bench under the olive tree and marched quickly over to the officers. They pushed him aside. Babbo staggered and almost fell to the ground.

This was Tommy's first rush of hatred towards authority.

"Where is your son, old man?" barked the taller of the two.

"He left yesterday to go back to Scotland."

The tall bearded man grabbed Babbo by the shirt collar and pulled him up towards his face. "Okay, now," the brute ordered. "Let's have the truth, Bertellotti; we know your son is still in Pietrasanta."

"I told you. He left before war was declared."

"You lie, old man." The officer slapped Arturo across the face.

Bruna had heard the commotion and was out on the veranda. "Leave my Daddy alone," she bawled in her distinct Scottish voice.

Mamma had also come out and was holding fast to her daughter in case the girl bolted down the stairs.

The man looked up at the two women and spat on the ground.

Mamma proclaimed loudly, "Irmo is gone. Leave us alone."

"How old are you, old man?"

"I'm sixty," said Arturo, rubbing the blood from his lip.

Again the bearded man grabbed Babbo by his left arm. "You are too old to be in the military, but not too old to beat." The officer raised his baton as if to strike Babbo, but fortunately his partner pulled the baton away.

"There is a child up there, you fool!" He spoke through tight teeth. "Mr. Bertellotti, my partner has a very bad temper as you can see. We only want your son. Our job is to watch the railroad station. Your son did not leave; we watched you both as you pushed through the crowd. Trains are for troops only. The army only wants to talk to your son. We are going upstairs to search your house."

~   ~   ~

I don't want to talk to them, thought Tommy, looking down at his suitcase. He listened to the heavy footsteps stomping around his father's house. He heard Bruna say, "I don't want you in my room." Tommy's heart beat so loudly in his ears that he was sure the men would hear it. His shirt clung to the sweat on his chest.

When the Carabinieri exited the house onto the veranda, Tommy heard them say, "When he comes back, you tell him we are looking for him. He is either a deserter or a spy. We know he is from Scotland. How convenient he is here in Pietrasanta when war is declared."

"He is a good son."

The tall man spat on the ground again. "Good sons make good spies. What is his *passaporto*?"

"It is an Italian *passaporto*, naturally."

"Perfect for a British spy! When we find him, he's going to jail or worse." They marched around the property. Tommy felt the vibration of their boots as they passed the trap door. When they exited the gate, Babbo waited until they were far away before he came to Tommy. He opened the latch and climbed down the steps. "You heard?"

"Everything, Babbo.," Tommy now had tears. "They hurt you, Babbo. How could they think that I am a spy?"

"Irmo, this is nothing. You must go from here to a better hiding place. I have friends—good partigiano people who know all about hiding."

"Babbo, I am amazed by your resourcefulness."

"I do what I have to do."

"Thank you, Babbo."

"My partisan friend lives high in the hills where the olive trees grow," Babbo went on. "Partigiani stick together. Giorgio Passaglia is a fine man, an honest soul. The Carabinieri will be watching this property, so I will send Bruna up to their house to alert him. You can trust both Giorgio and his wife."

"Bruna? She is so young."

"Here in Italy at this time the children know so much more than they should. Her best friend is Lena Passaglia. Giorgio will help you disappear, he is in the underground. He knows people who can help you. He knows the secret trails that the resistance fighters use. You will disappear from my house tonight."

"Will the Carabinieri come back to harass you?'

"I will be fine. I am too old for them to get too excited about."

"Remember, Babbo, he said you were not too old to beat."

Babbo waved the comment away. "Come indoors for a moment to eat and say goodbye to Mamma and Bruna, they are worried." Babbo handed him a thick roll of lire. "I am sorry, *mio figlio*. I know this was not what you wanted, but now it is war and nothing is the same. You will be with people I can trust."

Tommy kissed his mother and sister; both were dissolved in tears. "I am sorry, Mamma, I did not think it through when I decided to come to Italy."

"How were you to know the war would come?"

"Bruna, again we must say goodbye."

"Oh, brother, it will not be long." She ran quickly to her bedroom to find her bear. "Please, Tommy, Iggy is small; he can keep you company."

"*Grazie, mia sorella*, and thank you for Mariah, she did keep me company."

As the cat strolled away he realized that this was going to be one long *vacanza*, not the holiday he had expected.

8

"Collar the Lot"

1940

It was eight o'clock in the evening when Rudy and Peggy arrived at the Ideal Café. They were a striking couple; both wore only the most fashionable clothes of the day. They lived together, which was frowned on by friends and family, and both used black and gold cigarette holders for their imported fags.

"Let's talk, Andy," said Rudy.

The shop was not too busy, so Andy turned the gas down on the pans. "We'll take a break, Kathy."

The foursome sat around the table in Andy's living room sipping the amber liquid of Chivas Regal. "I've been saving this for a special time."

"It's so smooth, Andy, thanks. Peggy and I came to tell ye there's going to be a radio announcement tonight."

Kathy sat quietly, hands in her lap, not so interested in the golden liquid that sat before her. "What kind of an announcement, Rudy?"

"Churchill's on in fifteen minutes."

"I'm hoping for good news," said Peggy, blowing a perfect smoke ring.

"I'm glad Chamberlain stepped back to let Churchill be in charge," said Andy.

Churchill began in his booming English accent, "I wish I could bring good news, ladies and gentlemen, but in these sad times of war, good news is hard to find." He cleared his throat. "France has fallen and the Italian Prime Minister, Benito Mussolini, has thrown his hat in with Adolf Hitler. Great Britain has lost a valuable ally in the war against Germany. We are now at war with Italy."

Andy sat up straight. "My God, what will happen to Mamma and Babbo?"

Kathy shushed him.

Churchill was still speaking. "We must protect ourselves from the enemy within."

"What bloody enemy within?"

"Calm down, Rudy," said Andy.

"From now on all resident Italians will be known as *enemy aliens*."

"Enemy aliens?" Kathy stood up, hands outstretched, face pale.

Churchill's next words chilled all of them. "*Collar the lot.*"

"Collar the lot! What the hell?"

"Pour me another whisky, Rudy," said Andy, reaching out for Kathy's hand. "Ye'll see, hen, it will be all right."

Kathy burst into tears. "It won't, Andy, they'll take ye away!"

Rudy reached for the whisky bottle. "That damned Churchill. And I thought he knew what he was doing. We're not the enemy. The Italians who live here want to be here."

"Mussolini did this," said Andy. "Babbo always said he would."

"What will we do, Andy?" Kathy was crying and holding her stomach.

"Steady, girl," said Andy. "Don't get so upset."

Peggy had reached forward to touch Kathy's arm. "Kathy, are ye. . . ?"

"Yes. I'm pregnant, Peg."

"Oh my, this is not good timing, Kathy, I'm sure there will be trouble. This war will bring trouble to everyone."

"Tommy's already in trouble," Rudy interrupted. "I can feel it in my bones."

"Maybe he joined the Italian resistance, Rudy."

"I hope so, Andy. I would if I was in Italy. I always dreamed of being a soldier, like Babbo, but now there's no chance. If Italy had chosen Churchill I would have been able to go into the Royal Army."

"Maybe Tommy joined the Italian Royal Army," said Peggy.

"Not a chance, Peg. Tommy wouldn't fight for the Fascists, Babbo would never approve. Babbo saw more than his share of fascism in Austria during the last war! Hell, he immigrated to Scotland because of Il Duce's fascist policies. Mussolini is nothing but a damn dictator."

"None of ye are safe." Peggy spoke up. "Take me home, Rudy. Andy, Kathy, if ye need me, I'll be there for ye. My advice is to get yer suitcase packed and be ready for whatever is coming."

~ ~ ~

The newspaper boys yelled, "Enemy alien round up. Read it in the Glasgow Herald. Churchill says, 'Collar the lot!' "

No longer did Andy and Kathy's customers lean their elbows on the counter; their elbows and shoulders were frozen like their frowns. A brick shattered Andy's bedroom window, breaking the sink where Kathy bathed Aïda.

"Christ, Kathy," said Andy. "That brick could have landed on our wee Aïda."

Kathy sat pensive, her two-year-old on her lap.

He sat down beside her. "Kathy, what's happening? Our customers hate us now."

"What should we do? Do ye think we should close the shop?" Kathy put her hand on his arm.

"And go where?"

The wireless repeatedly blasted stories of looting in Edinburgh and Glasgow. Window after window was shattered; shopkeepers were beaten by thugs. In Manchester and Edinburgh, Italian shopkeepers were killed; others were herded onto boats to be shipped out to Canada. Andy and Kathy packed up all the cigarettes and valuables and hid them in a suitcase. Kathy packed Aïda's clothes and found the passports.

"Maybe ye and Aïda should go live with yer mother?"

"I'm staying beside ye, no matter what; come hell or high water."

"Ye realize they are rounding up Italian men, Kathy."

"Do ye realize I'm never leaving ye?"

He put his arms around her like a protective shield.

"Does the Government think that Italian shop owners are spies, Andy?"

"They just don't want to risk it. How I wish my folks had taken citizenship when we were just kids. Maybe we wouldn't be in such a fix."

"Somehow I don't think it makes any difference right now."

Andy

9

The Lorry

But pleasures are like poppies spread,
You seize the flow'r, its bloom is shed

Robert Burns, "Tam O' Shanter"

The army lorry with its dark beige canvas top pulled left onto Gilmour Street from St. Andrew's Street. A local police officer sat up front with the young corporal who drove. Two soldiers sat in back on the wooden seats. It was a cold night for June, wet and misty, the kind of cold that seeps into the bones and chills the spine. Police Constable Johnnie Millar hopped out, straightened his tie, put on his tall black hat, and strode into Andy's shop. He'd been there many a night, helping himself to nice hot steamy chips and delicious haddock. He had never paid, since he and Andy had been classmates in school and Johnnie had always kept an eye out for Andy's shop. He straightened out his shoulders and when the last customer left, he held his hand up. "No fish supper the night. I have official business. I am sorry to say this, but I have orders to escort ye to internment."

"What?" protested Kathy. "Get out of here, Johnnie Millar. What do ye mean by barging in here and bossing us around?"

"Missus Bertellotti, I'm sorry to be the one, but the two of ye now are enemy aliens. Don't give me any trouble. I have to follow the papers in my pocket."

"I'm no enemy alien, Johnnie," shouted Andy. "Ye've known me yer whole life and ye know for sure Kathy is not an alien."

"Get yer suitcases, Andy, and get a move on. If ye need something later, I'll try to send it."

"Ye're a bastard, Johnnie!"

"That may be, but ye know it's not my fault; orders are orders."

"Where are ye taking us?"

"To Darmellington, up the valley. Ye'll be housed there until Churchill eases off the restrictions. It's not my fault. Ye're lucky. Most of the Italian families have been split up, the men in one place, the women and children in another."

"Kathy's not Italian. Can she go live with her mother?"

"I'm going with ye, Andy," Kathy cried out, one hand at her mouth and the other on her belly.

"The orders were changed anyway. Women are being interned now. Come on now, man, get packed."

"But, Johnnie, Kathy is a Scotswoman!" Andy was enraged.

"Andy, it's a favour I'm doing ye. Ye don't want to be all alone for the duration. Ye'll be housed together. Kathy married a *Tally,* so she's goin' to suffer the consequences."

Kathy woke Aïda up and held her in her arms. "Andy, I have to be with ye."

The wee one howled as weans will do when snatched out of warm blankets in the night.

Andy was still arguing, even as they climbed up the metal steps into the back of the lorry.

"We'll freeze in here, Johnnie Millar," yelled Kathy as she climbed up, pushing Aïda ahead of her. Aïda was still bawling as she climbed the huge metal steps into the lorry. Kathy turned back for a minute. "I'll tell ye one thing, Johnnie Millar, I'm proud to be Andy's wife and if that makes me an enemy alien, so be it." But when Kathy saw the wooden seats she began to cry, "We'll be bounced all over, Andy. It could hurt the baby inside. Oh, my God, Andy, Rudy's in the lorry."

When Andy saw his brother, he knew that both of their worlds had truly come undone. They huddled together, Rudy, Kathy, Andy, and baby Aïda, glad for their overcoats. When the lorry started up, the breeze chilled them to the marrow.

Rudy whispered, "What in hell did we do to deserve this?"

"We did nothing, Rudy."

"Mussolini sold us out, Andy, sold us out when he chose Hitler. Imagine the minds of the lads who are fighting for him. Many are Partigiani, not Fascisti like his volunteer army in Africa."

"What's going to happen to us?" asked Kathy.

Rudy leaned over towards them. "Peggy said she would keep our shops open while we're gone."

"But how long will that be, Rudy?" responded Kathy, her tears choking.

"She said she would keep my shop open too?" Andy was astonished.

Rudy was too choked up to speak right away. He cleared his throat. "She said she'll try, Andy. That's all I know. I gave her the key I had for your shop. Did ye bring all the cigarettes?"

"Aye, I have them wrapped around my waist. We'll have some for a while at least."

"I have some, too," said Rudy. "No use letting the looters steal them."

Johnnie Millar stuck his head in, yelling over the noise of the motor, "I'll keep an eye on the shops for ye."

"Aye, for sure ye will, ye bastard," muttered Andy.

~   ~   ~

A dark, looming tenement was their internment quarters. It was very dark when they arrived and the only light came from a gas lamp. "My God, Andy, it's a bloody slum."

There was a gate at the opening to the long black entry. A retired guard sat there.

Andy's heart sank like a stone. "A guard! Kathy, this is a jail."

Their flat was one room off the shabby entry. It had a single bed in the corner and a double bed against another wall. The wallpaper was peeling and the room smelled of mould.

Kathy coughed. "Did we bring enough bedclothes? Where am I going to put Aïda to sleep? The Scots folk have turned their back on us," said Kathy, tears in her voice. "Our customers used to say how much they loved us. Now, because you two happen to be Italian, we are enemy aliens to be held captive."

10

Underground

Tommy spent a month in Giorgio's barn, sleeping upstairs in a loft filled with stinking hay. Giorgio was younger than Arturo; he looked to be around fifty, well built from his farm work, scruffy and dark bearded in his face and, Tommy found out, a sure hand at cards.

"You will be safe in my barn," said Giorgio. "The Carabinieri won't check my farm; we live too far from town."

Giorgio's wife, Adela, a small slight woman with early wrinkles and a tuft of hair growing at the tip of her chin, brought Tommy his meals. Adela was friendly and talkative; she was happy to have Tommy to talk to while her daughter was in school.

Many other scared young men who hated Il Duce came for shelter. They too would hide in the large red barn as they passed through. Most were headed to Pisa where an anti-fascist group was forming. These young men were not deserters or rebels; they simply wanted the best for Italy and were sure that Mussolini would ally with Hitler.

"Before I send you on, Irmo, you need to learn some skills. I know someone who can help you."

"What kind of skills?"

"He will help you become a *soldato*."

"Turn me into a soldier, Giorgio? I am a pacifist, not a warrior." Tommy walked around the old barn, thoughts raging through his brain. He was not one to argue with his brothers. He had not enjoyed the shoot-me games Rudy had played at the beach. Rudy was a natural to be a freedom fighter; Tommy only wanted to go home to his shop in Scotland. He was struggling to make sense of the complicated politics of Italia.

~   ~   ~

At dawn on the fourth day, the barn door burst open and Giorgio entered with a huge man by his side.

"Irmo, come on down; I want you to meet Giuseppe."

Tommy shook himself awake and climbed down the ancient ladder. He was dwarfed by the size of the man whose muscles rippled under his cotton shirt and whose arms seemed too big for his sleeves.

"So you're Irmo." Giuseppe had a shaved head and a low, melodic voice. He offered his hand.

Tommy shook it, feeling his warmth and strength. "I am."

"Giuseppe is a good man," said Giorgio.

"I will take your word for it," Tommy answered.

"Giorgio says I need to train you to be tough like me."

"I suppose I do need some help." Tommy stood as tall as his five foot seven would allow.

The large man smiled sideways. "Some help, son? Do you realize you are going to be on the run for the duration of the war?"

"I was afraid of that," the shorter man answered.

Giuseppe was a tough trainer and attempted to teach Tommy some hand-to-hand combat skills. Tommy's body ached from Giuseppe's punches and rough training. After a few weeks, Giuseppe sized up the Scots/Italian. "You're not much of a fighter, Irmo," he said. "I have a better idea for you. Since you are Italiano and Scottish, I'm going to get you to Pisa where the undercover organisation has an underground shortwave. I think you could be a radioman."

Tommy was relieved to stop the combat training and get

away from Pietrasanta. He was aching to go down the hill to say good-bye to his family, but he knew it would only put them in danger.

The two men, concealed under the hay in an open lorry, travelled to Pisa. There Tommy had his first glance at the many Partigiani who had joined the underground movement. Tommy realized then that Mussolini would make a disastrous mistake when he joined Germany against the Allies. As it was, Japan, who had been warring in China for several years, had already allied with Hitler. If Italy joined them, it would place civilization balancing on a precipice—it would be called the Axis.

~　~　~

Tommy, who was known as Irmo now, was a quick study on the shortwave and did not take long to master the equipment. His Italian had improved in just this short time, as had his resolve to help Italy against the madman Mussolini. Soon he was travelling with a resistance group. The band of men hid in basements, barns, and the like, any place that kept them away from Mussolini's forces. In July of 1940, as expected, Il Duce chose Hitler, and German troops appeared on Italy's streets. At this point, the announcers on the radio did not use the word occupation, but that's what it was. The Italian Army marched into France and by some stroke of luck defeated the French in only a few days. This clinched the occupation.

While the small band of resistance fighters learned counter-espionage, Tommy became expert on the shortwave, intercepting messages and sending code words to other groups around the country. The men and the few women who were involved would tease Irmo about his Scots accent. They nicknamed him "the Scottish-Italian," a moniker that would stay with him for the duration.

In Italy, life took a turn for the worse. German troops poured into the towns, commandeered buildings, stole artifacts, built war fronts, and checked constantly on the Jewish families. The Führer hated Jews, and his troops made sure the whereabouts of Jewish families were known. The SS was ready to ship all of them away to the concentration camps that were being set up in Germany. The anti-fascist groups were becoming better organised and by October they had obtained some weaponry. They also hid as many Jews as possible while they moved around the country. Italians were, at heart, a peace-loving nation, who did not appreciate Hitler and were uncomfortable with the Nazi SS who seemed to be on every street corner.

11

Labour Pains

Near and more near the thunders roll
Robert Burns, "Tam O' Shanter"

6 January 1941

"Don't leave me, Mummy. Have the baby here." Aïda's voice was a shrill whine lost in the Darmellington wind.

Kathy clasped her daughter's tiny hand as if to protect her from the approaching rain. "Come close, darling."

Graffiti decorated the walls of the entryway—the close, as the Scots were inclined to say. Someone had scraped *Tallies bugger off.*

The small family stood by the wrought-iron gate that was the only way in and out of the run-down tenement. Kathy had her back to the breeze and was hiding her large belly with a heavy wool coat; she was genteel about her condition, but pain was written on her tight lips. The baby was coming and something was wrong—there had been blood on the sheets.

Andy was pleased and relieved that the midwife would take Kathy to the hospital, but he wanted to go along. Annabel Webster, the County Nurse who had been attending Kathy for a few weeks, was gentle but firm in her decisions and sought no vengeance against them or any of the many Italians who had been placed in the makeshift internment quarters.

The rain began to splat. Annabel bent down to Aïda's level. "Wee lassie," she said in her broad Scots Glasgow accent, "yer Mum has tae go tae a hospital far away. Ye see, pet, Mummy is very small and she needs a doctor tae get that baby out."

"I can help," said Aïda, her little voice breaking. "Let Daddy and me come, Annabel."

Andy picked her up, pain registering on his face, his beard rough on the child's cheek. "Shush, lass, shush. See—" he said to the guard. "I need to be with my wife, even the child knows."

Jimmy McMurphy, the guard, was old, bent, and mean. His teeth clicked when he talked. "No, Bertellotti. Ye're not allowed tae leave this town, especially for a hospital on the coast. Tallies stay interned, that's what Churchill said. Don't get any ideas. The polis will send ye tae Barlinnie if ye try anything, and ye ken yer wife wid be all alone fur the duration."

Barlinnie was the biggest prison in Scotland, a place where many hapless Italian aliens had been interned beside hardened criminals. Andy did not want to end up in that hellhole. "Jimmy McMurphy, ye know I'm no threat. Do ye think I'm going to climb on a boat and set sail for Italy?"

"Orders are orders," the old man said.

"Andy, don't make trouble." Kathy's grip tightened around his hand.

"Come oan, sweet woman," said Annabel. She took the unsteady Kathy by the arm, guiding her up the steps of an army lorry that had been fashioned into an ambulance. Its brown canvas top did not provide much shelter for a wild January morning.

"Don't worry, Andy, there's a cot for Kathy tae lie on."

From the top step Kathy turned and took Andy's face in her hand, cupping his chin up. "Now don't do anything daft, love."

"Ye can bet I won't," Andy said, looking down at his tiny wife with her huge belly. But as she began to climb the steps, he decided that he had to. Aïda clung to his neck, so he held her out to kiss her Mummy.

Kathy choked and said, "Be a good girl, Aïda. I must go. Promise me, Andy, nothing daft."

He nodded, an audacious plan already forming.

"Will the baby be cold, Daddy?" Aïda whispered in her daddy's ear.

"No, pet," he answered. "Annabel has lots of blankets."

"I want to go with her," she went on. "It will be bumpy and cold in there, Mummy will cry."

"Mummy will be fine," he said, cold sweat running down his handsome face. "No thanks to yerself, Jimmy McMurphy."

"Following orders, Bertellotti, following orders."

The brown lorry with the Red Cross on the side started up. Annabel had gone in back with Kathy, and for that Andy was grateful.

"I'm closing the gate. Get back inside, wop!"

"I heard ye the first time, Jimmy," Andy replied, disgust in his voice. "What did Churchill say? Was it 'Collar the lot'? Bugger it, Jimmy, can ye no get it through yer thick head? We are not the enemy." Andy held his temper for Aïda, but he wanted to punch the old man. Instead he said, "I'm going to leave ye with Mrs. Scolatti next door while I go to work. Ye can play with Cara."

Aïda liked Cara; she and her mamma were forever making pasta.

"Uncle Rudy will take good care of ye tonight if I'm not there."

"Are ye going to go see Mummy, Daddy?"

He didn't answer, but he gave her a wink. He was glad, for once, that his brother Rudy was staying with them. The run-down flat was hardly big enough for two, never mind a whole family and a brother who liked more than his share of a dram. But now Andy needed Rudy to watch Aïda while he left to check on Kathy.

He hurried into the flat to change into his work clothes, careful to take an overcoat and hat. Thoughts and plans filled his mind. How could he get to Kathy? When he came back out to the entry to go to work, McMurphy repeated, "Hey, wop, don't do anything daft. Remember what yer wife said."

Andy ignored the slur and started up the hill towards the munitions factory where he and Rudy had been put to work. He walked head down, pulling up his collar to shield his neck and holding onto his hat so it would not blow away. He was glad it wasn't snowing; it was, after all, January. How was he to get to Irvine Central Hospital?

Bomb casings were made in the Darmellington munitions factory, a great, grey, imposing stone structure that sat on a hill above the town. Lots of internees worked there: Andy on the assembly line, Rudy loading finished casings onto a freight train whose rails came right into the factory. Their jobs were mandated by the war effort, Andy glad of something to fill the time but Rudy depressed because neither country wanted him to become a soldier, something he had dreamed of forever.

Andy thought and thought. Could he get onto the factory's freight train without being detected? The locomotive travelled to Kilmarnock, whose railway station was but one street length from the bus station. This was a Monday and the late bus left around seven for the coast towns, including Irvine where the maternity hospital stood.

The rain was pelting when Andy walked into the cobbled yard. As they often did, the supervisors, tough country women, spat at his feet when he walked by. Usually it angered Andy, but this time he was too pre-occupied to care. He nodded his head towards the nasty women and gave them a grim smile when he signed in. "*Buongiorno,*" he said to the hateful women.

He was forming a daft plan.

12

Escape

Wee, sleekit, cow'rin, tim'rous beastie,
O, what a panic's in thy breastie!

Robert Burns, "To a Mouse"

Rudy stood in the midst of a group of older Scotsmen. Andy approached him as casually as he could.

"How's Kathy?" asked Rudy.

The other men joined in. "Aye, how's the Missus?"

"On her way to the hospital," Andy answered. "Rudy, I need to talk to ye alone, soon."

Andy got into his spot on the assembly line and when the equipment started up, slammed his wrist between two metal plates.

"Be careful, wop," said a woman supervisor. "Ye might lose a finger."

When Rudy walked by with his supervisor, Andy caught his eye. The two men were not allowed to communicate while they worked. They couldn't anyway; the noise of the machines was so loud the men kept cotton wool in their ears. Andy signaled to Rudy with his head pointed towards the lavatory.

At noon the brothers met. Andy briefed him about Kathy, how her pains had started, how the baby was in distress, how he had to get to her.

"How can I be of help?" asked Rudy.

"Could ye leave a freight-car door open?'

Rudy raised his brows. "Aye, and I'll keep the guard busy while ye get on board."

"What time does the train leave, Rudy?"

"At five, on the nose; ye'll make the Irvine bus in Kilmarnock if everything goes well."

"It will. Ye can't win unless ye take a gamble."

"Kathy will be fine, Andy. I'll sign ye out."

"Oh, God, Rudy, I had forgotten about that. I was late in, so I can be late out. That'll work."

"Good luck, brother. Don't get caught." Rudy patted his back. "I'll cover for ye."

"When do the guards take their tea?"

"At quarter to five."

~   ~   ~

The light had already faded and the Scottish winter dark was closing in fast. The blackout shades were pulled over the grimy windows. At four-thirty, the whistle blew for the line workers to go home for the day. Andy slipped into the lavatory, washed the work-black from his hands, stuck his overcoat over his work clothes and hid in a toilet stall until most of the workers had left the building. The few who stayed behind were the loaders who trolleyed the boxes of ammunition casings out to the freight train where they were shipped to the Glenfield and Kennedy Factory in Kilmarnock. At the Glenfield the casings were fashioned into live ammo. Andy's heart hammered so loudly in his chest, he was afraid someone would hear it.

The train was due to leave at five o'clock. There were four railway guards: two were in a cubicle smoking, one was at the back of the train, and the fourth was talking loudly to Rudy. At exactly quarter to five, the two guards in the cubicle slipped into the building for a quick cuppa. Andy saw his chance and stepped onto the platform. The engine revved up, causing smoke to curl around his legs; Andy hoped it would obscure the fireman's vision. The fireman sat in the engine, which had a side mirror.

Rudy's voice was raised in an argument with the other loader. The guard at the rear of the freight cars moved up the platform to listen. Andy moved fast while Rudy kept the men busy. He ducked down as he passed the engine. He ran down the side of the freight cars. One huge carriage door was still open—Rudy had been as good as his word. Andy heaved himself up, grateful that he had kept himself in shape. He slid the door ajar and crept between large wooden boxes of ammo casings. He crouched down, waiting for his eyes to adjust, and then he sighed with relief. He was completely hidden. Sitting in the dark, cold, cramped, and determined, he went over each moment of the day in his head; every hair on his body on the alert. Soon the guards were back checking doors. Andy held his breath as they slammed the freight door on his boxcar completely shut.

At 5:00 p.m. exactly, the train chugged its way out of the yard.

Andy wrapped his arms around his body to keep warm, aware that his damp coat stank like wet dog. As the locomotive shuddered out of the factory, he grabbed onto the boxes to steady himself. Then as the train picked up speed he sat in the pitch black listening to the clacking rails saying, "*Enemy alien, enemy alien, enemy alien.*"

The journey to Kilmarnock seemed to take hours while he sat in the dark, craving a smoke, thinking about Kathy. How tiny she was. The blood on the sheets. Would the baby be all right? "Dear God," he said out loud, "let her be okay."

The brakes screeched when the train entered the Kilmarnock tunnel. Andy crawled forward, feeling his way towards the door. It seemed to take too long. He felt the cold of the train door. Where was the handle? What the hell? He couldn't find it, couldn't see a damn thing. His hands felt high and low on the metal door until he found a ridge. He stuck his hand under it and found a lever—it took several pulls to release it. The brakes locked onto the rails, screeching like a cat with its tail caught.

It took all his strength, but finally Andy slid the heavy door open just enough. The wind and rain hit his face all at once and he steeled himself for the jump. The noise of the brakes was a deafening screech. Sparks flew past the door and the locomotive slowed just a bit. He took that chance and leapt into mid-air.

The ground met him with a rush. Andy hit hard, rolling over and over on gravel. The wind gusted his face, taking all his breath with it. He picked himself up and found that his knee was stiff and scraped, but otherwise he was fine. He had to be, and he had to get a move on. Unbelievably his hat was still in his hand. The enemy alien ran towards the bus station, ignoring the pain that wracked his knee. The rain was pelting, making him move even faster. The bus station was at the bottom of the hill and around the corner on Portland Street. A row of double-deckers was parked facing towards the street; he heard the rumble of their diesel engines. A few drivers were perched inside their cabs smoking Woodbines.

Because of the blackout, there were very few lights on in the bus station, and each one had a hazy halo around it. A lone constable wearing his hard pointed hat stood inside the entrance, swinging his baton. Andy could hear two drunken soldiers as they swore at each other from the back of the station. The constable had also heard the disturbance and moved towards the noise. Andy took that moment to run and board the bus that had "Irvine" posted up front. He put a shilling in the conductor's outstretched hand and hobbled up the stairs. His knee had swollen and boy did it ache, but as Andy slid onto the back seat of the draughty double-decker he felt only relief. He lifted a newspaper that lay on the seat and pretended to read, hands shaking so hard that the newsprint danced before his eyes.

The constable jumped onto the bus to do a quick check and thumped upstairs. "Evenin', folks, everybody safe and sound? Gey wet oot there."

Andy answered, "Aye," from behind the paper.

An old lady turned. "Aye, gey wet."

The officer did not tarry; he stomped back down, calling to the driver, "Everything is fine, off ye go."

If it was cold, Andy did not feel it. By the time the bus reached the Kilmarnock Cross, he had reached into his pocket for a fag, inhaling it as if it was the last smoke he would ever have.

The bus pulled over three times for passengers—once in Prestwick, once in Ayr, and once in Troon. There was a police constable at every stop; Andy was sure that each one of them was looking for him. Each one boarded the bus, stomped up the stairs, and bellowed, "Is everything fine?" Not one paid attention to the man behind the *Glasgow Daily Register*.

The wind blew the tall bus back and forth as if it would topple over. The wind blows cold on the Ayrshire coast. It has salt in its very breath. The bus drivers were well used to the conditions and, with screeching brakes, the big red double-decker pulled up to the pavement right outside the hospital gate. Irvine Central Hospital had been newly built and was not yet completed. The locals called it "The Home." It was the Maternity Home for all of Ayrshire.

With his hat pulled down to cover his face, Andy limped down from the top deck and stepped off the bus heading towards the main gate. His knee ached, so he hobbled towards the gate whose sole light streamed from a lamppost draped with a black cover; it almost obscured the security guard at the hospital entrance.

"Evening, Governor," the man said, sounding very English. "Here to see the wife, are we?"

"Aye," Andy replied, heart beating in his throat. He wondered if the guard would arrest him right there.

"Straight down the path for maternity," said the Limey. "Watch your step, mate. It is particularly slippery. Sorry about the leg. Injured in the war, were we?"

"Aye," Andy replied, limping in a much more pronounced way down a wide path. The wind tore at his coat, but fear made his body react with sweat. His knee felt better with the walk.

There were buildings all around, long low buildings, each one with its own black and white sign. Andy hurried along, forgetting to limp, anxious to see Kathy. Then, there it was—the sign said Maternity. A side door opened and a black umbrella unfurled. A woman's voice said, "Come quickly, Mr. Bertellotti. Come this way. Ye didnae disappoint me, ye daft man. Come on in oot o' the pourin' rain."

"Thank you, Annabel," answered Andy. "Thank you."

13

The Visitor

My Mary's asleep by thy murmuring stream,
Flow gently, sweet Afton, disturb not her dream.

Robert Burns, "Sweet Afton"

"How is she?"

"Shh." Annabel had a finger to her lips. "Dinna talk."

Andy followed the nurse along a service corridor whose lights blazed. He adjusted his eyes, water dripping from his overcoat. "What about all these puddles?"

The midwife whispered, "I'll come back wi' a mop."

"Is Kathy all right, Annabel? What about the baby?"

They'd passed four or five doors when the nurse stopped, hand on the doorknob. "Kathy is still groggy from the chloroform, Mr. Bertellotti; she lost a lot of blood during the C-section, but we gave her a transfusion and she seems fine now. The baby's a bonny wee girl."

Andy's weariness melted away when Annabel said the word *fine.* "Can I see them?" he asked.

Annabel put her hand on his arm. "Afore ye go in, Mr. Bertellotti. . . ." She came closer and whispered, "The doctor kens that ye and Kathy are Darmellington detainees. He was very co-operative because Kathy is a Scotswoman, but I don't ken what he'd say if he found ye here. Ye canny stay a' nicht." She opened the door into a room that was dim and quiet and smelled like powdered milk. "I managed tae get her a private room because she had that C-section."

Kathy lay sleeping, hair matted and wet, her face a white mask.

"What is a C-section?" he whispered.

"It's like this, Mr. Bertellotti. Yer wee wife was in real trouble."

"I knew it," he whispered, a lump stuck in his throat.

"The baby was breech and Kathy wasnae dilated. We took her for an x-ray where they measured her pelvis and we found that she wouldnae be able tae give birth naturally; besides which, it was ower late fur that baby girl. Dr. Disoldinoff had tae give yer wife a full anaesthetic. He opened her belly and lifted the baby oot. That's when she lost all the blood. Neither Kathy nor the baby would have survived if that guard had made her stay in Darmellington. Mind ye, she's fine now"

"Thank God, ye were with her," said a relieved Andy.

The midwife handed him a handkerchief. He rubbed his face.

"Is that ye, Andy?" Kathy whispered.

"Aye, love."

"Thank ye, God, for a daft man."

Annabel slipped out of the room.

"Are ye all right, hen? Did it hurt? Is the baby?" Andy wanted to grab her up in his arms but was afraid she might break.

"I'm all right, and the baby is fine."

He took her hand and kissed it. "Thank God, thank God."

Kathy stirred enough to pat the bed. "How on God's earth did ye get here?"

"It was nothing," he lied, then his legs buckled and he sat in the chair, laying his head on her arm to kiss the fine hairs. "Oh, Kathy, it was murder. First, I hid in the freight train from the munitions yard."

"What! What if they had spotted ye?"

"I wouldn't be here if they had."

"I don't suppose so. How'd ye get off the train?"

"I'll tell ye all about that another time. Can I see the baby? Are ye goin' to be all right?"

"How'd ye get here from Kilmarnock?" she repeated.

"I took the bus. That was more frightening than the train. The coppers were at every stop, but not a one asked for papers."

"Oh, they were talking about that in the operating room. There's been lots of vandalism on the busses, so the policemen are patrolling for young thugs."

"Not looking for enemy aliens?"

"No, my darling, but I am happy that you made it. Come close."

He kissed her then, a sweet, soft, daft kiss.

"I'm happy that ye are here, if only for a short while." She held him tight.

Annabel tapped lightly on the door, pushed it open and walked in with a wrapped package of a child. "Look who I brought tae meet her daddy."

Andy lifted his child from the midwife's arms, "She is beautiful, Kathy, just like her mummy."

The midwife slipped away, saying, "Remember, Kathy, we have tae hide yer husband afore Matron does her rounds at nine."

"Andy, lie down beside me," said Kathy. "Place her here between us."

~ ~ ~

Andy smiled down at his second child, swaddled in a pink blanket, her pale cheeks blowing soft baby breaths. The smell of the child filled the room as she lay between them. It was a single bed, much too small for three of them. The terrible journey flowed away into a prayer of thankfulness to a gracious God who had helped them to be together; the child was their miracle of war. Kathy and Andy had been caught in the midst of a turmoil that had come too close—Scotland on one side of the battle, Italy on the other. For just a few minutes in time Kathy and Andy shared the deep bond that occurs when families are torn from the foundation of life by circumstances they did not create.

"Do ye know what day it is today?" Kathy asked him.

"Should I?"

"Aye, it's January 6, the Epiphany."

"On Epiphany we'd have a parade in Italy when I was a boy," he answered.

"When our baby was born, ye took a long journey to see her, just like the Wisemen in the Bible."

"Except I'm no very wise, remember?" he replied.

"What shall we name her, Wiseman?" she asked, her eyes on the baby.

"How about we name her after Annabel? She's the one who has helped us."

"How about Anna?"

"Anna it is, and to keep my Mamma happy, how about Anna Fiorina?"

"Done," she said with a grin.

~ ~ ~

Annabel found the three asleep. "Wake up, Mr. Bertellotti, Matron is comin'."

"Annabel," he whispered, "we named our baby Anna, after ye."

"Lovely. Now come on, come quick, Matron is a tiger and will hand ye over to the polis." Annabel hustled him down the hall and into a broom cupboard. "Thank ye, Mr. Bertellotti. That was a beautiful thing tae do. I'll pray every day for wee Anna."

~ ~ ~

Matron did her rounds, fluffing Kathy's pillow, asking if she felt well and then, without waiting for a reply, marching briskly away. Andy could hear her keys jangle as she passed by the cupboard.

"Mr. Bertellotti," whispered Annabel, "come on oot." They hurried back to Kathy's room. "I believe I have a way to get ye back to Darmellington without being discovered."

Andy couldn't believe it. "Ye do? I hadn't come up with that yet."

"Aye," replied the midwife. "There's a woman in labour at a farm up the road from Darmellington. She's a big strappin' farmer's wife and this is her third wean. Her pains have just started, but they are hours apart. I should have plenty of time to get there, and, if I don't, she'll be fine. Farmers a' ken how tae deliver babies. Ma driver is a different man from yesterday and he doesnae ken that ye are an Italian interned at Darmellington."

Andy nodded, unable to believe his good luck. This woman had to be sent from Heaven as his family's guardian angel.

"He only kens that Kathy had a C-section and the two of ye hail from there. I telt him yer last name was Neil; I used Kathy's maiden name. I asked him tae give ye a ride back to the road-end afore the Darmellington Road. From there it's only about two miles. Ye'll be riding in the back of the ambulance."

"When are we leaving?"

"It's almost midnight, that gies ye one mair hour tae be together."

"I'll be ready," he replied. He kissed his baby once more. Anna whimpered. Andy hated to leave, but he had to. If he got caught he knew the consequences.

~ ~ ~

"Come on, Mr. Bertellotti," said the nurse. "It's almost one."

"Are ye sure the man won't turn me in?"

"He won't," she said with confidence.

Andy kissed his wife one more time.

"Be careful, love."

"I will."

As they walked out into the bluster, Andy told Annabel how grateful he was to her for helping. He added, "Please call me Andy."

"Ye're a brave soul, Andy, but tonight yer Mr. Neil. I'm proud tae be of help."

He climbed into the back of the brown lorry, feeling guilty to have put the kind nurse in harm's way. She had left him a couple of blankets to wrap up in. He hardly noticed the bumps and the chill as he sat in the back figuring out how to get back into the compound through the fence. It would be easier to get in than get out, he tried to convince himself. He could try to climb over it, but what about the barbed wire? Maybe he could crawl under? Aye, he could dig a trench, but with what? Time slipped away and then he heard Annabel yell, "Wake up, Mr. Neil. We're at yer road-end."

He climbed out and walked up front.

Annabel rolled down her window. "Are ye all right, Mr. Neil?"

"Aye, I am. Thank ye, Nurse Annabel, and thanks for the lift, driver."

"Off ye go, then," answered the man.

~   ~   ~

It was much longer than two miles up the road and the wind was cutting his face. The rain had stopped, but for how long? The chill bit through him but he trudged along, left knee sore again. He was glad of the stars as he made his way step by aching step towards Darmellington. A lone bomber droned overhead. Andy wondered where the plane was headed. His confidence failed as he neared the dark town. How could he get back into the tenement compound without being spotted? The benefit was that the streets were pitch-dark. The street lights were out because of the blackout. He wished he had brought a torch.

The factory loomed ahead, so he skirted it in case the home guards were on duty, but it was so cold, they were probably inside. Andy moved stealthily along a side street that ran behind the factory and led down through a field towards their enclosure.

When he reached the fence, it was higher than he remembered. He had never really looked closely at it; the fence was to keep them from getting out. Now he wanted in. He walked the perimeter, looking for anything that would help him. The ground was muddy, his shoes were soaked. He thought about what would happen if someone spotted him. He inched along and almost fell into a drainage ditch, landing on a large pipe that was located in the culvert. The noise was really loud and he felt panic rising to his throat. He knew the guard was only there in the daytime, but had anyone else heard him?

A figure moved stealthily across the yard. "Andy, Andy, it's me—Rudy."

Andy couldn't believe his ears or his luck. He stood tall, two hands flat against the fence, watching Rudy as he approached. "God, Rudy, I'm happy to see ye!"

"I knew ye'd be back. I've been waiting here a long time. Hurry up, I'm about to freeze to death."

"But how do I get over?"

"Ye don't. Ye come through."

"What?"

"Go down into the ditch and crawl into the pipe. It was closed on this side and I loosened the grate so ye could crawl through. Don't make any more noise, or we'll both be in Barlinnie afore another day goes by." Rudy turned on his torch to show his brother where the end of the pipe was. "I can't leave the light on, someone will see it. Just hurry up."

"I wish ye could hold my hat."

"Stick it in yer pocket." He whispered loudly.

The ditch was so muddy that Andy sank up to his knees in

order to climb inside the pipe—it was wider than he had thought so he slipped right through, getting wet mud everywhere. Rudy pushed the heavy grate back into place as Andy stood up, brushing the muck from his coat and trousers. He shoved his hat on his head. The two men shook with nervous laughter.

"God, Andy, yer a mess."

They made their way around the rubble that lay there.

"How come ye're limping?" Rudy asked.

Andy waited till they were safely inside the flat. "I hit my knee when I jumped off the train."

Rudy laughed nervously. "I can hardly wait to hear the whole story."

The brothers embraced. "Ye made it, Andy. Ye made it, hat and all. Maybe we could have been spies?"

Andy stripped off his coat. "Where's Aïda?"

"She's with Mrs. Scolatti. Ye didnae want me to bring her along, for yer journey through the pipe, did ye?"

Rudy poured Andy a thimble-full of whisky. "I was saving this for an occasion."

"Kathy is fine, Rudy. We named the baby Anna. She's a healthy wee thing."

~ ~ ~

At dawn they readied for work, and Andy limped next door to see Aïda. He decided not to talk about the baby in case she would say something to the guard. She gave her dad a big hug, saying, "Where did ye go last night, Daddy? Did ye see Mummy?"

"No, pet," he replied. "I worked overtime. Ye were asleep when I got home."

"Is Mummy all right?" she asked.

"I'm sure she is. We should get word today. I'll tell ye when I get home tonight."

"Okay, Daddy." She was satisfied with that answer.

Andy went past the guard as usual, not forgetting what an

eagle-eye old McMurphy was. "Are ye limpin', Bertellotti? Did ye get drunk because ye couldnae go see yer bonny wee wife at the hospital? Did ye fall doon and get a bump?"

"None of yer damned business, McMurphy."

"Well, I'm glad ye didnae dae anything daft, Bertellotti."

14

Homecoming

The parent-pair their secret homage pay
Robert Burns, "The Cotter's Saturday Night"

Internment was purgatory. Andy had tried to be a good husband to Kathy, but the war had robbed him of that privilege. The tenement to which the government had restricted them was so run-down that he feared for Aïda's health, and now a new baby was coming home to this. "Aïda, we have to make this wee house cleaner than it has ever been."

"Okay, Daddy." Aïda was only three and a half, but she was a bright toddler. She and her daddy began to work. Andy scrubbed the brown dingy linoleum until his fingers bled. The toddler coloured pictures for her baby sister. Rudy baited the rats with bread crumbs dipped in lard; he caught fifteen! Then Aïda drew a robin with a fat red tummy sitting on an apple tree on a large sheet of paper given to her by the lady at the greengrocers. Rudy and Andy peeled off the tattered, once-sculptured, brown wallpaper and found some whitewash at work to paint over it. A nice Italian neighbour, Mrs. Ferri, presented Andy with a cradle and a lovely old wooden rocker where she had held her baby daughter. Andy polished it with a bit of lard until it shone like Babbo's counter. He found a soft pink woolen blanket at the odds and ends shop to go inside the cradle. Aïda put her doll in there to keep it warm for baby Anna.

~ ~ ~

The three of them could hardly contain themselves whilst they waited for Kathy and the baby to arrive. Andy pinned Aïda's drawing next to the old metal fireplace with the chipped tiles and the black iron grate.

"Look, Daddy," said Aïda. "The robin's red breast is the same colour as the teapot."

It was a red and white flowered teapot that Kathy had rescued from the Ideal Café. The Italian women were allowed to grocery shop weekly. Each family was given a ration book and could buy a few items with the stamps. If they had nothing else in the larder, they always had tea stewing at the fire.

When the brown ambulance pulled up to the gate, there was a celebration. The Scolatti women, the Ferri women and the Brazoli women came out to cheer. It was a Sunday. Someone was banging pots and pans together, and the Italian women sang lullabies. The tenements were filled with women and small children who crowded out to see Kathy and the baby. For a minute they all forgot they were behind a fence.

Annabel stepped down onto the cobblestones holding the baby tight, and when she helped Kathy climb down the two steps there was a great cheer from the small crowd. Kathy was bonnier than on the first day Andy had met her; her lovely hair shone in curls and her smile was huge. She looked healthier than she had in months. Andy supposed it was the good food at the hospital. He held her fast to his chest, while Annabel knelt down to let Aïda see her wee sister.

"Mummy, I drew the baby a picture of a robin."

"She will love it," said Kathy. If it hadn't been for the guard standing watching, that day would have been like any other home-coming from the Maternity Hospital. Andy kissed her tenderly, remembering their evening in her room.

"I'm glad yer a daft man," she murmured, and when they

entered their flat, Kathy's first reaction was amazement. "Ye cleaned it up, Andy!"

"I did. Rudy helped."

"It's lovely," she said. "And, Aïda, this fantastic picture is just what this room needed."

"Uncle Rudy killed all the rats, Mummy."

"That's grand, Aïda. That's grand."

But there was nothing grand about internment. Kathy cried for her mother, for clean sheets and good food. She grew thin from nursing Anna, hoping her breast milk was nutritious. Days became months and months became years, and still they were interned. Her pleasure came from her fags and from watching her two wee girls growing and making each day a play day.

Peggy Kempster, Rudy's girlfriend, kept in touch. She wrote to tell both Andy and Rudy that their shops were open and that their customers came in regularly for fish and chips.

"We have less fish now—there are not so many fishermen, most of them have become sailors and gone overseas. Also the older men who have boats are volunteering to pick up sailors lost at sea. And did ye hear about the seven hundred Italians aboard the *Arandora Star*? They were being shipped to Canada and the ship was lost at sea. At least ye are safe. I hired an old man to fry chips in both Andy and Rudy's shops. It should bring a little money."

Andy read Peggy's letter and was grateful. Rudy read Peggy's letter and pined. "I think that Piero, my friend, was on board that ship." Andy watched as his brother sank into a deep depression.

"No one wants us, Andy. We belong nowhere. Not to Italia. Not to Scotland." Any money Rudy had was spent on cheap beer.

If it hadn't been for the two weans, Andy might also have given up. All the radio news was sad and hopeless. War raged all around Europe. Bombs fell in London; they called it the Blitz. Coventry was bombed so much that the whole city center disappeared. Andy and Rudy were convinced that Great Britain was losing the war. What would happen to resident Italians if that happened? The two men fretted about their parents and Tommy and Bruna. What was happening in Italy?

Every day sirens pealed and planes droned as they passed over Ayrshire on their way to Belgium or Italy. Bombs fell in farmers' fields, others in the outskirts of Kilmarnock. If the Jerries had known about the armament factories in Darmellington and Kilmarnock, they would have bombed them.

Andy tried to keep his girls contented by telling stories at night. The toddler and the six-year-old wore their pajamas, Aïda curled in front of the small coal fire and Anna still in her cradle. He would describe in detail, as he remembered, Tuscany: the fields and the beach. Kathy leaned back in her second-hand chair holding a Woodbine, smoke curling above her head. It was the best they could do.

Their internment lasted for the duration—five long years.

15

Peggy, Peggy

We twa hae run about the braes,
And pou'd the gowans fine

> Robert Burns, "Auld Lang Syne"

My sister's smile was forever four inches from my face.

Aïda, who spelled her name with two dots over the *i*, had curls that grew wild all over her head and eyes as dark as coal. She was named for an Egyptian princess and loved me as if I were her child. My big sister treated me like a baby doll, holding me when I was cold, wiping my tears when I cried. I can still breathe her in, even now when I am older and she is gone. She smelled like apples dipped in caramel—I love caramel. My first real memories are of Daddy's hands lifting me high, his wet kisses raining on my cheeks, and Mummy's cigarette smoke circling the dark room. The smell of her fags always made me feel like the war would be over soon.

By 1944 they had lived for four years in that small damp tenement room with the green faded carpet and the ugly brown linoleum. There was a double bed in one corner and, in the other, was an alcove with a built-in single bed belonging to Uncle Rudy. It had a curtain made of beige taffeta, and when the gas light was lit, Aïda and I could see right through it. Our uncle thought it was private, but we knew better. At night, Uncle Rudy would whisper in his sleep, "Peggy, Peggy, where are ye, Peggy?"

Aïda and I would laugh out loud. He'd turn over and snore, his whisky breath stinking up the room.

Mum and Dad had two wooden chairs that they pulled to the fire in the evening, replacing them at night with our camp cots. The stove was a tiny, green, two-burner with wobbly legs, and there was a wee sink where Mum bathed us standing up. I'd howl because it was freezing cold to stand there naked. We ate at a card table that was folded during the day. Mum said the rats watched us eat. They were waiting for crumbs.

The toilet was the worst—we called it the loo. It was outside in the entry, and it smelled like rotten eggs. Italian mums were good with the scrub-brush and took turns cleaning, but it still reeked. I had to hold my nose. We shared with four other families. Mummy would knock real loud to see if anyone was in it, or to chase the vermin away. She'd sit me on the cold seat and wipe my bum with newspaper. There was a long chain to flush the toilet—that was my job; Mummy would hold me up, so I could pull it. Sometimes it forgot how to flush and Mum would say "Damn" under her breath.

For coal we depended on Jock with his horse and cart to come down the street in front of the two-story tenement. In the yard were coal cellars with flat roofs. They sat empty because each mummy was only allowed two buckets of coal per week in the winter, one in the summer. The buckets were brought straight into the houses instead of being dumped in the coal bins.

There was something about the Italian tongue and the Scottish tongue mixed together that made the weans talk really broad Scots. The women huddled together in the entryway while the older ones ran out in the street to fetch the coal.

They'd yell, "Gie us some coal, mister."

Jock threw lots of bigger pieces, which Aïda loaded into the coal bucket. We weans picked up the black dusty droppings when Jock missed the bucket. Aïda toted the bucket into the flat wearing an apron that Mum had made out of a burlap sack, then went to fetch another. Mum held me back, saying, "Come here, Anna, one filthy lassie is enough to wash."

Aïda and I were both covered in black coal dust when she was done. Mum was good at scrubbing the dirt off with stinky soap in that tiny sink. Dad was good at the lighting of the fire. I was good at watching.

Jock's horse was called Dobby; the poor thing had a scraggly mane and a sway back. I liked the brasses that shone around the wee horse's neck, and when I was old enough, Mum let me pet him. Jock told us that Dobby had once been a racehorse, a steeplejack runner.

Daddy knew a lot about horses. "Jock's tellin' a story," he said. "Dobby could never have jumped a hedge. He's not built like a racehorse."

Mummy often held her head and shivered, even when it wasn't cold. She'd murmur, "This is like a prison sentence," then she'd put on her straight-lip smile and say, "Mummy needs a lie-down."

Aïda would ask, "Mummy, do ye have the headache?"

When Mummy nodded aye, Aïda would take me by the hand to go outside to play. The cobbled yard was littered with limestone boulders and there were old, broken factory trolleys sitting around. I'd throw a ball against them, singing, *"One, two, three a leerie, I saw Bobbie Cleary, sittin' on his bum ba leerie!"*

Mum traded some ration stamps for black welly boots and yellow slickers, which we wore when it was spitting rain—and it was always spitting rain. When I was old enough to climb, we children made forts out of the rubble of war. We made up games; one of them came about from Uncle Rudy always moaning about Peggy.

We called our game *Peggy, Peggy. Where's my Peggy?*

The wee neighbour kids ran and hid, yelling, "Over here, over here, Peggy."

Uncle Rudy often chased us with a stick. "Cheeky wee buggers," he'd yell, but he never used that stick—he never caught us.

Aïda had a special game called *Captive Lorry*. She'd bark orders at me in front of the coal cellar. "All ye enemy aliens, get on this lorry now. Load up yer stuff and move it out." She knew I was scared of the dark, but I saluted in the way small girls salute and ducked my head as I marched into the coal bin. Aïda always made me go way in, further in, out of the light, then she'd holler, "Sit on the floor and face the back, enemy alien."

The brick floor was filthy from the coal dust, so I'd sit with my legs close together and try to keep warm by making fists. Aïda'd stand outside, pretending to drive a lorry through a cold windy night from Kilmarnock to Darmellington. Again she'd shout, "Bloody Italian buggers, enemy aliens." Her hands turned an imaginary wheel steering the lorry. It was in that dim coal bin that I met my imaginary friend, Mary, who kept me company on the cold floor—each of us pretending to rock with the rhythm of the lorry's wheels—each of us hoping Aïda would not keep us in there too long.

When she announced, "We're here, internment camp. Get out and stay out, ye Italian lot. Good riddance to bad rubbish," Mary and I would march out together, holding hands, relieved that the captive lorry game was over for another day.

I was sad when Aïda started school. She'd been given a pass like Mummy and Daddy. I had other wee pals, besides invisible Mary, and the good thing was the Italian children knew how to play *Peggy, Peggy*.

The only time I was really afraid was when the sirens went off. I'd put my hands on my ears and run to Mummy. She'd wrap her arms around me.

"Where's Daddy?" I'd ask.

"At the munitions factory, pet."

"Will he be okay? Will he, will he? Is Aïda okay? Is she under her desk?"

"Anna, Daddy is only a few streets away, and Aïda is safe at school." Mum knew that the bombers were looking for factories to blow up, but she never said it out loud. I thought my dad was brave enough to go to work there every day in a place where the women hated him and called him names.

"Are ye sure my Daddy's fine, Mummy?"

"Of course he is," was Mum's answer. "God will keep him safe."

"Aïda too?" It was a prayer—I was too wee to understand that if the factory went up, so would we.

16

Nowhere Safe

May 1943

Giuseppe's small band of resistance fighters, furnished now with military equipment, had been in the basement of a bakery, two streets over from the Trevi fountain in Rome, for over two months—a long time to stay in one place. The *panetteria* was owned by an older Jewish/Italian couple, the Freemans, who were Partigiani. Italian soldiers came in often for breakfast rolls, and they warned the couple that Hitler was sending Italian Jews to concentration camps in Germany.

"Will you keep us safe?" Mr. Freeman would ask the soldiers. The young men answered yes without assurance, the Italians flirting eyes at his lovely wife.

As the year wore on, more and more of the occupying Germans began to frequent the bakery. The increasing military presence made the resistance fighters feel safer, not more nervous, because the Jerries obviously had no idea they were in the basement. Giuseppe became angrier and angrier because every day the German officers sneered at the Freemans in their guttural German, asking the lovely Italian wife why she had married a no-good Jew. "I wish we could get them to a safe house," he said to Tommy.

"It seems there is nowhere safe for a Jew," answered Tommy,

hidden behind piles of flour sacks and bakery boxes where the sweet smell of challah bread baking in the ovens upstairs filled his nostrils. He had stayed glued to the radio and heard reports of Jews being herded into trains bound for "camps" in Germany. "These camps must be flea-ridden," he said to Giuseppe.

"Oh I think they are much worse than that," was Giuseppe's answer.

Japan had bombed Pearl Harbor in December of 1941, so now the allied forces included the United States, New Zealand, and Australia. Tommy used his English language more and more, and on the brief shortwave broadcasts he heard many other foreign tongues.

On a dreary Tuesday, he intercepted an American broadcast which stated, in code of course, that American and British troops were defeating the Italian Royal Army in Africa. "Listen, fellows, some good news at last."

He was interrupted when Sophia, Giuseppe's new woman friend who was a crack shot and loyal soldier, ran down the steps into the basement.

"Helena has been captured." Sophia leaned over to catch her breath. "We were walking on the Strada when two SS officers strode towards us. They were armed and looked like they were going to attack us. I ran, hoping Helena would follow. I spun around to check. She had fallen. She drew her gun but the officers grabbed her before she could fire."

"Slow down, Sophia," said Giuseppe. "Did they shoot her?"

"I dodged into a back yard and hid behind a wall. I heard no shots."

"Did they follow you?"

"I would have killed the Nazi bastards if they had."

Giuseppe reached for her hand.

She sobbed, "What will the SS do to Helena?"

"They will torture her to get information," he said in a low güttural tone. "She's tough, but she will break. Pack up! Pack up everyone. *Dare alle flamma*—burn the papers we don't need." Giuseppe threw Tommy a handgun. "Take this, Irmo."

He looked at it. "I don't want this, Giuseppe. I'm a radioman—you know I don't. . . ."

Giuseppe grasped Tommy by the shoulders. "Just point and pull the trigger, like I trained you to. Don't let them catch you, Irmo. You'll be hung like a dog!"

One of the numerous Roman water tunnels lay directly under the shop. Giuseppe pulled the grate up and the band of renegades climbed through. They had to crouch to wade through. Tommy held the equipment up to keep it dry, following behind Giuseppe and Sophia. The tunnel was approximately fifty yards and exited on the other side of the street.

"We will enter this building," said Giuseppe. "I have a relative in the upstairs flat—we can hide there."

They hustled up the narrow marble staircase, and Giuseppe knocked on a sturdy pinewood door.

"*Avanti, avanti,*" whispered a small old woman from behind the slightly opened door.

"I'm sorry to put you in danger, *Zia,* but it's only for a short time."

"*Bene, bene,*" she answered. "How can I turn away the *figlio* of my sister?"

There were seven renegades seated around the darkened flat. Giuseppe and Sophia whispered to the old woman. Giuseppe did not introduce his men; it was better if she did not know their names. It was twilight when a large black van drove up and parked in front of the *panetteria.* A group of SS officers stormed out and battered down the front door; glass flew everywhere. In a very few minutes two uniformed men carried out the flour barrel in which Tommy had burned the papers. The *soldati* poured out the ashes. Irmo watched through field glasses, holding his breath in case some had not burned. "Thank God," he whispered in English when he saw the pile of ash.

The other Nazis dragged out a man and a woman—the Freemans.

"Oh, my God, I thought they left when we did," Irmo whispered to Giuseppe.

"I thought so, too," he replied. "They told me they would leave by another exit. *Mio Dio*, I wish they had."

The Nazis shouted obscenities at the couple and pushed them around, then an officer wrapped a cloth around Mr. Freeman's eyes; the other backed off and took aim. The first man stepped aside. A single shot rang out, echoing from the tenement buildings. Seconds later the bastard turned and, as Maria Freeman's shriek pierced the night air, he shot her between her wide open eyes. Both bodies slumped, Maria landing partially on her husband's body. They lay, heads touching, a bullet hole in each forehead.

"Fucking bastards," whispered Tommy.

Another huge officer grabbed a petroleum can from inside the lorry.

"No," Tommy hissed as if to stop him.

This one tossed the can inside the door of the shop; almost instantaneously the flames leapt. Irmo saw the pack of Germans laughing as they hoisted the two bodies from the ground and tossed them into the fire as if they were rubbish. Tommy watched, horrified, as one of them opened the door to the van and dragged out Helena's limp form. The Nazi draped her across his broad shoulders; she let out one terrified scream as he flung her into the inferno.

Giuseppe stifled Sophia's wail with a hand over her mouth and caught her as she fainted. Irmo vomited. The smell of the challah bread invaded the air along with the stink of burning flesh.

The Nazis did not get into their vehicle right away. Remorselessly, they marched up the Strada banging on doors, swearing obscenities as a fire engine clanged past. Fortunately for the resistance fighters, the Germans presumed that they had moved on. At the top of the street the SS officers jumped back in the van, which exited north towards the Fontana di Trevi.

~ ~ ~

Later that night, several of Giuseppe's best guerrilla fighters left the flat, Sophia among them. "I know where those bastards hang out," she said. "They will be drunk by now."

Tommy held his head, heartsick. War brought out the worst in everyone, including his friends.

Next morning, Giuseppe announced, "We didn't get them all, but it is amazing what a few rifles can accomplish in a bar full of drunken Nazis."

Tommy thought he would vomit again.

~ ~ ~

A few days later, it was arranged for a lorry to pick up the small band of men. It was an ordinary grocery truck with *Droghiere* advertised on each side. The *camionista*, the driver, drove them all the way south to the Strait of Messina where they took a ferry to Sicily. Since Tommy had a portable unit, he could listen to the short broadcasts even as he bounced around inside the truck trying to stay upright. The *camionista* drove at breakneck speed through sleeting rain, over dirt roads littered with rubble, through small towns whose streets were so narrow it seemed the sides of the lorry would scrape the buildings, and over bridges made of wood that looked like they were too weak to hold the lorry.

Over the crackles of the radio, Irmo heard an English voice announce, "The Axis powers, Germany and Italy, have capitulated at Tunis. Two hundred fifty thousand Italian and German troops were taken as prisoners of war."

"Looks like Italy has surrendered in Africa," he reported.

His companions cheered.

"Perhaps now the Allies will come to Italia and kick Mussolini's ass," said Giuseppe.

Irmo prayed that an Allied landing in Sicily would happen soon.

~   ~   ~

In Sicily the anti-fascist groups had become very organised and were beginning to use the term Resistenza. Giuseppe's small band of resistance fighters hid in yet another basement. This one was below a sewing shop owned by two old Sicilian ladies who reminded Tommy of his mamma. This basement smelled more like a café than a sewing shop because the ladies cooked pasta very often. Tommy felt homesick for his café in Scotland. He assumed it was boarded up but hoped that somehow his cousin Vida had kept it open. The thoughts seemed insignificant in the midst of all he had seen and listened to.

17

Sicily

July 1943

Tommy intercepted a coded message from Allied Command regarding the British-Canadian-American Armies. He told the men, "The Allies, the Yanks, the Mounties, and the Brits will invade this island in early July. They're calling it Operation Husky; sounds like General Patton is in charge. Giuseppe, Sophia, the Yanks are coming!"

Sophia leapt into Giuseppe's arms and kissed him full on the lips. Tommy smiled for the first time in a long while.

On 10 July 1943, the Allied invasion of Sicily began. Thousands of troops descended on shores all over the island, and for the first time there was air support. Tommy only heard snippets of news, but it seemed to him that the young pilots often missed their targets in the dark. One hundred and forty British gliders fell into the sea, and the inexperienced naval gunners shot down twenty-three American transports by mistake. Tommy realized that the invasion was not going as well as predicted on the radio broadcasts. For the following thirty-eight days Tommy had his ear pinned to a crackling radio that told of battles all over the island. Thirty-eight days of fierce hand-to-hand fighting on every beach, in every village, on every street. The Germans knew the island's mountains so they used their positions to slow down the American troops, and they were able to spirit thousands of Italian and German troops across the Strait of Messina to Italy's mainland. The Nazis were not giving up. Giuseppe's band of resistance fighters stole out each night to kill German soldiers as they slept.

Little by little the Allies took control and took Sicily. Thousands of Mussolini's Italian troops surrendered without a fight, and the villagers were delighted with the foreign liberators. Giuseppe told Tommy, "You know Italy is still a political mess. My people are still *diviso*."

Just two days later Tommy grabbed Giuseppe's arm. "You won't believe this—the Grand Council of Fascism has limited Mussolini's power and the King has had him thrown in prison. He is in jail in Roma."

Sophia and Giuseppe danced for joy. "*Urrà*! About time the king deposed the bastard."

Il Duce had indeed been arrested and placed in a Roman jail; Marshall Badoglio was appointed as Mussolini's successor. Badoglio had orders to get Italy out of the war, any way he could.

Italy capitulated on 3 September 1943. But that was not the end of it.

~   ~   ~

Thousands of German and pro-German Italian soldiers had evacuated to the mainland and were retreating north, joining with others and building fighting fronts along the Apennine mountains as they moved. "God, Giuseppe, we are in for a civil war," said Tommy.

On the evening of September 8, the leader of the German Nazi Army, General Jodl, announced Hitler's newest command words: *Operation Achse*. The German soldiers were to burn the earth as they retreated north—they not only torched everything they encountered, they also brutally raped and killed innocent Italians, old and young. The German forces retook Rome.

"My parents are in danger," said Tommy to Giuseppe.

Giuseppe replied, "There are orders from the Italian government for mandatory evacuations, Irmo; your parents may have to leave the sanctuary of their home."

Just when Tommy had thought peace was at hand, Italy had become a Theatre of War. Just when the Resistenza could come out of hiding, the war had come face to face. The worst news of all was that Mussolini had escaped from his jail in Roma.

"Can you believe it, Giuseppe? Mussolini escaped. The Nazis grabbed him in a raid and whisked him up north to Lake Como where you are from."

"There are lots of Mussolini sympathizers in the lake district, Irmo. The bastard will regroup. The good news is the Partigiani have multiplied in that area also. Resistance will be high."

The damned war had split Italy in half; it had split Tommy in half. What he was unaware of was that it had split his Scottish family in half also.

Most of Giuseppe's resistance fighters left Sicily to continue their efforts further north, but Giuseppe, Sophia, Tommy, and a few others remained in their humble headquarters. Sicily was a hub of activity; bombers, both American and British, flew overhead night and day, their missions to bomb Mussolini's hideouts and to fly if necessary all the way to Russia. Tommy had earphones on, translating Italian directions and co-ordinates to the Americans and the British—relaying information about German placement and their retreat patterns. By fall, the early rains had begun and often Tommy was asked to translate pages of information for the American Army. There had been great losses on all sides. The war in Italy had become a scatter with small isolated units facing mud and mountains and moving very slowly up the peninsula. Documents arrived daily telling of casualties in the hundreds of thousands.

In July of 1944, Giuseppe came to Tommy. "We need to

talk, *amico*. The Commander of the 92nd Division of the American Army wants to meet you."

"What?" Tommy replied. "Why?"

"Maybe he wants you to join his army," he laughed. "I don't know that, but. . . ." He shrugged his shoulders.

"I'm no soldier, you know that, Giuseppe."

"The hell you're not!" He sat back in his chair. "You've been talking to the *Americani* and helping the anti-fascist groups for years now, Irmo Bertellotti. You are the best damn soldier that I know; there is nothing like a *Soldato Resistenza*, even one who doesn't like to carry a rifle."

18

The Interpreter

The United States Army had secured a Sicilian *pensione* for their headquarters. Tommy was to meet with the general there. He had visited the lobby many times, but as he climbed the carpeted stairs to Administration his heart hammered in his chest. He barely glanced at the huge American flag that hung from the balcony. The twang of the American soldiers milling in the lobby sounded like a chorus. A young sergeant stood on the landing waiting for him. "This way, sir."

Tommy was ushered from one room to another, introduced to one officer after another, until finally he stood in front of Major General Edward Almond, Commander of the 92nd Infantry Division. Tommy, a.k.a. Irmo, had a thousand questions.

"So-o-o," said the general in a slow drawl. "Irmo Bertellotti. You're the interpreter I've heard about?" He sat at a large, very tidy desk, an unlit cigar twirled in his fingers.

"Aye, sir," he said, saluting like an Englishman—it was the only way he knew how to salute.

"At ease, soldier," he said. "I hear they call you the Scottish-Italian on the shortwave?"

"They do, sir." Tommy stood on rubber legs.

"You ran the shortwave for the Resistenza?"

"Aye, sir, I did." Suddenly Tommy felt taller.

"The war has not always gone our way in Italy, as you know.

But now we're here, and many Italians are fighting alongside us. It is imperative that we be able to communicate with them."

"Aye, sir."

"We have a new division arriving soon, the 92nd Infantry. It's a segregated division, and it'll disembark in Naples early August. I would like to assign you there."

Tommy's eyebrows shot up.

"Yes, I am inviting you to help the U.S. Army." The general smiled a long slow smile. "You know, son, I need someone I can trust, someone the new Italy can trust, someone who is a Partigiano. Communication is sorely needed in this theater. I need you to translate documents and transmissions. Can you be a translator for me and handle the radio?"

All he could say was "Aye, sir." Tommy was overcome with emotion, heat radiating from his face.

"Since you are an Italian citizen, I can't draft you into the army. You'll be a civilian liaison, but you'll be issued a uniform with the 92nd insignia. If you agree to join us, you'll be assigned to the military police in my command, in charge of translation. Oh, another thing. I need someone who can get along with segregated troops. Can you do that?"

"Aye, sir." He felt bewildered but proud.

"I see," he said, looking at Tommy's papers, "you were born in Italy, but live in Scotland. Is that why you were never in the Italian Royal Army?"

"Aye, sir. I couldn't go back to Scotland and I did not want to lift a gun against either country, so I went underground."

"I hear you have done a fine job in that capacity."

Tommy felt more important than he ever had.

"Then, Irmo Bertellotti, welcome to the United States Army. We'll get you trained and off to Naples soon. I'll order transportation to get you there."

"They call me Tommy in Scotland."

"Tommy Bertellotti it is. Good luck to you, Bertellotti."

General Almond shook Tommy's hand and sent him off with an aide who drove him to the supply depot for a uniform with the 92nd Division insignia.

As Tommy tried on the jacket, the aide asked him a question. "Major General tell you anything about our unit?"

"Aye, he did."

"He tell you that the infantrymen are Negroes?"

"So that's what he meant by a segregated division. Fine with me," Tommy answered, shrugging his shoulders. "I'm fine with that."

"I'll assign you a jeep and a driver. You'll have to haul a lot of equipment."

Tommy gave him a half-hearted salute. "Aye, sir."

"There's a wounded soldier who will probably be well enough to drive you to Naples. He'll do."

"Thanks."

The aide handed Tommy a large rifle. "Can you use this?"

"I try not to."

The aide left him to try on the jacket. It felt good to be called Tommy again. He examined the insignia. The division's shoulder patch was a black buffalo on a green background.

On his papers was the motto of the Buffalo Soldiers: *FIRME ET FIDELI*. Tommy had taken Latin in school in Scotland. The words meant: *To the brave and faithful man, nothing is difficult.*

Tommy had proved to himself that he was faithful, but brave? That was another story.

What had he got himself into?

19

A Buffalo Soldier

June 1944

Henry was the tallest man Tommy had ever seen; he was a good six foot five, with skin as black as soot. The man with the handsome ebony face loomed over him and saluted. Tommy, who was only five foot seven in his stocking feet and short-sighted, took his glasses off, wiped his eyes, craned his neck and copied Henry's American-style salute, then had to shrug his rifle back onto his shoulder. He found the man's large, uneven features a little unnerving. "So I really am going to have a driver. When I was in the Resistenza we piled together in the back of a lorry."

"Yes-sir," said Henry, saluting back again. His words ran together. "Private Henry Washington at yo' service, sir."

"You don't have to salute, Henry, I'm a civilian."

"Y'ain't dressed like no civilian, sir."

Tommy smiled at his good fortune, realizing that it would be an adventure just talking to this driver. "Well, Henry. I'm Irmo Bertellotti, an interpreter and radioman. Just call me Tommy."

"Yes-sir, Tommy-sir," said Henry, standing as still as a statue. When he smiled, his face became a friendly tooth-filled grin. "At yo' service, sir."

Tommy stuck his hand out to shake Henry's and noticed

Henry's light-skinned palms. When Henry's large hand engulfed his, Tommy grinned, noticing that both he and Henry had dimples. In Scotland, Tommy had never seen a man of colour except for the Indians who peddled their wares from suitcases. His first reaction had been tinged with fear, but almost immediately Tommy felt the real softness and caring that radiated from the tall black man.

"I loaded the equipment in back, sir. We be movin' out next week. I'm drivin' yuh to Naples where the 92nd infantry will be landin'."

"So they'll ferry the jeep over?"

"Aye, sir."

"How did ye end up in Sicily, Henry?"

"I was with another battalion that was pickin' up bodies; the government thinks that's what we Negroes does best. A shell went off and threw me sideways and I broke mah collarbone. The doc fixed me up, and now I'm a jeep-driver. We'll be meetin' the Buffalo Soldiers. Like you, sir, I was reassigned. We be goin' to a real Negro fightin' unit."

"I saw their motto. Why'd they take on the name Buffalo Soldiers?" Tommy asked.

"The first unit of Negroes fought in the eighteen-sixties in the old West 'gainst the injuns. They wore buffalo skins to keep warm and that's why they was named Buffalos. They was smart. Them old skins kep 'em warm and hid their asses at the same time."

Tommy laughed at his accent and lifted the awkward rifle to prop it up in the jeep. He looked from Henry to the rifle. "Well, I'm glad you've got a pistol in your belt; I've never shot a rifle."

"I cain teach you. I hunted rabbits back home."

"I know how it's supposed to work, but I'm not much of a gun man."

"Like I say, sir. Maybe I cain teach you. Mah shoulder is all well now."

Tommy's first thought had been that a wounded driver wouldn't be much use to him, but now he was relieved. "By the way, ye don't have to call me *sir* with every breath."

"Yes-sir." Henry turned to Tommy with his cap at a jaunty angle. "Welcome to the American Army, sir."

"Just Tommy, Henry."

"Yes-sir." He paused. "I ain't neva been ask to call a white man by his first name."

"Hell, Henry, we're at war."

"Yes-sir." Henry's grin showed those dimples on each side of his mouth. He drove Tommy a few streets over to a large old stone building.

"This is yo' barracks, sir. Mess is at seventeen hund'ed hours." He parked the vehicle.

"Seventeen hundred hours I understand, but mess?"

"That'd be supper at five o'clock in the Mess Hall."

"Are ye billeted here also?'

Henry, with his never-ending grin, replied, "No, sir. I is in the tents with the other Negro infantrymen. Pardon me fur askin', sir, but I knows yuh ain't Italian and y'are sure not from the States. Where are yuh from?"

"Scotland, Henry. I'm from Scotland, but yer wrong, I am Italian."

Henry saluted again, that brief amusing American salute that lifted the brim of his hat. "Neva met a Scotchman before, sir."

Tommy's private quarters were situated right off the hall. The door had his name on it and inside he found a cot, a bedside table, and a gas lamp. These were infinitely better quarters than he'd had for several years. He rested on the cot, thinking about his entrance into Army life. *Next stop: Naples. That'll be interesting.*

~   ~   ~

When Tommy walked into the mess hall at 1700 hours. Henry was sitting at a large table with three other Negro soldiers. He got up and came over to Tommy. "Best yuh set with the white officers, sir, they be in the next room."

Tommy picked up a tray, helped himself to a plate of hash, and walked into the second room. Sure enough, there was a group of fine-looking white officers sitting at a table set with a tablecloth. They stood as Tommy walked up. He gave them as best a salute as he knew how and sat down. They seemed like a decent lot, but it seemed odd to Tommy that they had distanced themselves so far from the coloured men. He supposed it was the American way. He was a part of the American Army now and decided his place was in the background simply observing their ways. The conversations around him didn't include him, but he listened and learned. After all, that's what he had done for four years.

A tall mustached man in a captain's uniform approached him. "Are you Bertellotti? The interpreter?"

"I am, sir." Tommy answered.

"You speak Italian?"

"I do."

"I need your help. My name's Captain Bentley and I'm an interrogator. I need you to translate for me."

"Yes, sir."

Bentley led Tommy out a back door and across a dusty courtyard that led to what must have been a stable. It was dark inside and smelled of mould and hay and something else. Tommy's eyes had to adjust. Bentley led him to an old worn stall where two black soldiers stood guard. The only light was from a lantern suspended from a wooden stand; the smell of sweat and urine filled his nostrils.

"Evenin', Captain," said a thin, wiry officer with a filthy cloth wrapped around his knuckles, stepping out from the wooden stall.

On the ground, on a pile of stinking hay, lay a prisoner curled in a ball, his mouth bloody and one eye closed. His wrists were bound, and he was mumbling in Italian.

"Translate what he's saying," said Captain Bentley. "He's ready to talk now."

Tommy's heart sank, his stomach lurching from the stink of urine and blood. "Is he a prisoner of war?"

"Find out from the scum if his unit has escaped from Sicily," ordered Bentley through gritted teeth. "He could be part of Mussolini's Socialist Republican Army. I need to know if there are other Nazi sympathizers here in Sicily."

Tommy's legs went to rubber and he took an instant dislike to Captain Bentley. "Sit him up, please, so I can see his face."

The prisoner was hysterical. The American soldier with the rag had beaten him pretty good.

Tommy's anger rose. "Get him some water. I need to get the blood out of his mouth."

The man who had done the beating looked around and found an old tin cup. He dipped it in the horse trough in the next stall and shoved it at Tommy, who held it out for the bound man to drink. The prisoner swallowed the stagnant water and choked. Tommy grabbed a handkerchief from his pocket and wiped the man's face.

The Italian POW began to talk slowly. He was from Northern Italy so his Italian dialect was unfamiliar and Tommy had to listen carefully to make out that the soldier's unit had left him behind when they fled from Sicily. The man's unit had opted to join up with Mussolini again so he fled from them, making him a deserter. He had hidden in an old horse barn behind the town.

He told Tommy that he supposed his battalion was heading for Naples to be picked up and sent to the North, but he was not sure. He said, "I'm only a private and a partigiano country boy who wants nothing more than to go home. Ask them to stop. I'm no traitor."

Tommy translated the man's tale to Captain Bentley. "I don't believe he is a spy," he added.

"Thanks," said Bentley in a very brief manner. "I'll call on you again."

"Shit!" Tommy almost spat it out loud. Was this what he had signed up for? In his book the interrogator was an animal. "Captain," Tommy asked, "why do ye not speak Italian?"

"I was trained to interrogate the German POWs, not the Italians."

"What will happen to this prisoner? Will he be treated fairly?"

"Yes. We will take him to the holding compound and there will be no more rough stuff, if he cooperates."

The two soldiers standing guard came in and helped the man stand. Tommy untied the rope that bound the soldier's wrists, and they staggered him out.

"Next time, can I talk to the prisoner before your man beats him?"

"Depends, but I'll try."

Somehow, Tommy didn't believe him.

Tommy fortunately had other responsibilities and training. He was given a shortwave and asked to translate Italian commands and dispatches. Command Center was most interested in what Mussolini was doing in the north where he had been made the leader of the Italian Social Republic, a German puppet state. Northern Italy was now under German control.

Tommy was busy from morning till night—it seemed everyone needed an interpreter. It required that he be transported from unit to unit, and during this time Tommy confided to Henry how much he hated taking part in the interrogations.

Henry would nod his great head and sympathize. "Y'are a good man, sir. Interrogations is jest part of the job, yuh jist got to accep' that."

~ ~ ~

On the night before they were to leave for Naples, Henry drove Tommy around the small island to see Sophia and Giuseppe, who had holed up in a small house overlooking a sandy cove. They had managed to take a few hours off to have some vino with Tommy and wonder what they were doing in the midst of this war.

"God, Henry, it seems like yesterday I was in my wee café in Scotland without a care in the world," said Tommy.

"My mam was a strict woman," Henry reminisced. "Made us kids read and write. Said Lincoln died to make our lives betta. She'd whip us if we not do our homework. Many po' black folks in the South cain't read nor write. I went to school, even got to play a little basketball afore I joined the Army."

Sophia told her story. "I grew up in Poland, where my mother was murdered by the Russians. It was hell there. I fled to Italy to find a better life. Now look at me, in hell again. The only woman friend I had in the resistance was Helena, and she's dead. The only good thing in my life is you, Giuseppe."

They had become lovers as well as confidants.

"Giuseppe," Tommy asked in Italian, "what's your background? How'd you get so involved with the Resistenza?"

"Oh, I was a farm boy," said Giuseppe. Tommy translated for Henry. "We lived in northern Italy by Lake Como. It is so beautiful there," the Resistance leader sighed. "Mountains and pure clear water. My father was idealistic, a royalist. I grew up loving my life. We weren't rich, but we weren't poor. I wasn't about to let Mussolini destroy the Italy that I loved. I hated Il Duce's fascist politics and therefore. . . ." He shrugged his shoulders. "Here I am."

These four people had been brought together by circumstance. The vino helped. "Goodbye, Giuseppe, and be safe." Tommy hoped that he would see his friends again someday. In the meantime he thanked God that he had Henry to talk to.

20

Naples

1944

"I sure am excited, sir," said Henry.

They were driving through countryside that was once verdant with fruit tree orchards and vineyards. Now it was littered with the damage that war brings with it.

Henry turned his head slightly towards Tommy. "When the 92nd disembarks in Naples, it will be the first time that Negroes will be sent into combat."

"What'd they do before, Henry?"

"Oh, we drove like I do now or picked up dead bodies, like I used to. They did hospital runs, like that, but combat, that was for the white man."

"Ye must be proud to be a member of the 92nd, then."

"I am."

They passed Salerno. For miles there was nothing but rubble with a few church spires—all that was left from the Allied bombing. The two men spent the night in a tent. But even the ruins in Salerno did not prepare the two men for what was Naples. It was as if a giant saw had mowed down building after building. Rats ran in the streets alongside barefoot children who begged for crumbs, pennies, anything the two young soldiers could give them. The docks had been cleared, but there were crowds of

Negro soldiers and many others from around the world waiting for the 92nd to arrive. Tommy noticed a few Japanese-American troops.

A jubilant crowd cheered as the black men of the 92nd disembarked on July 30th ready and willing to give their lives for a world free from the Nazis. Two young men headed towards Tommy and Henry. "Well, I'll be darned," said Henry, "if it ain't Patrick Moore, mah old friend from Arkansas."

When Patrick came closer, he recognized the tall man. "Hey, Henry! Ma ol' pal, Henry Washington!" The two men took a brief moment to shake hands and slap each other on the back.

"Friend?" asked Tommy.

"Schoolmate," replied Henry.

~   ~   ~

The German Army did not give up; they were fighting in retreat, their very lives at stake. The Nazis held and built front after front. Because the American and British forces were fighting in so many other countries, there were not enough Allied ground forces to conquer each front.

By July, the Gustav Line just north of Naples was held by Field Marshal Kesselring.

The Buffalo Soldiers were assigned to the IV Corps of the U.S. Fifth Army under the command of General Mark Clark, whose reputation was that he would take men of any nationality under his command and turn them into combat soldiers. The 92nd marched and convoyed across the many miles that lay between Naples and the Gustav Line. The infantrymen, rifles and packs on their backs, walked grimly on the sides of the unpaved streets. Tommy and Henry, along with the white oficers, followed in their jeeps. Tommy's radio buzzed like a saw the entire time.

The foot soldiers crossed rising water fields of mud and traversed hills where insurgents hid in the bushes. The terrain was steep because the Apennine Mountains ran all the way down the spine of Italy, and the rain had started early. It was only August, but it blustered like winter. Soon the roads ran with mud. Tommy's radio repeated and repeated as he relayed all the necessary messages to the Commander, who was also in charge of an Italian Royalist Division. These troops marched alongside the Allied troops—there were Italians on both sides of every skirmish.

"Sir," said Henry, "explain it to me. Italians are fighting Italians. What the hell?"

How could Tommy explain such a mess? "Henry, Italy is fighting a goddamn civil war."

~ ~ ~

At Castelnuovo di Garfagnana, the men of the 92nd met a counter-attack by the brutal Fascist 4th "Monte Rosa" Division, who were aided by German forces. These forces outnumbered and overpowered the infantrymen of the 92nd. The Buffalo Soldiers had not long been on Italian soil, and too many lay dead.

~ ~ ~

The Spring Offensive did not begin until April of 1945. It had been a long hard winter in the hills of the Apennines for the 92nd Division. The Allies were fighting in many other parts of the world, which meant that the troops in Italy were stretched thin. Tommy stayed glued to the radio, praying to hear that reinforcements would soon arrive. The infantrymen had such faith that General Eisenhower would come through for them. They needed tanks. They needed manpower. They needed help.

Meantime, the Axis troops had formed a fighting front that stretched from Genoa in the west to the Adriatic Sea in the east, stretching over impassable terrain. The Fascist Italian and Nazi forces gathered on the northern side of the front, and the Allied troops pushed forward from the south. The fighting front was called the Gothic Line, but the Allied soldiers called it the Forgotten Front.

The German and the Italian Republican armies had a huge advantage. A large cannon that the Yanks nicknamed the Railroad Gun held the crest of an upper hill they called Punta Blanca. Rocky terrain made Allied advances difficult. By this time there were troops of every nationality fighting in the Allied forces. However, that huge gun killed and wounded thousands of brave men on every strike.

Injured soldiers lay hurt and dying in the makeshift hospital in the sanctuary of a monastery. Tommy translated for the doctors and nurses who tended the wounded. Henry took dictation for the black men who wanted to write letters home. "I'm helpin' these boys. Most of these men, sir, cain't neither read nor write."

"Oh, Henry, you are a good man."

"I'm glad I had the mamma I had."

Tommy watched him kneel at the injured men's cots, copying down the sweet sing-song words of the South. Tommy wiped his glasses, feeling his throat constrict as he too felt their pain. He wrote messages home for the wounded Italian and English-speaking soldiers who lay alongside the black men in the jury-rigged infirmary.

After one particularly bad night of combat, Henry came across his friend Patrick lying on a litter. Shrapnel had lodged in Patrick's left eye and his head was bandaged.

"Hell, Patrick, what happened?" he asked. Henry knelt down to speak to his old friend, words hoarse, eyes brimming tears.

Patrick mumbled incoherently. When Henry got up, he turned to Tommy. "What the hell are we doin' here in this country, sir?"

"It makes no sense, Henry, not now and probably not ever."

"Mah friend is dying and we was jist getting reacquainted."

Tommy took the big man by the hand. "Come, Henry, let him rest."

~ ~ ~

Patrick was gone on their next round. Wound infections took the soldiers away so soon.

"If we wanna win this damn war, w'all need more artillery and more medicine, sir," said Henry, his tears running unabashedly down his face.

"That we do, brother," Tommy replied. "But with the Allies fighting all over the world, I don't know when that will happen."

Whenever Tommy translated messages on the radio, Henry stood on guard, rifle to the ready. Tommy was forever grateful to Henry for backing him up. The two men were apart only in the mess tent and at night.

21

Refugees

August 1944

"Mamma, Babbo, listen, *pronto*." Bruna had run all the way from school in the centre of the village to her home on Ospedale Street. She caught her breath. "We need to leave Pietrasanta now! The Nazis are coming. Teacher said they have orders to burn down our town."

Mamma shook her head in the Italian way. "No, Bruna, no, no, no. Babbo and I have done nothing to anger the Germans. They don't know about Irmo. They won't harm us."

"Babbo, please tell her. Mamma doesn't understand. Tell her the Germans are no longer Italia's allies. They are retreating. Masses of people are evacuating. They are coming from all over, Viareggio and beyond."

"Bruna," said Mamma. "They fight together, Italia and Germania."

"No more, Fiorina," said Babbo. "Italia surrendered. Capitulation, they called it. Italians very confused. Troops are fighting on both sides. Germania is very angry with the Italian people. Bruna is right. Now we must hide. I will run to town to find out more."

Within the hour Babbo was back. "*O, Dio mio*," he said. "All of Lucca is evacuating. There are refugees everywhere. There

are no groceries to be had. We must go. Quick, pack all our food
and blankets. I will get the wooden cart that I take to market
with our vegetables and fruit. We will load our provisions on it."

"Where will we go?" asked Mamma.

"We will go up the path behind the *casa*. Many are already
on the trail."

"O, no, Arturo, it is so steep."

There were scores of women and children and fragile men
who were too old to fight, milling around outside the gate. The
crowd pressed together heading in the direction of the olive
trees on the hill behind Babbo's property. Bruna began to cry,
feeling like a child even though she was fifteen. Her father came
up behind her; she turned to him and pressed herself against his
chest. "O, Babbo, I am *in preda al panico.* Can we not just stay at
home?"

"We must leave. We have no choice."

Mamma fussed in the kitchen, tears cascading like a waterfall. "*Dio mio,* what is to become of us?" She carried a box of peaches and pears to Babbo. "There are so many people on the trail. The stones will trip me. It's too far for me to walk. *Prego,* leave me here."

"What about Lena?" asked Bruna. "She needs help with her Mamma. We must help her."

"Fiorina," said Babbo, "you have to try. Try to walk up the path as far as Farnocchia. Bruna will fetch Lena and her mamma. I will care for them on the way. It is the least I can do for Giorgio, who helped Irmo."

"You are wonderful, Babbo."

"Come on, Fiorina," he said, patting Mamma on the back-side, "pack only food and blankets and some clothing." He was gentle with his encouragement. "No knick-knacks, Fiorina. Take only your jewelry and hide it, just in case. . . ."

"Babbo, just in case what?"

"Sh, Bruna, just in case Germans come into our house."

"O, Babbo. No, no, no. We can't let the Nazis in our home." This was more than Bruna could bear. "Strangers, Nazis, *a casa mia!*" Tears ran.

The trio moved towards the gate with Arturo pushing the cart full of supplies, carrying his *medico* bag. He hoped the large rubber wheels would handle the steep dirt path. The trio was surprised to find Lena and her mother Adela right outside the gate on the dusty, busy street.

Lena stood tall, her black eyes steady. Over her shoulder was a pillow case stuffed with supplies. "We came to town today to find out what was happening with my father. Mamma needs you."

"What happened?" asked Babbo.

"*Mio papa* was killed in a Nazi raid a few days ago." Once her control broke, Lena's mouth worked unceasingly; she bit her lip as she spoke.

Adela, Lena's mamma, stood motionless, her eyes blank, her face expressionless.

"That can't be, Babbo," cried Bruna. "That can't be."

"I have to be strong for her," Lena explained, putting an arm on Adela's shoulder.

Villagers pushed past them, paying no attention to a grieving widow and three sobbing females.

"*Evacuazione, pronto!*" The words of the day.

Adela stared ahead, blind to her surroundings.

Babbo touched the small woman's face, strapped his first-aid bag around his chest and picked up the handles of the wagon. "Let's go." He was all business. "I wish I had *mia pistola*. Bruna, help Adela. We must leave now. We will grieve later. Come on, Fiorina."

"*Pistola*, Babbo?" asked Bruna.

"I carried one when I was in the Army, but that was a long time ago."

Adela remained motionless. Lena tugged on her arm. "Mamma, come on," and to Bruna she said, "Mio Padre was killed fighting for the Resistenza."

Babbo said, "I am so sorry, Lena, but we must evacuate."

~ ~ ~

"One more step, Mamma. *Uno per favore.*" Bruna's voice echoed off the olive trees, her mother gave a ghost of a smile and took another step. Bruna helped her, trying to be brave, but indeed she was terrified that someone would jump out of the old trees and vines that bent over the trail. Adela walked on without aid; she had said not one word nor cried one tear. It seemed that the whole world was headed for Farnocchia and the villages beyond.

Lena and Bruna had played hide and seek on this very walkway, now they each had mothers who needed their help. "Come on, Mamma," said Bruna. "This will take forever at this pace."

"Be patient, Bruna," said Babbo. "Your mamma has a bad knee. This climb is treacherous for her."

"*Mio Dio*, what is to become of us?" wailed Mamma.

Bruna said, "Mamma, courage. Babbo, why are the Germans so angry with the Italian people?"

Her father answered softly "It is *complicate*, Bruna. Everywhere there are whispers. *Fascisti, Partigiani,* no one knows who is who. The Germans are angry because we capitulated. Hitler has ordered his troops to burn Italia."

"I don't understand, Babbo."

"You are too young."

"I am not too young to know how sad Adela is."

"Thank you, Bruna. I am heartbroken for me and my mamma." Lena stopped for a minute to lean on her friend. "*Mio padre* helped your brother and other Partigiani escape from the Carabinieri; now *mio papa è morto* at the hands of the Fascisti."

"I am so sorry, Lena."

"They hung him like a dog in a playground. The children found him."

"Oh, Lena, that is *terribile*." Bruna and Lena hugged each other. "Babbo, do you think that Irmo could be dead?"

"No, Bruna, I would know in my heart if he was. Bastards," he muttered. "Mussolini split our country in half. Italians fight each other now. So much hate. How could they do that to Giorgio?"

"Babbo, we need you."

"I know, Bruna. I am here. I take good care of all of you, but I hate the German Nazis. Don't worry, Bruna, Irmo is fine." He spat on the ground. "I should have a-stayed in Scotland." That last he said in English.

The two mammas, one in pain, the other with no feeling, stepped one after the other up the trail.

Bruna watched the veins in her father's hands rise to the

surface as he pushed the wooden cart loaded with two families' provisions. How she wished they were not running from Nazis. How she wished that Irmo was beside her. How she needed Armando and Guido with the Scots names Andy and Rudy. She prayed for them all. Where were they? Were they alive?

The refugees had come from all over Lucca. There were many with small children. They trudged past Arturo's small group, pushing their way up the mountain path. Bruna overheard men speak of the *Americani* who had landed in Sicily: good men who had come to save Italy. Bruna wished that there were *Americani* on this path; there were only confused people seeking safety. "Lena, has your Mamma talked at all?"

"No, Bruna, she has said nothing since we were told that Papa was murdered. I do not know what to do with her."

"I am so sorry, Lena."

After many long hours, they passed a ramshackle farmhouse with but one wall standing. Many refugees were camped there, worn out from their trek. Mamma wanted to stop, but Babbo pushed on. "Too many people there, they can be spotted from the sky."

The large wheels of the cart creaked over rocks and debris on the road. Bruna, who loved pretty dresses, did not worry about what she had on or whether she was pretty or not. She had only enough energy to put one foot in ahead of the other, holding Mamma's hand when she needed it.

Her thoughts were with Irmo. Giorgio had found a place for her brother in the Resistenza. In her mind's eye she imagined Lena's papa hanging dead on the children's swings. In Pietrasanta she had once seen a dead woman hanging from a lightpole. She knew that resistance fighters were killed when they were caught. Was her brother hanging somewhere? When Irmo disappeared into the darkness he had asked her to take care of Mamma and Babbo. She wanted to vomit. Over and over she wished she and her parents had stayed in Scotland where they would have been safe.

"*Cara mia*, Mamma. Can you not move faster?"

It seemed like a lifetime. It was several hours of uphill struggle, Mamma moaning all the way, Adela walking like a stone woman, Babbo pausing only to encourage them. He whispered soft words and cursed the rocks under the wheels of the wagon. Step by step they climbed until they reached the large hill that led to Farnocchia, Stazzema, and Valdicastello. The shadows were lengthening.

Babbo said, "We must find shelter."

Lena's mamma had disappeared into her face, and Fiorina was crippled from the climb, her knees swollen and red. They had passed many families hiding in bushes, some in tents. Finally Babbo announced, "Here is a place for *riposo*."

It was a pile of grey stones and what was left of an old fireplace. There was still a partial flagstone floor where soft moss grew in clumps. Oak leaves covered everything. It was as if God had placed a carpet on the ground just for them. Babbo took blankets from the well-worn wooden cart, shook them and gently laid them down. "*Riposare bene*," he said in his softest voice to Mamma and Adela. "We are not far from Farnocchia where I was born and where my *cugino* still lives."

The two exhausted ladies settled down. Babbo took off his tattered *medico* bag. It was an old brown sack with a faded red cross that he had used in World War I. Bruna watched him, remembering when her father cured her blisters with his ointments and made a sling for her brother Armando when he broke his left arm. It gave Bruna a moment of pleasure, recalling Armando and his wedding to Kathy. It seemed so long ago. She thought about baby Aïda and the way they used to play in the shop.

Babbo rubbed a cooling lotion on Mamma's knees and wrapped them. She wept with pleasure and pain. Next he took a small bottle of *grappa* from the sack and gave each woman a taste. They grimaced, pulling their scarves close around their heads.

Afterwards Mamma whispered, "*Grazie, mio amore.*"

Bruna thought she saw a wisp of colour in Adela's cheeks, but if it was there, it disappeared immediately behind her blank eyes. Bruna wished she knew what to say to her. "Babbo," she asked, "can we light a fire to warm Mamma's legs?"

"No, Bruna, I do not want to attract attention."

Olive trees surrounded their lair, along with scrub and wild bay. Fear lived in Bruna's chest, but she had to put it away as Babbo wrapped a blanket around her shoulders to keep her warm. "Don't be scared, Bruna," he said, sensing the young girl's trepidation. They ate cheese and bread with home-grown olives. It filled Bruna's stomach but did not take away her feeling of unease.

Babbo gave Lena and Bruna a taste of *grappa* before they laid their heads down on the mossy pillow. "Drink this; it will help you to sleep."

The brandy scalded Bruna's throat like hot licorice. "Perhaps we can make it to Farnocchia tomorrow to get more food," she said to Babbo.

"That would be good," he answered.

Maybe it was the *grappa*, but suddenly Bruna was ready for sleep. "Is Farnocchia far from here, Daddy?" Her Scottish word for Babbo came tumbling out.

Her daddy put his arm around her and held her tight. "The hamlet is just over the ridge, and my cousin will take us in for a few days. His house is small, but he is generous. I am sure of it, *mia* Bruna." In the Scots tongue he said, "Ye'll always-a be my wee lassie and ye must-a be brave." Bruna was comforted by her father's words. Her mamma was almost asleep. "Do you think I can make it to Farnocchia with these knees?" She spoke in Italian, of course. Mamma never tried to speak English; it was too difficult for her.

"Perhaps, Fiorina," replied Babbo. "It is not very far. We just have to climb this hill."

~ ~ ~

The early rain had come and gone. The breeze from the Mediterranean sifted through their simple dwelling place. Adela took a huge breath and sighed. It was the biggest sigh Bruna had ever heard.

Lena sobbed quietly for both her father and her mother, and said, "So this is what it's like to be a refugee."

22

Sant' Anna di Stazzema

12 August 1944

"Wake up, Bruna!" Babbo's voice broke through the haze of Bruna's dream.

"It's too early, Babbo. The sun is not up."

"Mamma has *la febbre*. I need you to go find some spring water."

They had awakened Lena with their whispers; she wiped her eyes and stretched her tall, lean body and said, "*Buongiorno*. I will go, Bruna. I saw a spring on the path as we passed by. I'll fetch the water."

Bruna curled up to get few more winks on the soft grass. Soon Lena was back, urging her, "Come on, Bruna, let's take a look around."

"Girls," said Babbo. "Mamma is too ill to move this morning. I would like you to go into Farnocchia and try to find my *cugino*, Piero Bertellotti. The people who live in the *villaggio* will know him. Ask him if he has a safe place for us to hide because these two mammas are exhausted. Come back when you talk to him, and don't go too far."

The teenagers ate the last bites of cheese and bread, and set off up the rise towards Farnocchia. The sun had not yet risen. Bruna had to hurry to keep up with Lena. Bruna was the shortest girl in class, Lena the tallest. They climbed in the early mist of dawn; it took two hours to crest the hill and then what a vista! The sun was an orange ball in the grey-blue sky. Sun-kissed rolling hills whose grass was tanned stretched for miles below them. In the distance were rows of vines hanging with grapes. There were a few houses and the dot of a church steeple not too far off in the distance. On any other morning it would have been a joy. For sad Lena and worried Bruna it simply said hurry into the village.

"That's the spire of Sant' Anna di Stazzema," Bruna said quietly as if in prayer. "Mamma has told me of the *padre* who leads the worship there."

"*Sì*," answered Lena. "*Mio papa* told me the *padre* is named Marcello and is loved by the people. Today is Sunday—perhaps there is an early morning mass."

To the right, and closer, was a stone wall that told them Farnocchia was not so far. They took a small winding path that led past two stone farmhouses, each with a scrawny milk cow grazing on the side. No one was stirring. They trudged on, anxious to find out if Babbo's cousin was home. Bruna was jumpy; she had never been that high in the hills, and she was terrified that Nazis might be hiding in some of the houses. Lena acted brave, so Bruna held hands with her to give herself more confidence. The cobbled street took them to the center of a seemingly deserted hamlet. A door opened in one of the stone buildings and an old lady dressed in black shouted, "*Rifugiati*, refugees, what do you seek?'

"Piero Bertellotti. Do you know where he lives?"

"Of course I do. He lives here, *a casa*. You know him?"

"He is my father's *cugino*."

"He has gone with the others to Sant' Anna di Stazzema. Today *molti, molti rifugiati* attend mass to pray for peace. They pray for the end of the war. They pray the German *soldati* go home.

Amen. The only people left here are old like me. You youngsters belong in the holy place also."

"Is it far?"

"Just walk down the hill. Go quickly, mass is soon."

"Bruna, we should ask your Babbo first," said Lena.

"It is so far to go back," Bruna answered. "Babbo will not mind. He sent us for his *cugino*. Let's go find him. Let's go listen to Padre Marcello; Mamma says he is the wisest of men."

"You heard your Babbo. He told us not to go far."

"But, Lena, we could pray for Mamma and Babbo."

"Me, too, I fear my mamma might die from her grief."

"Okay, then, Lena. Let's go to mass. Let's go find Piero and say our prayers."

~ ~ ~

Blackberries lined their path as they descended. They stopped every once in a while to eat some berries. Bruna told Lena that they were called brambles in Scotland. Just that mention made her homesick. "I miss *miei fratelli* so much, Lena. My brother Andy has a baby daughter named Aïda. She is growing up, and I no longer know what she looks like."

The bells pealed in the steeple below. "We must hurry if we want to get there in time for mass," said Lena. "It seems the only thing we girls can do is pray that the war will end."

Lena pushed Bruna forward and they began to run. It was still quite a long way. The trees were thicker now and the air was filled with the scent of bay. They stopped at an opening where they could see the courtyard. "Look, Lena, look at all the people."

They looked like ants at first, but as the girls grew close, they could see the expectant faces of the faithful. There was such a multitude they spilled out from the church into the courtyard, and still more were coming in the gate. There were ladies with black shawls over their heads and babies in their arms, boys and girls running and playing, old men and women huddled together for warmth, and of course the priest in his robes. He stood on a podium that raised him above the people. His arms were out-stretched in love.

"That's Padre Marcello, Lena. He must be delighted that so many are there for mass. Let's hurry; maybe we'll get there in time."

They hastened their pace, but in only a few moments stopped to catch a breath. It was then that the first shot rang out, then a second, then a barrage of noise.

"*Mio Dio!*" Bruna jumped, hands on ears. She saw the priest topple from his perch.

Lena pulled her behind a bush. Shots rang out in rapid fire—rat-a-tat-tat, rat-a-tat-tat, over and over and over again. Both girls craned to see. Padre Marcello lay on the ground, blood everywhere. Bodies toppled all around him. Their cries for help filled the air. Bruna and Lena watched in horror as the Nazi *soldati* trained their rifles on the mass of people. The sound of the machine guns was deafening. The SS shot over and over, walking through the crowd, killing everyone in their path, even the ba-bies who were scrambling towards their already dead mothers. The weapons of death took their toll.

"*Sono tutti morti,*" Bruna whispered through tight lips.

The wailing of the innocents hung in the air like prayers. The gunshots continued until the voices ceased. Most of the multitude was dead—the boys, the girls, the women in their shawls, the old men, and the babies, *o, mio Dio*, even the babies.

"*Correre!*" Lena ordered Bruna to run.

Bruna was paralyzed. The scene unfolding below her was unspeakable. The Nazis came with their bayonets drawn. O, *mio Dio*, the bayonets. She heard a few baby cries, some anguished prayers, some pleading words from dying men. The bayonets stabbed over and over and over until there was no further talk or scream. The stench of death filled the valley. Bruna fell to her knees and retched. Lena strong-armed her to her feet. "*Correre, Bruna. We must run. They may come after us.*"

The sickening smell continued as they ran from the slaughter. They had gone only a few yards when there was a crashing in the bushes. They stopped, hands on mouths, afraid of what it could be.

A young boy of around ten pushed his way through the thicket, seemingly unaware of the thorns. He bolted towards the girls.

Bruna held her hand up. "Stop, *aiutare!*"

The boy did not pause; he ran like a hare past them, blood leaking from his shirt. The girls chased him. Seconds later, a young girl of around their age burst out. "Did you see *mio fratello?*"

"Keep going," cried Lena. "He is ahead of you. He is bleeding." The boy had disappeared around a bend.

Bruna had tears running down her face. "*Così terribile.*"

"Come on, Bruna. We must go on, it is not safe here."

"Will the boy be—what is that stink?"

Another, more pronounced odor burned their lips and nostrils. A cloud of smoke suddenly appeared in the sky, obliterating the sun. "*Dio mio, Bruna. Sento odore di bruciato.* They are burning the bodies."

Suddenly, boom, boom, boom, one after another, one explosion followed another. Flames shot to the sky from below.

"*Mio Dio,*" said Lena. "First they murder and now they burn."

The two young women held each other tight, unable to move, unable to comprehend what they had witnessed, unable to even think. Minutes flew by. The brambles parted, and a man appeared. He was burning. His hair and beard blazed. The man collapsed at their feet, his face blistered and raw, his hair melted to his scalp. His eyes begged for mercy. As he collapsed at Bruna's feet, his face turned upwards toward God with his beard still smoldering. Bruna and Lena stood paralyzed with fear. The man raised his burned hand for help, skin dripping from his fingertips. With his last breath he said, "Padre, help me."

Bruna knelt by the man. "*Dio mio,*" she prayed, "save his soul and all the others too." Bruna made the sign of the cross on her chest. Later she would say of him, "I saw the shadow of death in his eyes as he died."

"Bruna, we must go *now,*" urged Lena. "The SS may come here."

They gasped for air and coughed with the smoke as they loped up the path, away from the stench of smoke and the picture of death.

They were almost to the top of the hill when they heard sobs and cries for help. The girl who had run past them was kneeling over a small body. "Help me, help me," she cried out. "*Mio fratello è ferito.*"

The boy was sprawled on the ground, arms splayed out, blood drenching his shirt.

"*Mio fratello è colpo,*" she sobbed, holding the boy's head in her lap. "I'm so afraid he will die."

"Were you in the courtyard?" asked Lena.

"How could those bastards do that? They murdered my papa. I can't lose my brother as well. *Aiuto mi.* Help my brother."

"Where was he, when they shot him?" Bruna asked her.

"We were outside the wall. Marco was in the oak tree."

"Lena, you are faster than me, run for Babbo. I will stay here."

It seemed like an hour, but it was only minutes until Babbo and Lena were back. Babbo had come looking for the two girls when the shooting began, and was almost upon them. His bag with the faded red cross hung over his shoulder. He caught his breath. "I heard the call for help. I thought it was you, Bruna, I thought it was you!" He touched his daughter on the head. "Lena says it's a young boy. Let me look at him."

"Babbo, help him," Bruna pleaded. "Don't let him die, Babbo. I saw a man die. Babbo, his beard was on fire, he spoke to me just a few words and then he died."

"*Dio mio*, what did he say?"

"He said, 'Padre, help me.'"

Babbo's breath stuck in his throat. He knelt beside his daughter and kissed her ever so gently on the cheek. "Shh, Bruna, I am so sorry. Now we must be quiet. The Nazis might hear us. *Gesù*, what happened at the church?" He lifted the boy's shirt and placed a pad over the bleeding. "Help me carry the boy away from here. We need to take him to our safe place where I can bandage him." He picked the boy up and cradled him in his arms. "Support his legs."

The boy's sister took hold of the young boy's legs; her teeth clamped tight over her bottom lip.

"That will help, young lady. Let's go."

Babbo was so strong that he was able to carry the boy all the way to where Mamma and Adela were waiting. Worry was written all over their faces. On the way, Lena and Bruna sobbed out what had taken place at Sant' Anna di Stazzema. Babbo sighed over and over, mumbling something about war and massacre. His mumblings were like prayers.

The boy's sister had not spoken for a long time. Adela came towards Lena and wrapped her arms around her as if she would never let go, but still Lena's mamma did not speak.

"I am all right, Mamma," said Lena.

Adela burst into tears for the first time since she had heard her own terrible news.

23

Marco

Babbo laid the injured boy on the mossy bank.

His sister cried, "Will my brother live?"

Mamma reached for Bruna and hugged her gently, murmuring, *"Mia bambina, mia bambina."* She had become a softer, more caring mamma than Bruna had ever known.

"Come here," Mamma addressed the boy's sister. *"Cara mia,* come here." She patted the moss by her knee.

The girl sat whilst Babbo unpacked bandages and iodine from his pack. Bruna paid close attention while he cut away the boy's shirt.

Mamma held tight to the girl's hand. "Go ahead, cry, little one."

"Mio Papa è morto." The girl could hardly get the words out.

"Was he in the courtyard?" asked Bruna, always with her eyes on Babbo.

"He was." The girl was inconsolable.

Bruna turned, took her mamma's hand and told her about the shootings at the church and the murder of all the innocents in the courtyard.

Mamma moaned, "And Padre Marcello?"

"Padre Marcello è morto, Mamma, he was the first to die."

Mamma cried, holding her daughter to her ample breast.

"What is your name, little one?" Adela spoke for the first

time since the news of her husband's death. Lena could not believe her ears.

"I am Maria, *mio fratello è* Marco."

"I think, little sad one, that your father is gone to his Father in Heaven like my Giorgio."

Lena reached for her mother; the two of them hung together and wept.

"What is to become of us?" asked the girl, Maria, tears rolling down her cheeks.

"Where is your mamma?" Somehow the child's sadness had shocked Adela out of her own despair.

"We live in Farnocchia," Maria answered. "My mamma is very ill. That is why *mio* Papa went to mass. He went to pray for her. I was supposed to watch Marco, but while I read, the bad boy slipped out to follow Papa down the hill. I ran to find him. I had just reached the wall of the *cappella* when. . . ."

"Don't cry, Maria. See, my husband is tending his wound," said Mamma.

Bruna was on her knees helping Babbo. She rolled the injured boy gently from side to side as Babbo wrapped his wound. A moan escaped from the boy's lips.

"See," Mamma Fiorina said to Maria. "Marco is waking up. He felt the *iodina* in his side. That is a good sign. Our blessed Mother Mary will not take two from you this day. She has so many others to care for."

Lena already knew what it was like to lose her papa. She was hugging her mamma as if she would break. Lena reached out a hand to Maria. Maria took it gratefully.

"So you followed your brother, Maria?" said Lena. "Tell us the rest, *per favore.*"

"I did. I ran down the hill and saw Marco hiding up in the tree. I saw Papa and many others go through the only gate into the courtyard. I stopped because I saw the SS pushing people, forcing them along. Then the German *soldati* aimed at the crowd and fired; *Dio mio,* what a noise, the shots, the killing, the gasps of pain. Marco fell like a stone from the tree, then got up and ran through the brush shrieking in pain. I chased him. I could not bear to see the suffering in the courtyard any more. I knew my Papa was *morto.*"

"Who is taking care of your mother?" asked Mamma Fiorina.

"The *dottore* who lives in the *villaggio.* Every evening he attends *mia mamma.* He will know what to do with Marco. Mamma will be so upset; she has the cancer."

"We will take Marco to the doctor as soon as morning breaks," said Babbo. "I have given him something to help him sleep."

Bruna was sure it was *grappa.*

Babbo added, "*Il dottore* will have taken care of your mamma."

They sat so quietly, huddled in their blankets to stay warm. They ate little; no one was hungry. It was dusk before they were aware that time had passed. Bruna was petrified that the Nazi bastards would come their way when they left the area. She and Lena had seen such horror, they could no longer speak about it.

The smell of burning corpses filled the atmosphere all through the night. Fires smoldered in the olive groves, but the wind was soft so they burned themselves out. Babbo asked each girl to keep watch. Bruna went first, then Babbo, then Lena. Not one German came by. Maria was curled up like a baby, one arm touching her brother, her sobs muffled and sad. Bruna listened to the distant keening that sounded like the howls of wolves. It seemed the mountain itself grieved.

Next morning Babbo said, "The Nazis must have taken the road south towards Sienna. Thank the Lord that they did not come north towards us."

They learned later that the SS had indeed gone towards Sienna, leaving death and destruction in every quarter.

~ ~ ~

Marco awoke in pain. His face was a cold sweat and his lips were dry and cracked.

"We have to get to Farnocchia, no matter what," said Babbo. "The boy looks like he has infection, he needs medicine." Babbo laid olive branches on top of the wagon to make it softer and longer; Bruna put blankets on top for cushioning.

"Bruna, you and Lena will have to help me push," said Babbo.

"I should help," said Maria. "I am Marco's *sorella*."

"*Bene,*" said Babbo. "Then, Bruna, you help Mamma and Adela."

It was a weary, tear-stained group that finally arrived in Farnocchia after hours of struggling up the steep road. Bruna's clothes, a white shirt over a brown skirt, were stained and filthy. The small party looked and felt like vagabonds. The two mothers were exhausted, their long skirts black with dirt.

~ ~ ~

Farnocchia was a walled mountain *villaggio* with limestone houses built together in somewhat of a circle. Villagers stood outside in the small square, armed and ready for Germans. What they saw was a band of weary refugees pushing a wobbly wagon. The small group of villagers walked forward, and when they saw who was on the wagon, they called out for Marco's mother, "*Mamma Mia*, it is Marco and his sister, Maria; they are alive."

A small woman pushed through the crowd. "*Bambini,*" she cried.

"Mamma," sobbed Maria. "Mamma, I am so sorry."

The two fell to their knees hugging and kissing. The round-faced doctor came from his home. "Bring the boy *a qui.*"

Babbo pushed the wagon across the cobblestones with help from two older men. They lifted the boy and carried him inside. Maria and her mamma followed them into the house, which was set up like a doctor's surgery. Bruna, Lena, and their mammas stayed outside with the villagers who gave them fresh water and food. One old lady took Bruna inside her house to wash in her sink. The water felt like it might wash away Bruna's soul.

A few hours later, the *dottore* came out and proclaimed, "The boy will live, thanks to the good care given him by Arturo."

Babbo was embarrassed when the people crowded around him, congratulating him and thanking him. He was very sad, however, to find out that his *cugino* Piero had been in the court-yard at the church. No one knew how many people had been there. Many of the dead were refugees from all over Tuscany who had crowded into the courtyard at Sant' Anna to pray for peace. The villagers knew that many of the murdered had been mothers with babies and small children. Bruna could feel the grief hang like thunder.

The doctor said that Marco had survived because the bullet had not gone into an organ; it had lodged in the muscle, but Babbo had saved the boy's life by cleaning and wrapping the wound. Babbo explained that he had been trained to care for wounds in the First War. Dottore Tognini removed the bullet and gave the boy some herbal medicine; together the two men had saved the child.

~   ~   ~

The last two days had pulled Bruna's heart out. Many in the village had lost family and friends. It was hard to console. Mamma, Babbo, and Bruna stayed with Delia, the wife of Piero Bertellotti who had died with the others; she was good to them, even though she wept every day for her husband. Lena and her mamma stayed with Maria and her mother. Caring for Marco and his mamma helped Adela to heal.

~   ~   ~

When the smoke stopped, the old men and women who were left in Farnocchia marched down the pathway to Sant' Anna. What a scene of horror! There were others from neighbouring villages and farmhouses helping with the sad task of burying the dead. When Babbo returned, he explained that there were so many bodies it was impossible to count. Mamma and Adela cried together for their lost souls.

"Did you find *mio padre?*" asked Maria.

Babbo said, "*Sì*, we buried him with the rest." Later Bruna overheard him tell Mamma that he had said that to put Maria's mind to rest, but the burning had made it impossible to identify anyone.

~   ~   ~

Farnocchia was the saddest place in the world to be, but as the weeks went by the four young people found that grief can turn into ambition. Marco was soon well and recovered his naturally happy disposition. Bruna watched as each day Marco tried to make his mamma smile; even the tragedy that was this war could not dampen his spirit, which in turn bonded the four young people togather. They became close friends sharing every secret wish.

Lena's Mamma, Adela, became a new woman. She put her grief aside to help the villagers who had lost loved ones. Bruna's mamma became the village cook; she could make meals from next to nothing, and she taught others to do the same. Babbo was the strongest man in the village. He cut wood for the approaching fall weather and helped Dottore Tognini with the sick.

Bruna, Lena, Maria, and Marco were not afraid to go out into the woods. They had witnessed a massacre; nothing would ever be as traumatic as that. Fighter planes flew overhead every day. The youngsters waved to them as they passed over. They believed the Yanks were getting the upper hand in their fight against the Germans. The war itself confused them, and they discussed it as they gathered brambles for pies. An idea began to form in Marco's head. "We are the only ones who know about this massacre," said Marco. "No one knows how many died or who they were—perhaps we could find out."

"How would we do that, Marco?"

"We could make a list."

"How?" asked his sister.

"We go from village to village, from refugee camp to refugee camp to find out."

"Let's ask the *dottore*," said Bruna, "and Babbo, they will help us."

"This is a very big task," said the doctor, scratching his ear. "I think that your mammas will not allow you to go so far from this village. Some of the people who grieve live in remote areas. What do you think, Arturo?"

"I think it is a brave and courageous idea, but Mamma will not approve. You must tell her that you go to gather herbs and berries," he said.

Bruna was delighted that her father would keep their secret.

"I am so proud of you all," he said to the group. "Just be home each day before dusk."

Dottore Tognini gave Marco a large heavily-bound journal to record the names of the massacred. Marco alphabetized the pages and began by writing in his own father's name, Leo Shampa, in a beautiful script with large swirls. He had a line for his name, and date of birth. The next name to be memorialized was Babbo's *cugino*, Piero Bertellotti. So it was that the four young people began to visit many families in the area. The teens were no longer children afraid of the bushes; they searched those bushes for refugee families who were grieving for loved ones. The refugees hid in barns and tents, and it was there they visited them.

Marco recorded the names while Lena, Maria, and Bruna spent time with the women and children. They came back each day with food for the villagers.

Mamma asked, "Where do you go to get this food?"

Bruna answered, "When we walk we meet refugees and sometimes we find a farm house. The people are so happy to see our smiles that they give us treats to bring back to our families."

"You should return the compliment," Mamma decided, so

she made small cakes filled with berries to share with the refugees. Perhaps she suspected that the teens were sharing more than smiles.

~ ~ ~

News filtered up to Farnocchia from the main towns as more and more refugees climbed into the hills of Capriglia. Always Bruna could hear the sound of distant gunfire. She and Lena were informed that most of the fighting was occurring on a fighting front just south of Genoa—it was nicknamed the Gothic Line. Mussolini had formed another Fascist Army in Northern Italia. Babbo shook his head. "I was so afraid of this. Our country is fighting within itself."

~ ~ ~

In Capriglia, a very small *villaggio* far up in the Pietrasanta hills, the four young people met a woman who had actually escaped from the courtyard at Sant' Anna.

"I was there for prayer," she said. "O, *sì*, children, I was there. I hid under a trap door in the ground when the shooting began."

"How did you escape?" asked Bruna.

I stayed under the ground with my infant child until the SS left. It was hell." She said no more; her burned hands with no fingers told the rest.

"So, the *soldati* were SS," said Marco.

"*Sì*," she said. "Himmler's SS. They informed us that we were going to a prisoner-of-war camp after mass. We were herded in through the only gate, the only escape. We believed them. I saw the trap door and immediately lifted it and saw there was room for me and my daughter. We hid in the dark; the gun-fire started. We could hear the screams."

"Is your daughter still alive?" asked Marco.

"No. We did all right until they threw the petrol. We had to leave because there was no air. We ran, but the flames killed her." She looked down at her hands." I am alone now. But please put her name in your book."

The woman's pain burned in Bruna's gut.

"Do you know how the Germans found Sant' Anna?" asked Lena.

"The story is that a *fascista* brigade, an Italian brigade, escorted them there, but it is simply a story."

Marco wrote the child's name in his book with his tears staining the page.

~ ~ ~

The refugees called the four youths the *peace-collectors;* in Italian *i collezionisti di pace*. Bruna had found understanding in her heart, even though the images of the massacre and the man with his beard alight stayed with her. At night, into her pillow, she prayed that her brothers were safe, promising God that next day they would find two more families who had lost loved ones.

24

The Forgotten Front

American Command assigned the Buffalo Soldiers to the IV Corps of the Fifth Army in two areas of operation, the Serchio Valley and the coastal sector along the Ligurian Sea. The troops faced mountainous terrain and tremendous resistance from the German Fourteenth Army and the 90th Panzergrenadier Division which had many Italian-Fascist soldiers; there were many man-made defensive works that had been built by the Germans using Italian laborers and Slovaks. There were bunkers, tank emplacements, tunnels, and anti-tank ditches. The Germans had reinforced castles and had carefully designed mine fields as they retreated up the Italian peninsula.

Tommy anguished that his country was now in a state of full civil war. He knew that his friends in the Resistenza were still at work, staging guerrilla war on Nazi strongholds. It was now 1944 and the numbers of Partigiani had multiplied, but so many—millions—had died for Mussolini's misguided policies.

Tommy struggled to keep up with the orders and instructions that kept on coming. The Buffalo Soldiers had been split into two units, one moving inland to the Apennines and the other moving towards the coast. Tommy and Henry advanced with the coastal unit moving towards Lucca. The infantrymen shot and killed resisting enemy fighters along the roads as they waited for the Fifth Army to move up. The main attack on the Gothic Line did not begin until September 10th. Three days later both units of Buffalo Soldiers, along with a tank division, stood at the base of the northern Apennines ready to advance.

The inland unit had entered the Serchio Valley, moving slowly forward towards Massa. The weather was beastly and the unit could not be reached by motor; pack mules carried their supplies just like Hannibal's, two thousand years before. It was a long winter in the Serchio area with the 92nd moving slowly forward, fighting the enemy and evacuating civilians. The men were hit hard, but despite many attacks by the enemy they continued on, even on Christmas Day, pushing past grueling terrain and enemy gunfire. It took until March to hold the town of Lama.

Tommy' shortwave radio blasted news of victory after victory in France and Africa, but there was little to celebrate in Italy. Tommy guessed that the tank divisions and heavy artillery weapons were engaged elsewhere. Finally, on March 28, there was word from overseas that more tank divisions would be sent to Italy. The men celebrated, but it took until April of 1945 for Allied Command to organise the huge variety of forces to fight as one—the language barrier was immense when dealing with troops from all over the world. Tommy was only one of many interpreters trying to relay orders and news. The units were jokingly called the Rainbow Brigades.

Tommy and Henry followed the 92nd unit when they crossed the rising river Po and marched along the Ligurian Coast towards Turin. It was one constant battle. The 92nd lost numerous soldiers. Tommy was sick with the news and spent a lot of time in the jeep with his equipment turned high to hear the movement of the other divisions. Henry helped the medics bandage wounds and tend the dying. The two men felt that the fighting would never end.

~ ~ ~

It was a brutal spring. The weather and the Nazi guns continued to kill the men of the 92nd. Many of the white officers were replaced as they died or were injured. The infantrymen were often confused as to who was in charge. Tommy could hardly sleep at night, worrying about pleasing the officers, and always in the back of his mind was the safety of his parents and sister. The battle raged on with the huge coastal gun, nicknamed the *railroad gun,* battering Massa and Forte dei Marmi.

As they drove close to Massa, Henry cried, "Watch out!" He swerved, but the jeep dumped into a crater that was big enough to swallow a tank. The two men hung precariously on the edge until one of the tanks came up behind, threw them a tow, and pulled the vehicle out. Fierce rain battered their heads, but Henry and Tommy broke grins when they regained solid ground.

"Amen, Henry, we made it!"

The Germans were determined to hold La Spezia, so the black troops were totally relieved when the tanks of the 4th Army arrived. The tank division travelled along the edge of the Mediterranean, riding in the water because the beaches were treacherous minefields. Henry and Tommy could watch from their higher vantage point. The tanks landed north of the Cinquale Canal and began their advance. The continuous noise of battle roared incredibly loud. Infantrymen of various nationalities climbed foot by foot as the tanks rolled forward; even the ground below their feet was treacherous. Tommy's radio popped and shrieked; it was as if he could hear blow after blow until the tanks eventually took out the railroad gun. Polish, Russian, Spanish, and Italian voices bellowed in unison. "By God, they did it. They took it out," gasped Tommy.

~ ~ ~

Meantime, in the Serchio Valley, the black soldiers had pushed forward after a savage fight at Castelnuovo and were able to hold off the Germans as they retreated. Of the twelve thousand Buffalo Soldiers who saw battle, three thousand had died.

~   ~   ~

By the end of April, the Axis forces retreated in defeat. Finally the battle was over. Hitler and Mussolini were defeated in Italy! Tommy and Henry danced in the street with the others.

~   ~   ~

On the 27th of April, Tommy and Henry drove behind the infantrymen as they entered the port of La Spezia. For the Buffalo Soldiers, this was the end of the fighting, the resolution of the battle. For Tommy it was bitter-sweet to be in his home town for the end of the damned conflict.

Old men, women, and children poured out of their houses to greet the soldiers. They didn't care what colour the Americans were; their cheering filled the sky and the people wept for joy. The line of tanks and trucks became a spontaneous parade—the celebration lasted all day, and the soft evening air was pungent with the glad sobs of women and the screeches of children who ran freely for the first time in years.

Henry picked Tommy off his feet and swung him around.

"Don't ever do that again, you big galoot!" Tommy slapped his shoulders.

"Yes-sir." The tall man stepped back, saluting.

"Henry, this is where I was born."

"I know that, sir."

"Henry, I couldn't have survived this without you."

"Glad to be of service, sir!"

Tommy laughed and saluted him back. "If we can get some leave, will you take me to Pietrasanta?"

"Why, Tommy, of course I will."

25

Reunited

Division office had been temporarily set up in a vacant *pensione* off the main square in La Spezia. Tommy had orders to see Lieutenant Wilson; he opened the door to the lieutenant's office cautiously.

Wilson's big voice boomed, "Where have you been, radioman? The general's aide has been looking for you. Get over there ASAP."

"Do you know what for, Lieutenant?"

The man, whose forehead was as big as his voice, drawled in his Yankee tone, "The general doesn't need a reason, soldier."

"There are pricks in every man's army," Tommy muttered to himself as he climbed into the jeep.

At Headquarters, a very young-looking Captain Anderson sat squarely at his desk talking on a field telephone; he put a hand on the receiver. "Bertellotti, right? Interpreter?"

"Aye, sir."

The captain pointed to a seat and when he hung up, he said, in a much gentler tone, "General Wood wants to speak with you." He motioned Tommy to follow him. They walked down a hall that displayed portraits of assorted Italian government officials, including one of Mussolini that had been drawn on. They entered a high-ceilinged room where several captains sat around a table. Tommy swallowed, wondering what in the hell General Wood could want with him.

The general smiled, giving a quick wave of his hand that was half salute, half welcome. "Sit, young man. You must be the interpreter they call the Italian-Scot."

Tommy saluted nervously and sat in the only empty seat. His mouth was dry.

"Well, Bertellotti, I'll make this short," said the general. His voice was calm. He sat ramrod straight, uniform starched and clean as if he'd never been to war; the man was known to be a brilliant strategist who was fair to his men. Tommy held his breath. Andrew Wood tapped the ashes off a fat cigar. "My officers and I have been discussing the Liberation speech. We have decided—" There was a pause. "That is, we realized that it needed to be translated for the Italian people. After all, they are the ones who are free from the tyranny of the Germans and Mussolini. You may not know this yet, Bertellotti, but Mussolini is dead. He and his mistress, Claretta Petacci, were executed on 29th April by the council of Partigiani in the village of Giulino di Mezzagra. They took his body to Milan where they strung him up upside down in the Piazzale Loreto."

Tommy could not believe his ears. "Barbaric!"

"Perhaps, but necessary. This meeting is not about that."

Tommy saw faint smiles around the table.

"So, even though you are a civilian, I would like you to translate my speech."

"Me, sir?"

"Yes."

"Aye, *sir*," Tommy said, a grin appearing. "What an honour!"

"I know you will do well. We will get it prepared; you will receive all the details from Captain Anderson. We will make the speech together on May 3rd at 1300 hours. That's all, interpreter."

"Thank you, sir, and thanks for your confidence in me."

"Thank you for all your good work, Tommy Bertellotti. It has not gone unnoticed by those in charge. Dismissed."

~　~　~

Tommy followed the captain back to his office, where Anderson briefed him. "I'll know more day after tomorrow when the general has the speech finalized."

"I am honored, Captain. I do have a request, though."

"Go on."

"My family lives close by, in Pietrasanta. If you don't need me till day after next, may I have a twenty-four-hour leave?"

The young captain's face softened. "God, I wish my folks were close by. You can certainly have leave, interpreter man. Be back in my office by 1100 hours April 30th and be safe."

~　~　~

When Tommy saw Bruna in Pietrasanta's crowded square, he waved so much he almost fell out of the jeep. She wore a pink dress and waved a white handkerchief at the row of army vehicles. Tommy believed she was the prettiest wee lass he had ever seen. She had not spotted him. He was riding in an American jeep, wearing an American uniform, with Henry at his side; why would she look for him?

Pietrasanta's main avenue swarmed with cheering troops of multiple nationalities and citizens from all over Lucca. The noise was ear-splitting. The news about Mussolini was out. Many men carried banners saying *Mussolini é Morto.* Liberation had not yet been announced, but everyone could feel it coming.

Tommy removed his hat and waved it at Bruna; she waved back as one would to any Yankee soldier passing by, then her hand went over her mouth and her big brown eyes filled with recognition. She jumped up and down, screeching, "Tommy, Tommy, it's yerself, it's really ye!" Her Scots words just rolled off her tongue.

"Pull over, Henry!" Tommy jumped from the vehicle. Bruna ran full tilt towards him, almost bowling him over.

"I don't believe it." She jumped up and down, her breath coming in gasps. "*Mio bello fratello*! Ye're alive."

Tommy wrapped his arms around her to keep her still. "*Sì*, Bruna, it's me. I'm here."

She clung to him while a mass of people jostled by, pushing them sideways. The brother and sister held each other tight as if they were the only people on earth. From somewhere, Bruna's voice returned. She took two steps back, looked Tommy up and down, and asked in Italian, "What are you doing in an American uniform?"

"It's a long story." He pulled her close again. "*Mia sorella*, ye've grown up." He ruffled her hair the way he did when she was little.

She grabbed his hands. "Och, Tommy, dinna do that."

He laughed at her Scottish accent. "Okay, lassie. Are Mamma and Babbo well?"

"*Sì, sì*, Tommy, but life has been difficult." She threw her arms around his neck and became still; sad deep tears welled in her eyes. "Come, come to the house! Are ye a Yank now?"

"Not quite, but I'm here now, *cara mia*, I'm here now."

"Oh, Tommy, you will never know how glad I feel. Come on, right now. Come home." She dragged him along the crowded pavement.

"Wait," he said. "We'll go in the jeep." Henry had stepped out of the vehicle and was smiling ear to ear, surrounded by admiring girls. "That handsome guy over there is my driver. Hey, Henry, this is my wee sister, Bruna."

"*Buongiorno*, Henry," Bruna shouted over the noise of the crowd. "My goodness, but yer a tall man." Bruna, at four foot nine, came only to Henry's waist.

"Henry, take us home, and that's an order."

"What? You want me to leave these lovely women? Okay, Tommy." The tall man's dark eyes flashed with pleasure.

Bruna jumped into the back of the jeep with exclamations and questions, giving Henry directions to her parents' house on Ospedale Street.

"I never met a black man, Tommy," Bruna whispered.

"You will like him," Tommy whispered back. "He's my best friend."

~ ~ ~

Babbo's property was not as Tommy had last seen it. Black swastikas were haphazardly painted all over the garden wall that faced Ospedale Street. The gate dangled on one hinge. As they walked up the path towards the house, Tommy noticed that Babbo's prize grapes hung on broken trellises. The fountain's top had tipped over, the baby boy with the arrow cracked. There were no goldfish in the bowl of the fountain. Another swastika was painted on the front door.

"My God, did the Nazis live here?"

"*Sì*, Irmo," she answered, slipping into Tommy's Italian name. "They moved into our house when we evacuated. We were told it was their headquarters."

Tommy felt deflated, guilty. He had left his family alone, unprotected, his parents who were more than middle-aged and his baby sister Bruna. How could he have done that?

"Is Babbo . . . ?"

"They are both fine; see, here comes Mamma."

His mamma was limping. She looked worn. She moved down the steps very slowly. "*Irmo, Irmo, mio figlio. Venire, venire.*"

They embraced, tears running free.

Arturo had not aged. His back was as straight as a rod. He seemed younger, stronger, and more agile. Tommy felt relieved.

"*Mio figlio,*" Babbo said over and over as he patted the back of his youngest son, kissing him on both cheeks, weeping openly.

Henry had stepped back and was looking at the jeep outside the gate.

"No, Henry," said Tommy. "Stay here with us."

"Il benvenuto, benvenuto," Mamma encouraged.

"Mamma says you are welcome in her house, Henry." Tommy put his hand out to him and together they climbed the seven steps up to the veranda.

"I neva been in a white man's house, Tommy."

"You heard my mamma, Henry. This is Italia, and you are my friend. All my friends are welcome in Mamma's house."

Henry swallowed with pride when Babbo poured him a glass of Chianti and Mamma put a plate of her *pasta asciutta* in front of him.

"Tommy, this is fine," Henry repeated over and over. "Are y'all sure?"

"We're sure," answered Tommy with a grin.

Mamma smiled and said, *"Mangia, mangia."*

"Tell you mamma that her spaghetti and meat balls is as delicious as my mamma's mashed taters."

Tommy's mother, of course, did not understand a word he said, but she laughed anyway.

Babbo patted both men on the back. *"Eroe, eroe,"* he repeated, proud and admiring.

Tommy looked around, hating that the SS had chosen his parents' home for their headquarters. The bastards had scraped maps, pictures, and swastikas all over the walls.

"I try-a clean the walls," Babbo said in English for Henry's sake. "My fingers they bleed."

"Did they steal your dining room chairs, Mamma?" asked Tommy.

"They burned them, the bastards." Her speech was of course in Italian. "They took photos and paintings and threw away our clothes. Such a mess."

"Did they take your oil painting from the living room?"

"*Sì*," she said with a sob.

"Germans steal for the *lire*," explained Babbo in English so as not to upset Mamma any more.

"This is a disgrace; I will ask the guys if they will help you to get this place back as it was. What do you think, Henry?"

"They'd be happy to, Tommy."

"Henry, what is guys?" asked Bruna, smiling at his twang.

"Oh, Bruna," Tommy laughed. "It's an American word for men."

"Are all the guys in your unit *senza latte* like you, Henry?"

"Yes, ma'am," he said to Bruna. "The troops are Negro, the officers are white." Henry was very matter-of-fact about the situation. "It will be our pleasure to help you, ma'am—" he bowed towards Mamma—"and git your home back together."

Tommy translated, but Mamma had already understood Henry's well-intententioned words. "*Grazie, Irmo, raccontare tuo amico, grazie.*"

"Mamma, tell me about the evacuation."

"*Ah, Irmo, ho perso il mio la fiducia nella provvidenza.*"

Tommy translated for Henry. "Mamma said her faith was tested."

In Italian, he said to his mother, "Mamma, you have more faith than the mountain."

"*Innocenti perirono al chiesa terribile,*" she answered, her hand on his.

"What innocents? What church?" Tommy looked at Bruna, who sat as still as stone.

"Not now, *mio Irmo*. Not now."

"What church, Bruna? Please tell me."

"Tommy," she said in her soft Scots lilt. "There is no time to tell of such sadness this day."

Henry leaned forward across the round kitchen table. "We have all seen and felt so much sadness, little lady. One day y'all kin talk it over—some day when it don't hurt so much."

"Thanks, Henry," Bruna said, reaching out to touch his huge hand; her tears fell on it. He smiled that huge grin of his.

Tommy looked at Bruna's small white hand encased in Henry's large black one and thanked God for both of these people at his mother's table.

"We Italians owe you *Americani* so much, Henry," said Babbo.

"Y'all have already paid me back by askin' me in to break bread in yore house." He stood up. "By the look on all of yore faces, we Yanks is not the only ones who put up a good fight."

"Thank God ye did," Bruna said in a whisper.

Tommy realized how much Bruna had matured during his five-year absence. "How long did you live in the hills?"

"Three months, one week, three days, and two hours," Bruna answered with a grin.

Tommy gulped, "And when you came home, the house?"

"It was a mess," answered Babbo, who again spoke in English for Henry. "At first I-a stormed around and Mamma, she cried. Bruna went wild, running from room to room out of control. I had to calm her down. It was a complete mess, and my hatred for Germany and fascism boiled over, but we were alive, *mio figlio,* alive. So many people die in a massacre at Sant' Anna and many old people perish in the hills from the cold. We were lucky. *Mio cugino* from Stazzema, Piero Bertellotti, was killed in the square by the SS *bastardi. La mia casa,* my house, she just-a needed paint." He ran out of steam and collapsed in his chair.

Henry sat with his head in his hands, taking it all in.

Tommy knew Henry was thinking about his friend Patrick. In his mind Tommy saw all the faces of the injured men in the hospital cots who knew they were going to die. They were buried on foreign soil. There was so much sadness in the air around this little family, and each had a story that might never be told.

"I will help you, Babbo, after the Liberazione Ceremonial."

Henry stood up then as if on cue. "Thanks for dinner,

ma'am," he said. "Tommy here needs to share something important with y'all."

Tommy stopped him. "You're staying here with us tonight."

"Thanks for the invite, Tommy, but I suspect there might be dancin' in the streets tonight. I'll be back tomorrow to get yuh." With that, Henry tipped his hat and slipped out the door.

Tommy turned to his father, his face breaking into a huge smile. "Babbo, *il Liberazione* will be on May second, day after tomorrow." Now he was speaking in Italian so Mamma could understand everything.

"*Bene, bene,*" she said.

"General Andrew Wood has asked me to interpret his speech for the people of Italy."

"*Tuo!*" Babbo's face was flaming red. He put his arms around his son. They stood up. And after kissing Tommy on both cheeks, he said, "*Mio figlio,* I am so proud."

The years and years of separation and pain left.

Bruna could not contain herself. "Can I tell my friends? Can I tell Lena?"

"*Sì,* tell them to listen on the wireless. The speech will be given in Genoa."

"Perhaps Henry could take me there to listen, Tommy."

"I think that would be against regulation, Bruna."

The Bertellottis did not sleep that night. There were years of catching up to do. They were relieved that Mussolini was dead. Mamma held her rosary beads and prayed as Bruna and Babbo told Tommy that Giorgio, Lena's papa, had been killed for being in the Resistenza. Bruna told Tommy the horrible details of the massacre at Sant' Anna, but went on to talk about Marco whom Babbo had saved. Tommy listened and in return told Bruna of the actions of the brave Buffalo Soldiers and the courage and skill of the Resistenza fighting men and women.

2 May 1945: Tommy as he translated for Brigadier General Andrew Wood. He was very proud. What a privilege it was. Could that be Henry on the third chair?

26

Visitor Sunday

The youngster's artless heart o'erflows wi' joy
Robert Burns, "The Cotter's Saturday Night"

Something happened to change the Bertellotti luck—Mum called it Visitor Sunday.

Daddy said, "Girls, Mussolini is in jail now; the war has changed, Italy capitulated."

"Hooray!"

"America has sent lots of soldiers to Italy to help Mamma and Babbo."

"Hooray!"

"Imagine this," said Mummy. "We're going to have visitors on the first Sunday of the month."

"Hip, hip, hooray! Then can we go home?"

The tenement buzzed. On the first Sunday, grouchy Jimmy McMurphy, the guard, announced that any internee who had a visitor could walk to the Presbyterian Church Hall up the street, so off we went with me skipping.

The Protestant minister stood at the door of the big hall, wearing a black suit and a round white collar. Daddy murmured as we stood in the queue, "Watch this, girls, ministers never miss a chance to sway a Catholic to be a Presbyterian."

"Catholic or Protestant?" the Minister asked.

"Pick me up, Daddy," I said, anxious to hear.

"Catholic," answered Daddy, reaching down to get me.

"Protestant," said my Mum.

"Well, well, well," said the man in the white collar. "That's a predicament. Why are ye in internment, lass? Ye sound very Scots."

"I'm married to this man."

"Is that so? I suppose ye were married in the Catholic Church? That probably didn't help yer predicament." He didn't seem to care if he was hurting Mummy's feelings.

"No, sir," answered Mummy, hanging onto Aïda. "We were married in the Registry Office."

"Well, now," the pastor said. "So ye didnae convert, missus? Maybe yer family could start coming here, to this church? Ye could come with her, mister. 'Twould get all of ye out of that damp tenement for a bit."

"Ye know, sir," said Daddy, "right now, in this life, in this place, I've not much time for God."

"Perhaps, as I said, if ye started coming tae church on a Sunday?" The minister in the white collar puffed up like a balloon, his face red as beetroot.

"I've no time for God on a Sunday, sir, because He has no time for me through the week," Daddy answered.

"Oh, lad," said the minister, "God aye has time for ye, sometimes ye just don't ken."

As we walked into the hall, Mummy patted Dad's arm. "They never miss a chance for a conversion."

Inside the hall, tables were set up with tea and—joy of joys—biscuits for the kids. There was a great black board shaped like a church steeple that had all the times for the church services and passes for those who wanted to attend.

Mummy said, "See, I'm right."

That Sunday our Aunt Jean came to visit, and Peggy came to

see Uncle Rudy. Mummy had been so excited that she'd pressed our worn dresses twice with the big iron heated at the coal fire. "Anna," she said, combing my fly-away hair, "I've not seen my sister since afore ye were born."

They hugged as if they'd never let go. Aunt Jean looked so much like Mummy that I just stared and stared, especially when their tears came running.

"Do ye remember Jim, yer cousin?" Aunt Jean asked Aïda.

"I think I was too wee to remember him," she answered. "Is he my age?"

"Aye," said Aunt Jean. "And ye have another cousin called Violet. She's the same age as Anna."

"Oh, boy," I said, dancing around. "A cousin, a cousin, I have two cousins. Can they come next time?"

"No, pets. Ye'll have to wait till ye come back home to Kilmarnock."

"That's a long time to wait for a cousin."

"Ye never know, girls. The war might be over soon. The Yanks are helping us now."

Aunt Jean turned to Mummy. "Kathy, remember when we thought our only problems were that we were marrying Catholics?"

Mummy looked sad. "Aye, Jean, life is difficult in internment, but I hope yer right. Perhaps the war will be over soon. Then we can go back home to Gilmour Street."

"Aye, soon," sighed Aunt Jean.

The ladies lit their Woodbines. Mum said it was the only fags she could afford.

~   ~   ~

Daddy and Uncle Rudy sat at another table with Peggy. I curtsied over to gaze at her red lips and fancy cardigan. Mum was pretty, but I couldn't take my eyes from Peggy with her rosy rouged cheeks and her silk stockings with seams up the back.

Her shoes were red. I had never seen red shoes. Uncle Rudy was kissing Peggy's ear and rubbing her arms and hands. Her brown cardigan with the Fair Isle border was moving up and down, up and down, and the pink bow in her hair bobbed each time Uncle Rudy rubbed her arms.

"Can I have that bow, Peggy?"

"Don't be cheeky, Anna," said Uncle Rudy.

"Of course ye can," said Peggy and pinned it on top of my head. "I wish I'd brought two." She was looking at Aïda, who was looking down at the floor.

"Here's a penny for ye, lass."

Aïda smiled and took the large brown coin.

"Ye know, girls," said Dad, "Peggy worked for Uncle Rudy in the Ritz—that's where they fell in love. On the night the soldiers took us away, Peggy promised that she'd take care of both of our shops. She loves yer Uncle Rudy, but she is taking care of all of us."

"How come Peggy didn't get interned, Daddy?" asked Aïda.

"She and Uncle Rudy are just friends—that's why, nosey-parker."

"But. . . ."

Dad put his finger on his lips.

"The shops are doing so-so," said Peggy, her red hair tossing. "Sometimes the fishmongers canny get whiting because the boats are being used for the war effort, but I always have tatties for chips, thanks tae the tattie-howkers."

"What are tattie-howkers?" asked Aïda.

Peggy laughed. "Men and women that howk the spuds from the ground and bring them tae market. They are hard-working country folks."

Uncle Rudy was kissing her neck, listening to her tinkling voice. "Where did ye get the pretty silk stockings, Peg?"

"Oh, a Yank gave them tae me."

"Yanks, in Kilmarnock?" Uncle Rudy sat bolt upright.

"Aye, Rudy. There are Yanks in yer shop. They're keeping yer business going."

"Imagine that? Yanks. Do they look at ye?" He had a funny look on his face as he stared at her buttons. "Yanks in my shop, looking at my woman, and I'm here, stuck here."

Aïda started laughing, so I did too.

"Don't be so jealous, Rudy," said Peggy, handing Daddy and Uncle Rudy extra rationing stamps. "I need yer bank books for the deposits. Do ye trust me tae take care of them?"

Dad said, "If we can trust ye with our businesses, Peggy, we can trust ye with our bank books."

Uncle Rudy had scooted his chair up close to her. I watched him stroke her hair as I twirled the bow on my head. "Of course, my darling, but promise me that ye'll stay away from the Yankee boys."

"I promise. I love ye, Rudy. Don't be jealous. I'm a good girl."

"How are ye managing both shops, Peggy?" asked Daddy.

"I have help—mostly women. I take Tuesday and Wednesday off."

"What do ye do on yer day off?" asked Uncle Rudy.

"Yer an awfu' man, Rudy." Peggy gave him a big smile and reached for my hand. "I play with my children."

"Yer a wonder woman, Peggy," said Dad, shaking her right hand. "Rudy, don't be foolish."

Uncle Rudy pulled Peggy away to a corner so they could snuggle in private. We watched them kissing.

"Aïda, let's play *Peggy, Peggy* when we get back."

On another Sunday, a wet one this time, Granny Brice and Aunt Violet came to visit. They had sewn dresses for Aïda and me out of brown velveteen material that was left over from drapes that Granny had made for the windows of a rich merchant. My

Grandmother had soft old cheeks and wild fly-away grey hair that often escaped from her hairnet. Aunt Violet was tall, with fingernails that were painted pale pink. I had never seen anything like her nails; they were an inch longer than Peggy's. Aunt Violet was sixteen, and I wanted to be like her when I grew up. Aïda and I danced around like Cinderella in our soft-brown dresses. It felt so good to meet both a granny and an auntie. This turned out to be Mum's best day during internment; it cheered her so much that she had no headaches for a fortnight.

27

Storytelling

His clean hearth-stane, his thrifty wifie's smile,
The lisping infant, prattling on his knee,
Does a' his weary kiaugh and care beguile,
And makes him quite forget his labour and his toil.
              Robert Burns, "The Cotter's Saturday Night"

Our daily life included Mum reciting Rabbie Burns's poems to us by heart. She knew "To a Mouse" and some verses of "The Cotter's Saturday Night." She also read from an old copy of *Grimm's Fairy Tales*. Aïda and I loved Hansel and Gretel. Aïda would chase me around the room, and I'd jump over my stool and hide in Uncle Rudy's bed. Aïda was the wicked witch who wanted to put me in the oven. She'd pretend to stuff me into the fire-place. When I was home alone and Aïda was in school, I played the same game with Mary, my invisible friend. In the afternoons, Mum tried to make a pound of potatoes feed all of us and fretted that she had no meat. The one pleasure Mum had was visiting with Mrs. Scolatti. They sat outside on a big stone smoking their Woodbines; Mum always seemed to have just one or two fags stashed away. The two ladies would chat, and sometimes they even giggled. By evening, she would have the headache again.

What I liked best was our Saturday evenings when we'd be

warmed by the extra lump of coal on the fire. Dad sipped on his Scotch whisky, bought with the extra stamps from Peggy, and told us about his childhood in Liguria. "Where should I begin?" he asked us, night after night, as if he was telling us a fairy tale. "Once upon a time, there were three wee boys who lived with their Nonno and Nonna in a teeny-weeny house in La Spezia. Their daddy, Babbo, was off fighting for Italy in the Great War. Nonno and Nonna were their mamma's parents. Their house was white with green shutters and had red geraniums that blossomed in window boxes. The sun always shone and the sky was bright blue."

We'd clap. We'd heard these words often and we never tired of them.

"I was Nonna's favourite; she taught me how to play the mandolin and she would sing along with me."

"Tell us about the beach, Daddy," asked Aïda.

"Well, pet, the beach was littered with blue glass. It was my job to find the best, bluest, and prettiest glass for Nonno, who had built a wall around his house."

"Was he afraid, Daddy?" I asked. "Did he need a wall to keep bad people out?"

"No, pet. Nonno was a sculptor. His wall was only about your height and was made of white clay. I would stick my pieces of glass into the soft clay as he worked. Nonno Peri called it mosaic. It was a masterpiece."

"So there was no barbed wire?"

"No barbed wire, my pets. Only love was poured into this wall. People came from all over the town to see it."

"Tell us the name of the town, Daddy."

"La Spezia. Yer Uncle Tommy was born there, but his name was Irmo then."

I rolled his name around on my tongue like a sweetie.

Daddy went on, "The three boys had a mamma who was a soft woman, very round and very proud. Her name was Fiorina, which means little flower."

"That's my middle name, Daddy."

"Aye, Anna, it is, and you are a wee flower. Nonno Peri was an old brown man, wrinkled from the sun, handsome nonetheless. Nonna was round like my mamma was, maybe rounder. Nonna's blue eyes were lined; the lines looked like the rays of the sun. Nonna loved to sing, she played her mandolin like an angel and she made scrumptious cakes for her three *nipoti*—us."

"What were the *nipoti* called, Daddy?" Aïda always asked the same question.

"Armando, Guido, and Irmo," Dad always replied.

"Those are the wrong names, Daddy. Ye know yer brothers are Rudy and Tommy, and yer name is Andy, can't ye ever remember that?"

"Of course I can, Anna, but remember the three boys lived in Italy then. Our real names were Armando, Guido, and Irmo. It was not till we moved to Scotland that those names were changed."

"Why, Daddy?" Aïda asked, even though she already knew the answer.

"The school teachers and the other children couldn't pronounce Italian names, so they gave us nicknames. Uncle Rudy was named after Rudolph Valentino because he was a flirt. Tommy and me, well, those were easy names for Scots boys to say."

"Time for bed," Mummy would say.

"One more story, Mummy."

"Okay, girls," said Daddy. "One more. When the boys lived in Liguria by the sea, they loved playing outdoors because the sun shone brightly, making their world bright and luscious. The wind blew softly from the. . . ." Dad stopped there. Our hands were already up in the air. We shouted, "Mediterranean!" I was proud to know such a big word at four years old.

"The Mediterranean Sea shone like a diamond, her waves breaking gently onto the beach with its pearly white sand, full of shells and blue glass."

"That's all for tonight, girls," Mum interrupted.

We gave Daddy a big hug, happy because, for just a little while, he had taken us away from Darmellington and its greyness to Italy and all the colours of the rainbow. As Aïda and I brushed our teeth, the adults murmured quietly, voices droning like a melody, but their talk had a serious note; Dad and Uncle Rudy were worried about the family in Italy.

"Does the sun still shine there, Daddy?"

"Yes, Aïda," he answered. "We just don't know what's going on. That's what makes us worry."

"How old is Bruna now?" asked Aïda.

"She'll be around fifteen," answered Mum. "She'll be quite the young lady. Come on now, girls, jump into bed and don't fret about Bruna. She's just fine."

"Aye," agreed Uncle Rudy. "The Yanks are there—Italy will be lots safer."

"Of course it is," said Mummy, tucking us into bed. She had the biggest smile. "One day all of us will be together again."

28

Hip, Hip, Hooray

Or like the Rainbow's lovely form
Evanishing amid the storm.

Robert Burns, "Tam O' Shanter"

It started out like any other day. Daddy went to the factory with Uncle Rudy. Aïda was outside with her friends, leaving for school, and Mum was cleaning up after a breakfast where Aïda and I had split an egg with toast and marmalade. I followed Aïda out, wrapped up in my warm jacket and a red knitted hat; I did not need my welly boots because Mum said it was not going to rain. We walked towards the main gate.

At first I thought the Jerries were after us, because a bunch of factory workers ran towards us down the cobbled street, jumping up and down, arms waving in the air. They roared, "The war's over, the war's over!"

The mums came out to see what the commotion was about. Mummy encircled us with her arms. Daddy and Uncle Rudy raced towards us, jumping up and down and bumping shoulders.

Over and over the men shouted, "The war's over—hip, hip, hooray!"

The women joined in. "The war's over—hip, hip, hooray!"

The old grouch swung open the gate. Even he wore a smile! Daddy rushed towards us. I had never seen him run before, and I thought it was very funny. Uncle Rudy was right beside him. I knew he could run—he chased us when we played *Peggy, Peggy.*

Daddy seized the three of us, hugging so hard it hurt. He twirled us, lifting my feet clear off the ground. "We beat the Krauts! Germany has surrendered. It's done. It's *over*. We can go home!"

The mums banged their pots and pans; the drumming of their wooden spoons echoed off the chimney stacks. One or two pots flew through open windows. The mixed-up clatter of Italian and Scots words soon turned into the songs of Italy and Scotland. Accordion music filled the air. Daddy's face was wet with sweat and tears. Uncle Rudy danced with every girl he saw.

For one minute there was silence, and someone said a prayer of thanks. One Italian asked for forgiveness for the Scots who had locked all of us up for five long years. I craned my neck trying to see who was speaking.

Someone shouted, "Churchill is on the wireless."

Mum put a finger on her lips; every wireless was turned on high.

"First I want to thank all the men and women who laid down their lives for victory as well as those who fought valiantly on land and sea." He went on, "We may allow ourselves a brief period of rejoicing, but let us not forget for a moment the toil and efforts that lie ahead. Japan with all her treachery and greed remains unsubdued. We must now devote our strength and resources to the task both at home and abroad. Advance Brittania. God bless you all!"

The people sang, *"For he's a jolly good fellow, for he's a jolly good fellow."* When they got to *"And so say all of us,"* Mum started crying.

Aïda asked her if she had a headache. "No, dear, I'm crying

because I am so happy. Daddy and I used to hate Churchill, but he did a good job. He did a good job."

"So now we can go home," said Aïda wisely.

"Now we can go home," answered Mum.

"It will take a few days, though," said Dad. "They need lorries to take us all back to Kilmarnock."

Aïda saw my scared face and told me quickly that these would be *rescue* lorries.

Mary, my invisible friend, was quite relieved!

The singing continued all evening while the Darmellington rain spattered the roof. Dad and Uncle Rudy were drinking Scotch whisky—even Mum had some. All three ran outside in the rain as if they were children.

Aïda whispered, "They're drunk."

Mum came back inside, shaking her wet hair in happiness. She made up our cots and put three lumps of coal on the fire. "May as well use it all up; oh, dear God, I canny believe it." She sat then and told us about our house in Gilmour Street. "Ye'll love it there, Anna. Ye'll have lots of playmates."

"I've got pals here, Mummy."

"How many rooms does it have, Mum?" asked Aïda.

"It will seem like a palace."

"Will we have a real bed?"

"Aye, a double bed with a satin bedspread."

"Can I still cuddle with Aïda?" I asked.

"It is dark green with pink roses embroidered in the middle, and there are two lovely brown easy chairs by the fire in the living room."

After hearing all this I thought I would never sleep again, but she hadn't answered my question, as usual.

Next day, Mummy dressed us in our nicest frocks: the brown velveteen ones that Gran had made for us. When we went outside, we saw Mrs. Scolatti and her two lassies just staring at the open gate; it was if they couldn't quite believe it. Mrs. Scolatti smiled and took me up in her arms. "Anna, my darling, soon I will see my Federico and my Piero."

"Can I still play with Cara and Roberta?'

Mummy joined us outside, her fag glowing in the breeze. "Anna, pet, we live in a different part of Kilmarnock."

"But, Mummy. . . ."

The Darmellington neighbours were arriving at the gate, carrying plates of Scotch eggs, salmon, and boiled tatties.

"That salmon was poached out of the river," said Mummy.

I didn't know what poached was and I felt left out the fun.

They set up tables in the courtyard to have a feast.

"Why is everybody here, Mummy?"

"Maybe they just feel sorry for us and want to make amends."

I didn't know what mends was, so I gave up on the questions and tucked into the food. Mary sat quietly beside me.

A man in a suit and tie came over to Daddy. "Let's let bygones be bygones," he said. "Guid luck tae ye all. We are very sorry that ye were interned for the duration." He slipped a pound note in Dad's pocket. "Tae get ye started, mate."

The Protestant minister and his wife brought scones and tea. Aïda and I ate those black currant scones till our tummies hurt. The best part was when someone in an army uniform passed out wee Union Jack flags. We waved them, and soon there was one in every hand. Now I was really having fun.

Next day, the soldiers loaded all the internees into a big army lorry with wooden seats on both sides. We bumped and rolled from side to side with the Scolattis, the Ferris, and the Brazolis, who all lived in Kilmarnock.

Mum started the singing. *"For ye'll tak' the high road and I'll tak' the low road, and I'll be in Scotland afore ye."* Soon, everyone was singing and rolling with the lorry as it pitched from side to side around the green corners of the Ayrshire countryside. That was when I saw my first sheep.

Dad sang, "*I'll take you home again, Kathleen.*"

I didn't know Daddy could sing. I laughed because he was so out of tune.

He had Mum's hand in his while he crooned into her dark eyes. "*Tae where yer heart will feel no pain. And when the fields are fresh and green, I will take ye tae yer home, again.*"

The words made Mum cry. Mum had kept her tears inside even when she had her bad headaches; these tears came from her insides. "Just think, pets," she leaned over to whisper, "tonight we'll be home."

The lorry bumped through Kilmarnock town, packed full with townspeople waving those same wee flags. Dad said, "I hope they don't notice us."

"Why, Daddy?'

"Oh, I suppose I don't know if they like Italians yet."

At least it was an answer.

It took a long time to wind through the crowded streets to Gilmour Street to reach our shop with its big windows that curved around a corner. I had never seen anything so grand. It was time to say *ciao* to our friends. Darmellington had lasted so long that it had felt like we would always be there.

"Can't Cara and Roberta come here to Gilmour Street to live?"

"No, darling," said Mummy. "Ye have to say goodbye to yer friends. They go to a different school."

"The Catholic school," added Aïda.

"But. . . ."

"Just give them a hug, Anna," said Mummy.

The Scolatti children and their Mamma kissed us on our cheeks, and Mrs. Scolatti cried into her hanky.

"Thanks for everything," said Mummy. "For taking care of

Aïda when Anna was born, for being my friend. Och, this is so hard."

Dad helped Mum down the steps, and the people in the lorry began to hum "Auld Lang Syne." By the time they got to *"We'll tak' a cup o' kindness yet,"* the hankies were out again.

The whole group hung out the back of the lorry, waving and crying. *"We'll meet again some other nicht for auld lang syne."*

"Wave goodbye, girls, this is the end of an era." Mum pushed us towards the front door of our corner shop, and the lorry pulled away.

I dried my tears, and when I turned my head there was Peggy Kempster, wearing a bright pink jumper covered by a Fair Isle cardigan with pearl buttons. She wore silk stockings with the seam down the back and black high heels. I couldn't believe my eyes. Her gorgeous red hair was wound on top of her head where a black and gold Chinese pin looked like it was stuck right into her brains.

Uncle Rudy leapt forward and grabbed her; I thought they'd never be done with the kissing. Mary and I giggled, and I almost forgot about my Italian friends who had just pulled away. Peggy pushed Uncle Rudy away, took a breath, and handed Dad a large bunch of keys. Next, she took a black book from her pink handbag and handed it to him. There were tears on Peggy's cheeks and tears on Dad's moustache. Uncle Rudy looked like he was in a trance. I turned away to look up, up, up at the tall tenement that loomed over me like a mountain. So this was my home!

"Welcome back, Andy," Peggy said.

Daddy took the long silver key and opened the shop door. I took a big breath and pounced in. The windows gleamed. The silver cooking pan shone. The long counter was polished and the walls were white.

"Peggy, the place looks perfect," said Daddy. "And," he went on, turning the pages of the black book, "Peggy, ye took nothing for yerself."

"Ye can pay me whatever ye think I earned. All I ever wanted was my Rudy back and yer bairns safe and sound, and just look at all of ye, home at long last."

"Hip, hip, hooray!" Aïda and I chorused.

It was Dad's turn to hug Peggy, "Thanks, lassie, thank ye," he said. He held her out away from him so he could talk right into her face. "Ye saved this family from disaster, Peggy. We owe ye everything."

"Not just me, Andy. Ye might not believe this, but Johnnie Millar kept an eye on both shops. He sent his constables round often tae check the doors and the windows and made sure nobody bothered me or this shop."

"I can hardly believe that," said Dad. "He kept watch, did he, the bastard?"

Aïda and I ran to the counter to feel the shiny wood, running our fingers around the carved roses on each end and stretching up tall to rub the top. Daddy had told us about the magic when he and Mummy touched their fingers together, so Aïda and I touched fingertips. There was nothing, no magic, nothing. I didn't feel a thing, just Aïda's sticky fingers.

We ran into the kitchen where a giant empty pot sat on a stove. "What's this for, Mum?"

"We boil dried peas all day until they're soft. We call them mushy peas."

"What else do ye cook in here?"

"Daddy fries the fish and chips in this big pan; ye can never eat just one. Ye pick up a salt shaker and cover the chips with salt, and then ye pour enough vinegar on the fish so that it is not too sweet and not too spicy. Sometimes ye put peas on the side. Girls, we will never be hungry on Gilmour Street."

I knew that meant no more headaches for Mum.

~   ~   ~

The two rooms that were our living and bedroom were huge. Large brown armchairs sat in front of a lovely green tiled fireplace and a small square table with a white tablecloth was set for four. Peggy had put a bunch of daisies in the middle of the table. They were the prettiest flowers I had ever seen.

I followed Aïda into the bedroom. "Wow, Aïda, look at this."

We lay on the double bed. I spread out my arms and legs like a starfish so I could feel how big it was. It was ten times bigger than a cot and I could sleep next to my sweet-smelling sister. This made me very happy. We sat on our elbows to peer around the room. There was a tall wardrobe and a dressing table with a stool. I jumped down to look in the mirror, "Aïda, look. Look, how pretty I am. My eyes are big and brown and Mummy's right, I do have long eyelashes."

Aïda pushed me away to look at herself. "Aye, yer bonnie, Anna, but I have curly hair and darker eyes."

We did some pushing and shoving then, and went on to discover another tiny room off the bedroom. It was green and had a light bulb hanging down over a large black box.

"What is this big thing, Aïda?"

"It's got a dial. I think it's a secret safe," she answered.

We went out the side door into the entry, where we found the loo. When we pushed open the big brown door, we saw a stack of newspaper for bum wiping in the corner. The toilet didn't stink like the one in Darmellington, but it was so cold I knew I wouldn't stay long. Next to the loo were stairs that led up to the second and third floors of the dark grey tenement. The long entry opened up onto a huge square that Dad called the barracks. There were lots of doors into lots of flats, and I could see two landings high above me. Aïda said there would be lots of kids to play with. The entry from Gilmour Street was long and dark, with a black floor with whitewashed strips down each side; I later learned it was a magic place to play in on rainy days.

When we went back into the bedroom, Uncle Rudy and Peggy were kissing and hugging.

"Kiss her again, Uncle Rudy," I called out.

"Away with ye," he answered.

"Hey, Uncle Rudy, do ye want tae play *Peggy, Peggy*?"

"What on earth is that, Rudy?" asked Peggy.

"Oh, Anna, ye are a wee bugger," replied our uncle as he chased me back out the door.

29

An Ideal Corner Shop

When chapman billies leave the street,
And drouthy neibors, neibors meet

Robert Burns, "Tam O' Shanter"

When folks walked down Gilmour Street towards our chip shop, their noses were entertained by the smell of fish frying and chips sizzling in our deep fat pan. Every day at four o'clock, after school, I was hungry for a bag of Dad's warm chips.

Mum would say, "Wait till teatime, Anna."

My tummy flipped and I knew I had to have just one or two chips or simply die. I would beg Daddy, who'd glance at Mum and slip me a midget bag of hot chips with vinegar all over them. I'd step out into the entry to eat them and get my fingers all greasy from putting the yummy tatties into my mouth one by one. I didn't even share them with Mary.

That same smell made all sorts of feet march into our shop at teatime. The fish frying in the pan would grab their noses and steer them out of the freezing Ayrshire wind and into the shop's warmth.

Aïda and I could watch from our stools behind the counter. She did homework and I coloured. Dad had a big silver basket filled with wet chipped tatties which he placed on the left side of the huge pan. They'd sizzle whilst he dipped the whiting in a lovely, white, silky batter and gently, without splatter, dropped each fresh fish into the boiling lard on the right. The fish splatted and bubbled, making the customer's lips twitch in anticipation of their spectacular taste. Dad's moustache had grown thick and black and his hands had softened from the grease. All of his ammunition calluses disappeared but he'd been left with a case of the gout from standing on the rough floors of the munitions factory. When he had the gout, Mum had to do the frying.

Daddy had a smile for each customer, whilst Mum was more serious. Dad was called Andy by adults and children, but Mum was Mrs. Bertellotti to everyone.

Folks said, "Those mushy peas warm up yer cockles on a windy day, Missus Bertellotti."

Mummy would smile at us and say how happy she was to be out of Darmellington and in the warmth and comfort of her own café. Aïda chattered with the customers. They made a fuss over her dark eyes and her charming mouth. I would push her aside and entertain them with a poem or a song.

A thin man with a limp came into the warmth one day. "Hey, Andy, guid tae huv' ye back, mate." Aïda told me that the man had a club foot, whatever that was.

"Hello, Ned," said Dad. "Long time, no see." He wiped his hands on his apron and leaned over the counter to shake Ned's long-fingered hand. It was as if there was nobody else in the shop. "Those years are best forgotten. How are ye, Ned?"

Twelve people craned their necks to listen.

Ned whispered loudly, "It was a crying shame that the government locked ye Tallies up."

"It's over now, pal."

A sad-looking old man with baggy trousers barged into the shop, pushing people aside; his eyes were wild and his hair stood straight up with no hat. He pushed his way to the counter, then, from between his brown teeth, the sad man hissed right at Dad's face, "enemy alien" and "damned bloody wop" in the same breath.

I grabbed Aïda's arm, afraid to look. Was this man going to hit my dad?

"Whoa, Mister, what's yer problem?" said Daddy.

Who should come in, right at that very moment, but Officer Johnnie Millar?

Mum turned white as a sheet. Dad was speechless. He stepped back, almost on top of us. I hid behind Aïda.

The police officer turned towards the angry man. "Ye can reckon wi' me if ye want tae sling names, Jock, and we'll take it outside. Andy and Kathy have had enough." He turned to Daddy. "This old man's son was killed in Italy, Andy, and he hasnae been right since. I'll take care of him." The officer in his great tall hat took the old man's arm, and together they moved through the crowd of customers. The man sobbed as he stepped out onto Gilmour Street. I heard him say, "The Tallies killed mah boy."

The customers shook their heads, and the old fellow walked away down the street muttering to himself.

Ned, the newspaper man, said, "Ye see, Andy, they say war is inevitable, but what does it ever prove? One day ye hate a whole race because of one lousy evil man, and the next day it's over and what the hell was it all about? What was the damned war for, I ask all ye?" He was speaking to the crowd that had gathered in front of the counter.

"We had tae stop Hitler, that's what it was all about," said Johnnie Millar. He had stepped back in and was at the rear of the crowd. "We followed orders whether we liked them or not. That damned Hitler would have turned this country into a hell-hole, but we won. Andy, Kathy, I'm glad yer back. I'm sorry for what I did, and I'm asking yer forgiveness. If there is anything ye need, don't ever hesitate tae ask."

All the heads in the shop nodded in agreement. Then there was a great murmuring amongst the customers. My mother's face was whiter than the sheets on her bed and her thin lips were working full time. She came forward and, in front of everyone, she said, "Johnnie Millar, I have hated ye for five years. I took the war out on yer back and here ye are apologizing. I was told ye helped keep the toughs away from the shop and helped Peggy when she needed ye. Let's let bygones be bygones and get on wi' getting this country back on its feet."

The murmuring turned into *ayes* and *maybes*, and Officer Millar came forward to shake Dad's hand and take his hat off to Mum.

I grabbed Mary by the arm—she always showed up when I needed her. The two of us scooted out from behind the counter to play hide and seek among the customers. The big work boots tapped a song of the Highlands, the high heels with the nylon stockings scratched out *"Comin' thru' the rye,"* and the coats, stinking of wet wool from the rain, made Mary's nose run. I began to sneeze, making the customers laugh as they called out their orders, each one pushing forward to be first.

"Two fish suppers, Andy."

"Peas fur the wee one, Mrs. Bertellotti, and lots o' vinegar on my chips."

"A bottle of Currie's Ginger Beer and three bags of chips, please."

A sailor came in, looking sad as sad could be. He held his white hat in his hand. "Hey, Mister, I jist got discharged but my pay didn't; could ye gie me tick, Mr. Bertellotti?"

"I'll help ye, son."

The sailor lifted his eyes to look at my dad, and took off his watch and handed it over.

"I'll put it in my safe, son; ye can come back for it when ye get paid."

So that's what Dad did with his safe. It was his secret box.

"Okay, sailor, here comes yer dinner." Mum had wrapped up a nice fish supper with lots of salt and vinegar for the embarrassed man.

Dad handed the sailor the brown-paper package; Mummy did not like our fish suppers wrapped in newspaper like at the other fish and chip shops. Daddy also slipped two half-crowns into the man's hand. "That'll get ye a room for the night."

The sailor's face reddened. "Thanks, Mr. Bertellotti. I heard ye were a kind man, I'll pay ye back just as soon as I can." The man opened up the warm chips and fish and stuck a greasy, vinegar-soaked chip in his mouth with a great big sigh. "This is smashing, best I ever tasted."

Mum noticed the crowd was getting bigger. "Now, now, Andy, let's get back to business. We have a huge order from the folks at the Saxone shoe factory." She looked relieved that the sailor and the policeman had left and she fussed around in her high heels that clicked and clacked. "Isn't it nice to be busy," she said, in her best Scots voice.

30

Gilmour Street

Now, auld Kilmarnock, cock thy tail,
An' toss thy horns fu' canty

Robert Burns, "The Ordination"

Aïda and I were delighted with Gilmour Street. It was newly tarmacadamed, no more cobblestones. Now it had deep gutters for playing marbles and broad pavements which were perfect for hop-scotching kids.

"One, two, three, skip; two, two, three, skip; three, two, three, skip!"

Dad's shop was on the corner of Gilmour and St. Andrew's Streets, and to me it was the most important place on earth. I had made new friends and immediately forgot what it was like to live behind a gate with only Italian children to play with. At the far end of Gilmour Street was Miss McConkey's Wool Shop and the Co-op Grocery. The three-storied, limestone tenements that lined each side of the street had hundreds of smoke stacks on slate roofs, which meant warm homes for Scottish children. We kids never felt the cold, even in our short skirts. Girls wore tartan socks that kept legs from chafing in the wind and sometimes mittens that grannies had knitted. Boys wore short grey pants and hand-made woolen socks that came up to their knees.

Saturday was my favourite day of the week because all my play-mates—Mary Beattie, May McNair, and Eleanor Gordon, Aïda's pal from next door—were home from school. We girls skipped up the pavement, running our fingers across the lime-stone walls, scratching our nails on the sandy surface, stopping often to visit young mothers with their new babies. The mothers smoked their fags and shook the pram handles to keep the bairns asleep.

Aïda whispered, from the back of her hand, that when the men came home from war they must have been busy with the baby-making; she seemed to know a lot about baby-making.

We often visited Miss McConkey's shop. She had a huge red birthmark that spread all over the right side of her face from her big lip to the edge of her bright-blue right eye. She was a spinster, that's what Mum said, but we believed that Miss McConkey had had a husband who was a spy for the government. Our story was that he died on assignment in Egypt. Miss McConkey did have statues of the pyramids on her counter, so I believed the story. She was kind to us kids, but we were heartless. "Hello, lassies," she'd say. "Would ye like a wee cup of tea?"

"Yes, thank ye," we'd reply, and while we drank our tea from her dainty white cups with our pinkies in the air, we'd stare at her birthmark. Once I stared so hard it made my eyes water.

"Don't cry, Anna. I was born like this, I'm used to it," she said.

She didn't realize I wasn't crying.

One particular Saturday was sunny and brisk, and we kids had the feel of mischief. While we sat drinking our tea with Miss McConkey, we gazed across the street. There was a black and white sign on the red-tiled building opposite that read "*MEN.*" A Cheshire cat grin spread like marmalade over my sister's face, and when we all said "Goodbye and thank you" to Miss McConkey, we stepped out on the pavement.

Aïda looked directly at me. "I dare ye."

"What?" I asked.

"I dare all of ye," she repeated, turning her head and tossing her black curls.

"Dare us tae what?" asked May Beattie in broad Scots.

"Dare ye tae tak' a gander intae the men's toilet," said Aïda, laughing and pointing across to the black and white sign.

I suddenly remembered the enemy alien lorry game and held back.

~ ~ ~

Five kids sped across the street as if the bogey-man was after them and stood in a row in front of the red-tiled toilets. Five sets of hands crept over their mouths to stop the giggling. Five pairs of feet mounted the tall step. Five faces skimmed around the dark marble doorway. Twelve eyes (including Mary's) saw a grey marble trough that looked like it was made for horses. It gurgled as water ran from taps into the basin. Five noses crinkled at the smell of Dettol. At first they thought no one was there, then one of them spied a pair of brown shoes with beige-coloured trousers hanging around them under the door of the stall.

They heard "ugh" like the sound of a horse blowing air through its lips. Then they burst into peals of laughter.

A man's voice roared, "What the hell!"

~ ~ ~

We girls were bent double, unable to move or run, laughter boiling out from our stomachs. We realized in an instant that we had to get out of there. We ran, hiccupping, holding our bellies. When we craned our necks the man was outside, pulling on his pants, shoving his braces over his shoulders. "Damn it," he swore. "What are ye doin', ye naughty wee lassies?"

We ran like rabbits getting chased by greyhounds. Mary ran ahead of me.

"Get back here!" he ordered.

We bolted to the *Bleachie*, a playground where a small patch of green grass grew and mums hung out their sheets to dry while their children did tricks on a rickety old roundabout. Once we got there, all of us felt safe. We clambered on the roundabout, running to make it spin.

"Who was he?" May said.

"Don't ken, don't care," answered Aïda.

"Do ye think he'll tell Daddy?" I asked.

My older wiser sister said, "The man couldn't see our faces. We're all right."

My invisible friend, who sat beside us on the roundabout, sighed with relief.

Then we heard the skirl of a pipe band. Soon all of us were back on Gilmour Street, parading alongside the marching band as if we had done nothing at all to make a man angry—there was no sign of him. There were about twenty men in the Killie Band; some banged the drums, some blew on chanters that puffed up the bonnie bagpipes, and some just marched. The Sergeant Major tossed the long baton high in the air, leading the band up the street. The pipers played and the drummers drummed. We marched innocently along to the music. Oh, how I loved Gilmour Street.

~ ~ ~

Dad was at the shop door, smoking his Craven "A" and enjoying "Scotland the Brave." We piled around him, breathless and panting.

"What have ye been up to, lassies?" he asked, a big smile on his face.

"Oh, nothing." The standard kids' reply.

"When we lived in Ayr, I played in the street with my wee sister, Bruna. We'd play hide and seek and go for walks on the dunes at the shore. She loved the smell of the ocean and the skirl of the pipes, just like yerselves. I sure do miss her."

"Me, too," said a deep Scots voice from around the corner. "Me, too."

"Look what the wind blew in! Girls, this is yer Uncle Eddie, Mummy's brother."

I could not take my eyes off my Uncle Eddie's large hand. It was twice the size of his other one and very red. It was even more interesting than Miss McConkey's birthmark.

"Go get Mummy, Aïda. Eddie, how are ye, my man?"

"I've missed ye, Andy."

"How great to see ye." Daddy shook Eddie's good hand fiercely. My uncle looked like Mummy but was darker skinned.

"How beautiful yer weans are, Andy. Aïda looks like Bruna."

"She does, doesn't she? So, Eddie, how's our greyhound?"

"Ye would not believe how he's grown. He is quite the racer."

My uncle saw me staring at him and bent down. "Don't be afraid of my hand, Anna, I was born with it."

I was glad that I wasn't born with a red mark or a big hand.

Eddie turned back to Daddy. "We've got a real racing dog this time, Andy. And yer weans are lovely. Welcome home."

"Thanks, pal."

"I bet yer glad that internment is done."

"Ye don't know the half of it, Eddie."

"Have ye had word from Italy?"

"Not a peep. The papers don't tell us much, either. Maybe we'll hear something after America beats Japan."

"Do ye think it's sunny in Italy today, Dad?" interrupted Aïda. "Do ye really think that I look like Aunt Bruna?"

"Aye, ye do, hen. Aye, ye do."

I wondered who I looked like.

31

Love at First Sight

When the fighting was over, the Buffalo Soldiers stayed in the Pietrasanta area to mop up, clearing rubble from buildings with large moving equipment. The young black men had won the hearts of the Tuscan people.

At Babbo's house, Henry, Tommy, and a few others painted, repaired windows, cleaned out gutters, and trimmed trees. Mamma cooked many different types of pasta while the men laughed, worked, and enjoyed each other's company. The motto of the Buffalo Soldiers was *Deeds, Not Words.* Indeed, Henry and his comrades certainly followed it to the letter at Babbo's house in Pietrasanta.

"Tommy, some of the men say they'd like to stay here in Italy."

"Why's that, Henry?" For such a serious conversation, Tommy put down his shovel and motioned for Henry to join him for a beer.

"Folks like Fiorina and Arturo respect us. Here in Italy, we can go into any café. At home, it's not like that."

"Didn't your country fight a civil war to stop Negro discrimination?"

"White gov'nors make the rules in the south; we call 'em the Jim Crow laws. It's all about segregation. Someday, someday in America, the people will understand that here in Europe we'all fought for their freedom and our own. Most black folks in mah state cain't even vote because they are illiterate. It's black-only schools 'n' white-only bathrooms."

"Henry, all I can say is this. You're welcome in this house until the Army says you have to go home."

~   ~   ~

In a few months it was time for the 92nd to demob and return to America; their job in Italy was done. This time Tommy drove the jeep south to Naples.

Henry leaned over to him. "Tommy, I think teachin' yuh to drive was scarier than this whole dang war." They laughed as only friends do.

They convoyed south to Naples, where the men were to be dispatched to the States. Tommy felt such a loss when Henry boarded the troop ship; he had learned so much from his tall dark friend. Tommy knew it would be years, if ever, before they would meet again, but he prayed that somehow they would. As the ship pulled away from the pier, Tommy stood for many minutes, waving and remembering.

~   ~   ~

He had orders to remain in Napoli; his obligation to the American Army was for several more months. Naples was at capacity with returning soldiers, men of every nationality living a crazy, drunken life. It was October and the war was completely over, even in the Pacific where the war had ended with a bang in the form of the atomic bomb—the likes of which Tommy could hardly believe. The newspapers showed the great grey mushrooms of death that had hovered over Hiroshima and Nagasaki in Japan. Tommy realized that the destruction was complete and irreparable. It made his heart break.

~   ~   ~

Most of Naples was war rubble, but the dock area was a throng of bars and pubs. Tommy knew that his brothers would have loved whooping it up in those places, but that's not who he was. He enjoyed watching the hubbub, but his thoughts were about Scotland and his bonny wee café. Even as he waved goodbye to Henry and the others, Tommy was engrossed by the future. Would he go back to Scotland when his tour of duty was over? He was an Italian/Scotsman but was he a Scot? He wandered the narrow cobbled streets attempting to figure out who he really was. Would he stay here in Italia or go back to the Scotland that had been his home for so many years? He whistled, missing his chats with Henry, fascinated by the tiny alleyways where the sun managed to sneak from behind red chimneys to heat his head. The ancient stones that lay below his feet had been smoothed by time. He was, after all, only a few miles from Pompeii, where Mount Vesuvius had spewed its lava centuries before.

Tucked into a corner of a narrow cobbled lane was a tiny shop called Il Negozio di Scarpa, the shoe shop. The windows were fashioned with small panes of thick glass that gleamed from tiny facets woven into the thick glass. Tommy stepped up the three worn stone stairs into a small, dimly lit shop. The remembered smell of leather filled his nostrils. He decided at that very moment to buy some new shoes. There was the sound of laughter from behind the small counter where a young woman stood; her voice sounded to Tommy like the bells that tinkled on the sheep in the hills of Scotland. He smiled from the inside out. A strip of sunlight streamed through the leaded glass and gleamed on the young girl's hair. It made a rainbow halo over her blond curls. Tommy's heart jumped into his mouth—was this an angel?

The days of war melted away into his subconscious mind as he gazed unabashedly at an enchantress who stood in front of him. He breathed in the deep Mediterranean blue of her eyes and noticed her full red lips. Her skin glowed soft and light; somehow he knew her voice would be *dolce soprano*.

"*Posso aiutarla?*" she said in a dove tone. "May I help you?"

Tommy thought for a moment that this place was heaven. Even the smell of her light perfume pleased his senses. A silly grin made his dimples show.

"*Americano?*" she asked.

Tommy did not answer. Of course she would think that he was American—he was in uniform.

"*No, sono un Italiano.*" He finally found his voice and put his hand out. "Irmo Bertellotti." He had slipped into his Italian without thinking.

She shook his hand firmly.

"I was an interpreter for the *Americani* and I am in Napoli for only a short time." Tommy used his best Italian for the incredible young woman. "I came to see the young *soldati* off to the United States. Soon, I will be allowed to go back to Scotland where I lived before the war, so I need a good pair of shoes."

Where did all that chat come from? Why was he telling this young woman, this vision, so much in such a short space of time? He had had no conscious thought to get shoes until he entered the magical shop. Now he was bound to stay. He realized that he had not released her hand.

She smiled, "*Mi chiamo Lea*," and slid her hand from his grasp. "I will look for you some comfortable shoes."

He watched her move. Her soft blue dress moulded around her curves. He was breathless.

She picked out a few pairs and beckoned Tommy to a fine old leather chair with a sloping box in front. He placed a foot on it to take off his army boots. Lea sat on the end of the box, a pair of soft black loafers on her lap. When Tommy bent down to untie his laces, she leaned forward to slip off his boot. Their heads bumped.

"Did I hurt you?" Tommy asked, rubbing his forehead.

The young woman laughed, shaking her head no. That sound went straight to Tommy's heart. Could he already be in love? "Are you from Napoli?" he asked.

"No, I'm from Viareggio."

"Viareggio! *Mio papa* lives in Pietrasanta."

"I know it well," she answered in a soft tone. "Papa and I are here in Napoli for a month or so to sell shoes to unsuspecting soldiers like you."

Tommy laughed a bit too loudly. "Did your family evacuate like mine did?"

"*Sì*, we were in the Capriglia hills, hiding from the Germans. It was awful."

And so it went with Lea and Tommy, or Irmo as she called him. He was enchanted with her voice, her blondish hair, her violet eyes, and her faint perfume. It was as if they had known each other forever.

She slipped several pairs of shoes on his feet and spoke of her college days, before the war. "I teach small children now, but school is not yet ready to begin. So many children run like urchins in the streets, begging and with no shoes. I want to make a difference for them. My father was a well-known cobbler, but his business was closed all during the occupation. As I said, we are in Napoli only a month maybe two."

"I am so glad that you are here."

She blushed.

Tommy had always been shy with girls, but this woman was easy for him to talk to. Had she been sent to him from heaven? He'd been in her shop for over an hour and it seemed like a minute. Lea's father, a tall handsome man who was slightly greying, stood behind the counter smiling and listening.

Lea looked up at him. "*Mi scusi*, Papa. Irmo, this is *mio papa*, Stefano Genovesi."

Tommy stood up and shook the man's hand; he was taller than Tommy, with steely blue eyes that smiled in his wrinkled face; his daughter looked like him. "Why are you wearing an American uniform?' he asked in Italian.

"I am with the American Army," Tommy replied. He explained that he had grown up in Scotland and was bilingual. Stefano seemed impressed and expressed his gratitude to the American boys during and after the fighting; he must have immediately taken a liking to Tommy because when Lea interrupted their conversation to ask, "Would it be okay with you, Papa, if Irmo and I went for a short walk?" her papa answered, "This is a nice young *soldato*. You may go for a short time." Tommy did not explain that he was a civilian.

As the couple left the shop together, Stefano watched at the window. Young women were chaperoned in Italy then, but somehow, that day, the war had made the old ways not so important. Being alive was all that counted. Lea and Tommy wound through the maze of cobbled streets towards the beach.

They strolled along the sandy beach in bare feet, shoes long-forgotten. Their hands hung loose, almost touching. Tommy wanted so much to take her hand in his, but his shyness had returned. When the sun dipped, they returned to the shop.

Lea's father smiled. "I believe you are a gentleman, Irmo."

"Papa, can Irmo and I go for dinner now?'

"I suppose it will be all right. The old customs do not seem to count in Napoli."

~   ~   ~

In a *taverna bistro* near the pier, they sat facing each other across a round table, sipping Chianti. Each time their fingers touched, Tommy's heart leapt. As the level of wine in the bottle lowered, so did their voices. They spoke seriously about what had happened to each of them during the war.

"I could see the glow from the fire at Sant' Anna di Stazzema," said Lea. "The blaze lit up the sky until well after dark. The smell of the smoke was acrid. It wasn't until the next morning that we found out that it had been bodies burning." Tears sprang from her eyes. "How could a massacre like that happen in the quiet hills of Tuscany?"

"Only in a terrible war," he replied. He told her of the bravery of the black American soldiers. Then as he explained his translating and radio communication job, Tommy realized that his war experiences had changed him for life. Their conversation fell silent. They were alone in their thoughts.

Tommy gave her some time before he reached for her hand. "Lea," he began, "I have never felt like this before." He hesitated for only one moment. "I believe I am in love with you." Their hands were gripped so tight that all their knuckles were white.

"How can that be?" she asked. "You only came in for a pair of shoes."

They laughed, but when they stood up together, they were in each other's arms.

"I feel the same way," she whispered in his ear.

"So you will see me again?"

"I will."

They spent most of the week together. Lea's father understood; he manned the shop alone. As they sipped espresso in a café, Lea and Tommy made plans for the future. His new job entailed driving up and down the Italian peninsula. He had been asked to remain as a courier and interpreter for the Americans who were working to rebuild Italia. "I will visit you in Viareggio."

"When will you go back to Scotland?" she asked.

"It doesn't seem to be as important now," Tommy replied, gazing into her bright eyes.

"It sounds like an interesting place to visit."

"One day, perhaps, Lea. One day."

She smiled and said nothing more.

He leaned across the white tablecloth and kissed her lips. "I have to leave in a few days, but I will see you very soon."

"I will be waiting for you."

~ ~ ~

In mid-December, communications were finally allowed between the two countries of Italy and Great Britain. Tommy went immediately to the telegraph office in Genoa to send a yellow telegram to his brothers in Scotland:

Mamma Babbo Bruna safe now STOP
Hope you are all fine STOP Miss you STOP
With American Army STOP In love with Lea STOP
Hope to come back to Scotland STOP
Merry Christmas STOP

                                                        Tommy

32

A Bertellotti Christmas

"I've got a telegram fur yer daddy," the telegraph boy called from his perch on a bike. "It's from Italy. Go fetch him."

Aïda and I were playing hopscotch on the pavement outside the shop door. "Daddy, Daddy, come quick, it's a telegram from Italy."

Dad stopped his fish cleaning and wiped his hands on his white apron. "I bet it's from Babbo."

Mummy came quickly to the door. "Is it bad news?" she asked the young man with the bike clips round his trousers.

He shrugged. "I don't ken."

Dad opened the yellow envelope slowly and took a quick look, and then read it out loud. A huge smile spread over his mouth. "Listen, girls, this is what Tommy says: 'Mamma, Babbo, and Bruna are safe.' He misses us. He's with the American Army—how on God's earth did that happen? Kathy, he says he's in love."

"Ooh," said two wee girls.

"Andy, I'm so pleased," said Mummy. "Does Tommy say his girlfriend's name?"

"It's Lea."

We were all hugging. Dad even hugged the telegram boy! The boy turned red and rode off on his bike; he turned his head to say "Happy tae be of service, Mr. Bertellotti." His second thruppenny piece jingled beside the other one.

Mum and Dad were in each other's arms.

Aïda and I giggled. "Does Uncle Tommy know about me?" I asked.

"He will soon, pet," answered Daddy, "I'll send him a letter."

I had only Dad's stories to go by. I knew about Italy and the sunshine and the Mediterranean and my Auntie Bruna. I knew that Daddy had been worried, and now I loved the look that was on his face.

"Imagine, my brother in an American uniform. Imagine that. He's a Yank."

"Tommy was so shy, Andy. I can't believe he met a girl so quickly after the war." Mummy looked so surprised.

"Dad," said Aïda, "can we pin the telegram up on the wall?"

Daddy put the telegram up where the customers could see it. A telegram was a very important item to receive in those days. Some were good. Some were very bad.

"How did yer brother end up looking like a Yankee soldier, Andy?" customers asked.

Constable Johnnie Millar read the telegram while he was in the queue for his fish supper. "Good for Tommy."

"I suppose yer right, Johnnie," answered Mum, still cautious around the moustached policeman who had ordered her out of her own shop.

~ ~ ~

Two days before Christmas, Johnnie was back in the shop. "Kathy, Andy, I have news."

It looked like Mummy held her breath, her eyes suspicious.

"I was at the pictures last night. They had a newsreel about Italy from months ago when the Brigadier General announced the Liberation. I think the town was called Genoa. I could swear yer brother Tommy was the interpreter."

Daddy wiped his hands on his apron. "Are ye sure, Johnnie?"

"His round glasses gave him away. Of course he was speaking in Italian, but there was something about those glasses, and I could hear his Scots accent even in the Italian words. Aye, it was Tommy all right, in a Yankee uniform. Tommy and I sat next to each other in school, I'd know him anywhere."

"That's terrific news, Johnnie. He must be famous in Italy. Imagine, girls, yer Uncle Tommy an interpreter. It makes sense. It makes sense." Daddy lifted me up to sit on the counter and gave me a big kiss on the cheek. "No wonder he's got a girlfriend."

I said, "Hip hooray!" This was going to be a fantastic Christmas.

Next day Daddy brought home our first Christmas tree. He bought it outside Woolworth's. Mum said it was very scrawny and could he not find a better one? Aïda and I loved our very first wee tree; when we hung our decorations on, it came to life. Dad was absent—he'd gone to the pub to cool off from his scolding. Aïda had cut a star from cardboard and covered it with small pieces of silver paper she'd saved from the inside of Mum's packs of cigarettes. She'd folded the thin sparkly paper till it was flat, and glued each piece carefully on. Her star glistened. Mum placed the small tree on a card table, so Aïda had to stand on a chair to pin her star on the top of the tree.

Mum tied small electric lights from America, via Woolworth's, onto the branches. Those lights were all different colours and glowed like candles. She helped us make wooden dolls from clothespins, painting their faces with rosy red lips like Peggy's. She scolded me when I made a mistake with the paint, so all I got to do was the red rosy cheeks. Aïda glued yellow yarn on the top for their hair. We threw small balls of cotton wool all over the branches for snow and covered the whole thing with silver tinsel. When Dad came home from the pub, he slid the tree to the end of our bed so we could watch it as we fell asleep.

On Christmas Eve, Mum kept the lights on for Father Christmas, and she put a wee dram of whisky and two shortbread biscuits on the table to help Santa on his way. She read us the story of the Three Wise Men who never let anything get in their way on their life's journey to find Jesus, the baby. She told me that Daddy also followed a star on the night I was born. She had wet eyes when she told me about Daddy. When Dad came in to say goodnight, he whispered that because I was born on January sixth, I was a gift of the Magi.

When the lights went out Mum and Dad fell asleep in their double bed across from ours, with Daddy snoring like a train engine coming through a tunnel. He'd told us that this would be the best Christmas ever because his whole family was safe from Hitler and our chip shop had been very busy, what with the feeding of the factory workers and the folks who lived around Gilmour Street. Aïda and I cuddled together, her black curls smelling of Sunsilk shampoo, her brown Italian eyes closed but moving around under her lids. She was pretending to be asleep.

I took peeks around the bedroom, pink from Mum's lampshade; the fringe made shadows on the wall, and the glow of the Christmas lights made Scottish magic. I squirmed around in my bed, wondering what Father Christmas would bring and dreaming of snowflakes and silver sixpences hidden inside the Christmas pudding that had boiled on the stove all day.

The night was crisp, like most Christmas Eves. In my dreams I saw Father Christmas in a long ruby red coat, sitting on his sleigh, hoping to visit all the children in the tenement. I could hear the tiny feet of the reindeer pacing three stories up, their hoofs echoing on the slates. Mum had said that Father Christmas could come now because the war was just a memory, but he had so many chimneys to climb down on the Gilmour Street tenements, I prayed he would find ours.

Then I saw him! There he was, in his red jacket bumping and jiggling in his sleigh.

I heard a "Ho, Ho, Ho!"

"Hi there, Father Christmas," I whispered to the night air. "Can ye see Mum and Dad's satin bedspread? Can ye hear my Dad's snores? Can ye see the electric lights glowing on the tree?

Mummy bought them at Woolies and then she made Aïda and me wait outside the door, with an ice-cream cone, while she ran back in for other special gifts. Can ye see Aïda's star shining on the top? Mum left ye a piece of shortbread. If yer not hungry, give the biscuits to the reindeer, but drink down the dram—it'll keep the cold out. Can ye see Mum's left arm draped over Dad's shoulder? That's so she can tap him when he snores too much. I am over here, Father Christmas, scooted right up to my sister because my hot water bottle is cold now."

I shook Aïda's shoulder. "Wake up."

"It's not time yet," she whispered.

"Didn't ye hear him?" I whispered.

"Who?"

"Father Christmas."

"Go back to sleep," said my older wiser sister.

~ ~ ~

Then it was daylight and I could see my breath. The room was filled with frosty air, and Daddy's snores still echoed around the wallpapered walls—between each snore was a puffing noise from somewhere in his throat. I looked out the window. It was snowing. Maybe the noise I had heard in the night was snowflakes drifting on the slate-covered roofs? No, I knew it was reindeer. I could see frost sticking on the windowpanes like waves. It was Christmas outside and inside the glass.

I pinched my sister.

"Ouch," she said, "I'm already awake." Then she said loudly, "Ready! Set! Go!"

"Mummy, Daddy, wake up. Father Christmas came," we sang out together.

"A bike! Look, Anna, he brought me a red bike."

I didn't care about her bike. I had a baby doll dressed all in pink: pink hat, pink rompers, and pink rosy cheeks. She was sleeping in her very own pram with her eyes closed; I knew they would pop open when I picked her up. Her pram was grey with white swirls painted on the sides, and it had big wheels, just like the big prams the posh ladies pushed when they walked up-town every afternoon. My pram bounced when I pushed on the smooth white handle. I gave my baby doll a name immediately, just like Daddy did for me when I was born. I named her Bruna, because I imagined Aunt Bruna looked just like this walky-talky doll. I asked my imaginary friend Mary if she liked the name, and she said she did.

Aïda and I leapt together onto our parent's bed where Mum was reaching for her first cigarette. "Easy, girls. Did Father Christmas leave any presents?"

I showed her my gorgeous dolly. "Look, Mum!"

Mummy made a big "Oh" with her lips and pushed gently on the doll's tummy.

The dolly said, "Mamma, Mamma," and winked her gor-geous big blue eyes.

"Oh, Mummy, did ye hear her? She said Mamma."

"I did," answered my mother with a big smile as she stroked my fly-away hair.

"Wake up, Daddy. Stop yer snoring. It's Christmas. I got a bike," said Aïda. We leapt onto him and Mum blew out her first puff of grey smoke; that familiar smell made everything in my world seem right.

"Happy Christmas, pets," said the man in the striped pajamas.

"Look Daddy, look at my dolly. Her name is Bruna."

"What a nice name, Anna. I wonder if my Bruna got presents today."

Mum spoke up, "I'm sure she did. *La Befana* is the Italian Father Christmas and she must have come." She leaned back and took another puff of her fag. "It's so good to be in my own bed for Christmas. No more war. No more internment. Amen."

My Mum was good at speeches.

33

New Year's Eve . . .
Hogmanay

That Sense and Worth, o'er a' the earth,
Shall bear the gree, an' a' that.
                    Robert Burns, "A Man's a Man for a' That"

"Here's tae us," cheered Dad, raising his whisky glass.

It was almost midnight.

"Tae us," was the answer from the grown-ups in their blue and white party hats. They sipped the golden Scottish whisky; the smell made my nose wrinkle.

"Thank God the war is over," said Dad. "Thank God we're home."

Our steamy front shop smacked of Dad's lovely fish and chips served with a few drops of vinegar. There were all sorts of folks packed into the front shop at Number Two Gilmour Street. There were so many aunts and uncles I got mixed up who was there and who wasn't. There was Aunt Jean and Uncle Jimmy and then there were two uncles I had never met. Uncle John and Uncle Bill were home from the fighting in Africa and Burma; Mum called them her stepbrothers. Uncle John, who was already bald, picked me up and swung me around—I liked him immediately. Uncle Bill had dark hair and dark eyes like Mum; he just shook my hand.

Next through the door were Uncle Rudy and Peggy. Peggy was wearing a black dress with gold earrings, and Uncle Rudy wore beige spats over his black patent shoes. He had cufflinks that matched Peggy's earrings. I thought the two of them were the bee's knees.

At ten minutes to twelve, everyone blew party horns that sounded like bagpipes, and Aïda and I danced the Highland fling in our black patent shoes with the silver buckles on top. The lovely shoes were presents from Father Christmas.

Mum had been right. She had said, "When the war is over, Father Christmas will come."

Daddy lifted us up on the dark mahogany counter to watch the lovely ladies and the tipsy men singing "Auld Lang Syne." He whispered, "The two of you look smashing in your corduroy dresses."

The party people sang with their arms crossed, *"Should auld acquaintance be forgot . . . and. . . ."*

It was exactly midnight.

"I would like to make a toast," said Mummy in her wise way; earlier, she had sat in front of her dressing table brushing her hair until it shone. I had watched her till my eyes watered. Now she looked like Rita Hayworth, with the gleam from the shop lights making her bonny lips glow and her dark eyes spark with flickering lights. Her purple heather brooch lay on the soft green material of her dress lapel as if it were tucked into the grass.

Daddy was showing Jean and Jimmy the telegram from Tommy; there was a titter of voices.

Mum stood, trying to look tall, behind the great rose-carved counter that had been Babbo's pride and joy. It was covered with meringues and black bun. Bruna doll sat beside me, and Mary watched, invisible to everyone but me.

Mum began, "Okay, here goes. It's been a long, long time since we've all been together like we are now, and in case ye dinna ken—we won the war."

"Hip, hip, hooray," the neighbours and relatives toasted.

Glasses were raised. Whisky was sipped. Aïda and I clinked our glasses of orangeade. Mum petted my wispy, brown hair— she was always doing that. "The government put my family into internment," she choked then, and stopped talking. The tittering stopped.

I slipped down onto the floor, taking Bruna doll with me; this was going to take a while.

Dad walked over to stand beside Mummy. "It's still impossible for me to understand why we were interned," he said. "We Bertellottis are more Scots than Italian."

"Had ye taken yer citizenship, Andy?" said Uncle Bill, Mum's stepbrother.

"No, none of us did. Mamma wouldn't hear of it. When the rumours of war began, I didn't think about citizenship. Tommy went to Italy on a visit just before the war actually got going. When he didn't come home, we were stunned. Rudy and I still don't know what all happened in Italy, but Tommy's telegram says that everyone is safe now."

"We're happy for that, Andy," said Aunt Jean.

"Rudy and I still feel that we are men without a country."

Uncle Rudy straightened up, nodded his head, and drank more whisky.

"Easy, Rudy," murmured Peggy.

It seemed to me that he and Daddy had already sipped too much whisky. I reached for the meringues that Mum had made with egg whites and rationed sugar. I stuffed two in my mouth— Mum took the third one away.

Dad blethered on. "Men without a country get carted off in the middle of the night. It was dreadful for wee Aïda, she was just a baby."

Now I paid attention. It was Aïda's captive lorry story.

Uncle Rudy said loudly, "The bloody British refused to give Andy and me a chance."

Peggy pulled him to the other side of the room. "Rudy, watch what ye say."

Daddy carried on. "The troops had tea and fish suppers in this very shop at five o'clock and came back with guns at nine. They loaded us up and pushed Kathy up the steps into the back of the lorry."

"They'd already shoved me into that cold damn truck," said Uncle Rudy.

Peggy was giving them both the shush sign.

I put my hands over my ears.

"Now, now, Andy, stop," said Mum. "Let's not dwell in the past. Look to the future. Thanks go to Peggy for keeping our shop open, and praise God for bringing my brothers home safe and sound." She put a finger on her lips to stop Dad from talking any more.

He took another wee dram and added, "I had to sneak out to get to Kathy at the hospital. Thought I was going to get pinched. Hell, I could have been put in Barlinnie. Bloody hell, no one should be treated that way." Daddy staggered and sat down heavily on a wooden chair.

Uncle John and Uncle Bill took big uncomfortable draws on their fags.

"I bet it feels wonderful to be back in the shop," said Aunt Jean.

"It does, Jean," said Mummy, "and it must be wonderful for John and Bill to be with Mum in Hurlford."

Bill's jet black hair was almost hidden by his pointed soldier's hat with the wee black and white squares on the sides. "Aye, it's great tae be hame."

"Where were ye stationed?" asked Uncle Rudy.

"Burma. We were on the Silk Road."

I thought about that word, Burma. It seemed like a place where they had elephants.

"How was it there?" Uncle Rudy sounded jealous.

"I don't dwell on it," replied Uncle Bill, looking at the floor. "I'm trying to forget the whole thing."

"What about yerself, John?" asked Daddy from his chair. "Where were ye?"

"I was in Egypt, then the Sudan. It was all heat and mosquitoes."

Was that another place with elephants? I wondered.

Dad asked in a very loud tone, "Did either of ye kill Italians?" My tummy felt sick.

"It was war, Andy. They shot at us and we shot back."

The two Scots uncles looked at each other with black piercing eyes that looked right through each other's heads.

Aïda whispered in my ear. "I think they did kill Italians."

"We did what we did, and it's over now," said Uncle John.

"Aye," said Dad, but he had a look that said he didn't quite believe him.

Mum coughed and raised her glass. "It's time the girls were in bed."

I held Bruna doll close. Mary and I got ready for another one of Mum's toasts.

"I'm glad that peace has come, especially to this family," she went on. "We're back in our lovely wee shop. Rudy, Andy, and I made it through our dark times." She coughed a funny noise. "Five long years we survived the damp, the cold, and the rats. Look at Anna and Aïda. They are healthy, and my brothers, John and Bill, are safe. As Rabbie would say, *'Man tae man, the world o'er, shall brothers be for a' that.'* Here's tae us!"

"For a' that and a' that . . . Here's tae us!" The folks raised glasses high.

Dad smiled. "It's past midnight, girls," he said, bending down to give us a wet kiss. His breath reeked of the whisky.

Mum said that even though the party would go on all night,

we needed to get into our bed in the alcove. She took us by the hand through the living room with its cheery fire to our dark, chilly bedroom, kissed both cheeks and tucked Aïda, me, and Bruna doll in. As she closed the door to go back into the shop, she switched on the bedside light above her pillow. The tiny, fringed lamp made the darkness pink, and the glow from the winter moon flowed through the frozen squares of the small window.

Mum said, "Look, girls, love is shining from both sides of the glass."

"Mum, do ye think Uncle John and Uncle Bill saw elephants?" I whispered.

"Go to sleep," said Mum.

"Aye, Anna, go to sleep," said my big sister, who fell asleep in a Scottish minute.

I was too excited to sleep. My head was full of black patent shoes, elephant tusks, and Daddy's eyes. My nose was full of the smell of fish and chips and the stink of whisky. My heart was full of love for my Mummy and Daddy, Bruna doll, my older wiser sister, and, of course, my imaginary friend Mary. It was comfy in our double bed with the heat from Aïda's back and the smell of her Sunsilk shampoo. The pink darkness enfolded me, and I fell asleep tangled in Aïda's curls. She reached out her hand. I took it and I felt safe.

34

Brothers Be for a' That

She tauld thee weel thou was a skellum,
A blethering, blustering, drunken blellum

Robert Burns, "Tam O' Shanter"

While children sleep, grown-ups think they never hear a thing!

I dreamed I was riding an elephant and wearing a golden crown, when suddenly there was a *bang*, then *another bang*. It sounded as if the ceiling had fallen in. Then there was a slap.

"What's happening, Aïda?" I sat bolt upright.

Before Aïda could answer, I heard "*John, damn it, John!*"

I grabbed for my sister. Next was the noise of pushing and shoving, boots scraping, chairs falling over!

Aïda and I leapt up from the covers and stood up. It was freezing in our nighties. Daddy's voice echoed through the wall as he shouted, "*What the hell!*"

We pressed our ears against the wall. There was another thump, an "*ouch!*" Then . . . CRAAASH!

"*Was that a bomb?*" I screeched.

I heard breaking glass and women's shrieks, as loud as sirens.

"What's going on out there?" Aïda wailed over the commotion. She was sobbing. I was scared.

Dad sounded like he was in our room. "Bill, get off me!"

We put our pillows on our ears and lay back down. I curled up like a baby; Aïda wrapped her arms around me like she did when the sirens went off.

Dad's voice sounded rough. Uncle Rudy swore, "Bloody hell," like he used to do when he chased us. This time it sounded like he was furious.

It was Uncle John's turn to bluster. "Jesus, Andy, ye and Rudy were enemy aliens. That's why ye were sent away."

Dad bellowed back, "John, ye'll never be a brother to me."

We could hear every movement through the wall. The men were pushing each other.

"Bill and I were following orders, Andy. Of course we killed Italians. War is hell."

"*Stop it!*" roared Mum. "This is a disgrace. Ye're brothers whether ye want to be or not. I married an Italian. I took the consequences. *Stop yer fighting now.*"

There was a loud thud.

"Now look what ye've done, ye silly buggers! I bet ye woke my girls." I'd never heard Mum's voice so angry.

We jumped down from the bed and ran to the door. The living room was empty, the fire was out. We tiptoed through to the shop. "Aïda, look!"

The huge mahogany counter lay on its side. Bottles were smashed. Glass was everywhere. Ginger beer puddled on the floor.

"They broke everything," I sobbed.

Uncle Bill had lost his pointy army cap and his mouth was bleeding. Daddy's face was beetroot red and he held his eye. Uncle John rubbed his elbow. Uncle Rudy had blood on his nice shirt and was trying to help Peggy, whose arm hung weird. Mummy stood, feet apart, arms crossed over her heart, chest puffed out like a rooster. She was the smallest person in the room but everyone was staring at her. "What in bloody hell do ye mean by tearing up this place with my children asleep in the next room? And look what happened to Peggy. She was just trying to separate ye idiots, and it looks like she got her arm broke."

I was afraid Mum would turn her head and see us, but she was just too angry. I could not stop staring at Peggy.

"Let's get this counter back up," said Uncle John.

"My God, Rudy, look what we did. We've hurt Peggy, and Babbo's counter is. . . ." Dad stammered. He was drunk.

"We'll fix it, Andy. Bill and I will repair it, I promise." Uncle John staggered and almost fell.

Uncle Bill leaned on the wall. "I'm sorry, Kathy, I'm sorry."

Uncle Rudy tried to take care of Peggy's hurt arm. She said, "Don't touch me, Rudy. Ye've done enough damage. I'm going home."

Aïda and I bee-lined back to the bedroom. We jumped into bed and hid under the blankets. It was darker now. The moon had left. The love was gone from the window. I tried to hold my tears. I liked it in bed when Daddy was snoring across the room and Mummy was sneaking a smoke in the night. I wanted my hot water bottle. I wanted my Mummy.

~ ~ ~

The door squeaked, flooding our room with light. Mummy's brooch had slipped, her hair was messy. I reached for her hand. It was cold and shaky. Aïda was crying softly, not like me.

"It's okay now, my pets. The show's over. I'm sorry ye had to hear it."

"Mummy," I said with my nose running. "Was that a war?"

"No, lass, just a stupid argument amongst a bunch of drunken brothers. That's what too much whisky does."

"We're sorry, Mum," said Aïda, as a scraping noise began.

"They are trying to pick up the counter, girls, but they'll never do it tonight, they're all drunk, and, lassies, don't say yer sorry; ye're not to blame." She rubbed our backs. "Children don't cause fights." She took a breath. "Adults cause fights. Drink causes fights. Grown-ups who think they're smarter than everyone else cause wars. Kids don't. They just get hurt."

We felt a draft of cold air come under the door and the murmur of voices saying good-night. "They're leaving now, girls. It's snowing, so they need to go home. If they can find their homes," said Mum. "Go back to sleep, my pets."

"Is Daddy all right?"

"He'll be fine. Everyone will be fine."

"Even Peggy?"

"Even Peggy. She hurt her arm, but I don't think it's broken." Mum tucked us in and then she sat quietly in the dark looking at us.

I could smell the smoke from her fag and knew that everything was going to be all right.

35

Making Up

We'll tak a cup o' kindness yet,
For auld lang syne.

Robert Burns, "Auld Lang Syne"

Mummy knew about forgiveness.

She would get angry when we didn't drink our milk, but then we were forgiven. She didn't like it if we skipped washing our necks, but soon it was forgotten. But how was she going to forgive Daddy?

It was early morning. I tiptoed over to his bed—sometime in the night he had crawled under his covers. I stood beside him, watching him sleep. "Ouch!" I exclaimed when I saw his swollen eye. It was black and blue, and dried blood was stuck to his nose. A tiny piece of cotton wool was entangled in his moustache. It was moving up and down with each snore. I looked over to see Aïda watching me with a grin on her face.

"What are. . . ?" she began.

I put my finger to my lips. "Shush," I whispered, and pulled the blood-splattered cotton wool from his nose. He snored but didn't wake up.

Mum was in the living room, sitting in her soft chair, drinking a cup of tea, smoking her morning fag, and gazing out at the pale morning light that streamed through each window pane and made dust drops dance in the light. Grey smoke swirled around her head.

Aïda whispered, "Look at the magic dust." We crossed the room to sit on our cushions by Mum's feet. Daddy trailed in a few minutes later, still in his pajamas and looking like a sad dog. His head drooped and the eye that was open watered. I ran to hold his hand, but he needed to sit down first. Mum handed him a cup of tea with two lumps of sugar and two aspirins.

"Kathy, ye know how sorry I am."

Aïda and I were crying again. I felt sorry for Daddy.

"Ye can make it up by shaking hands with my brothers."

Dad nodded his head, "Aye, Kathy. Aye, I will. I don't know what got into all of us. I suppose too much drink and the pressure from the war years." After Daddy had his tea, he got up and walked around in a state, wondering how he could put his shop back together again. Mummy had swept up the glass and mopped the orangeade, but the counter had a huge crack. The fish-fry pans sat cock-eyed, and grease had run down the side.

"Peggy kept it so well," he muttered. "I've been home just a few months and we wrecked the place. Babbo would be furious if he saw this, and Peggy is so angry with Rudy that I wonder if they can make up."

"I think he hurt her arm, Andy."

"Aye, he was just trying to keep her out of the fight, but she pushed her way in."

I got up from my cushion and took Dad's hand; it felt soft from the cooking of the chips, but it had a bruise on the knuckles. "Thanks, pet," he said. "That's nice."

~   ~   ~

In the afternoon, Aïda and I dressed all pretty again. We were invited to Aunt Jean's for a Hogmanay Feast. The four of us walked slowly up St. Andrew's Street towards John Finnie

Street, where Aunt Jean and Uncle Jimmy lived. The sky was a solid grey, and the snow had packed down to slush and ice. The town smelled clean and fresh because none of the factory chimneys were burning, and it was too cold for the cooking smells to drift out the doors of the tenements.

Aïda and I slipped and slid all the way up the street. "Are ye feeling better yet, Daddy?" Aïda asked, with one sock up and the other down, her breath puffing around her rosy cheeks. Our legs didn't feel the cold, they were happy to be playing.

"Aye, pet," said Dad, cocking his hat to hide his black eye. He held Mum tight, so she wouldn't fall on the ice, and I watched him pull her close to him in her brown fur coat. "I'm really, really sorry," he whispered in her ear and gave her a peck on the lips. That's when Mum forgave him.

There was hardly a soul in the town, no bagpipes played, no snowflakes fell on my lips. It was brisk and silent except for our footsteps echoing. The tenements stood tall, watching over all of us as we marched on the slippery cobblestones.

Mum whispered, "I think everyone in Kilmarnock has a hangover."

~   ~   ~

At Aunt Jean's, we kids sat on the long piano stool at one end of the table so we could swing our legs. I whispered to my cousins, Violet and Jim, about the *big fight*, and I watched my uncles, John and Bill, the boxers, out of the corner of my eye in case they needed a referee. Uncle Eddie Neil, Mum's real brother, had not been at the party, but he was at Aunt Jean's table. Eddie was Dad's best pal from before the war, and I was sure he could have stopped the fight with that big fat hand of his. He would have held it up like the boxing referee does and stopped all their nonsense. I had never seen such a big hand.

Daddy and the arguing uncles had moved out into the hall with drinks in their hands; Uncle Eddie went with them. We kids stayed on our stool like we were told to, so I couldn't keep an eye on them anymore.

Auntie Mary was Eddie's wife. She hailed from Glasgow and had a lovely broad accent. Her favourite song was "*I belong tae Glasgow, dDear old Glesca Toon.*" She sat down beside me on the piano stool, with her bum hanging off the end. Her face was so close that I could see the fuzz on her lip. "Och, ye silly wee monkey," she said. "Dinna ye greet aboot a tiddly thing. It a' happened last nicht and soon the whole rig-a-rimole wull all be forgot."

Before we could stop laughing, the men came back into the dining room with smiles on their faces. Uncle John was the spokesman. He strode into the small green dining room where the table stretched from one end to the other and said, "We're very sorry for the fight last night, and to make things right, Bill, Eddie, and I will repair Andy's counter. We'll work thegether and make the Ideal Café the best place it can be."

Mum raised her glass. "Cheers for guid brothers, and let by-gones be bygones. I suppose this proves that good Scots whisky can sometimes sort the very thing that it broke in the first place."

It seemed Mum was always making speeches.

We kids watched the rig-a-ma-role that was dinner. I had never seen so much food. One after another were courses served on Aunt Jean's willow patterned china: mashed neeps, tatties, cold meats, homemade pickles, and two big chickens; more food than we'd had in a month when we were in internment. We kids clapped when we saw the tiny white frills covering the chicken's claws. Granny and Aunt Violet had baked fairy cakes, small cup-cakes with the tops cut off and made into wings that stuck de-liciously out of the clotted cream. What a treat for our lips! All the bad feelings had been replaced with laughter, and we kids rolled off of our perch on the piano stool to say a poem or sing a song to entertain the family.

Mum called it "taking a wee turn."

Mary always gave me courage when it was my turn to sing.

~ ~ ~

True to their word and armed with all sorts of tools, our uncles arrived at our shop the very next day. There was much talk about how to accomplish the repairs. Mum came up with a smashing idea. "Why don't ye cut the counter in two pieces and move each into separate rooms? Make one the front shop for take-out and the other for a sit-down dining room."

And that's what happened. The uncles sawed the great mahogany counter in two, and set one piece in front of the kitchen door. The other went into the dining area to set the plates up. It looked as if they were always meant to be there. Dad polished each half till it shone. Next they moved the fry pan into the kitchen behind the counter. Dad decided that he would ask the town council if he could put in new linoleum. When the inspectors came, they decided that if our shop was to have a sitting room it should also have a bathroom for the customers. Aïda and I were excited. Now we'd have an indoor toilet! For days, the shop was filled with workers laying linoleum and putting pipes in.

Uncle John and Uncle Bill painted the walls, yellow for the front shop and pale green for the dining room. Dad ordered small round tables and curved-back chairs. He purchased glass boxes to sit on the counter to hold Cadbury's chocolate bars when the rationing ended. Our shop looked as posh as Uncle Rudy's Ritz Café.

Uncle Bill made me a doll house from the scraps of lumber. It was my birthday present, along with a nice cake from Mum and a trip to the pictures from Uncle John to see *The Bells of St. Mary's* with Bing Crosby. It was my best birthday ever!

To top off the remodel, Daddy ordered a new front door. The top was smoked glass with *The Ideal Café: Andy Bertellotti,*

Restaurateur etched in bold letters. When the door opened a bell rang. All my uncles were there for the grand re-opening, even Uncle Rudy.

"Where's Peggy?" Aïda asked.

"Peggy is not my girlfriend anymore," he replied.

"Is it because ye pushed her, Uncle Rudy?"

"Well, no, but that didnae help. She moved away, far away. She lives in Canada now."

"Don't ye love her, Uncle Rudy?"

"Aye, Aïda, I do. I miss her, but she says I'm too jealous."

"Maybe she'll forgive ye, like Mummy does for Daddy."

"I think it's too late, lass."

It was.

36

A Sure Thing

But pleasures are like poppies spread,
You seize the flow'r, its bloom is shed
                    Robert Burns, "Tam O' Shanter"

When Andy and Rudy were children, their mamma did not allow them to play after school; they were expected to study and then work in the shop every evening. But those two were rebels. They'd sneak out the upstairs window, down the roanpipe, to play soccer with the other boys. Their mamma tried everything, using a strap and even tying them to the bed, but still they escaped.

When they were in their teens, they sneaked out to the *Dug Races*, which were held in a large paddock down by the Ayr pier. That greyhound racing was illegal made it even more exciting to the two teenagers. Andy was probably only fifteen when the two boys first crept into the remodeled horse paddock with its rickety bench seats for spectators. A rowdy bunch of men hung out at the Dugs and thought nothing of giving the two curious boys cigarettes or beer. Soon the boys learned how to skim the till at their dad's shop to bet on those magnificent greyhounds with their long sleek bodies and tails that curled up over their backs.

By the time their folks moved to Hurlford, Rudy and Andy

were drawing a small wage from Babbo for working in his café, so they no longer had to skim. When Andy met Eddie Neil, Kathy's brother, they became instant pals. Eddie was a few years older and could easily buy beer for Andy. Because of his malformed, swollen left hand, Eddie had endured teasing all through school. He maintained it had made him tough. Eddie had finished school at age fifteen and gone to work on the railway to help support his family.

The one thing Eddie loved above all was watching the greyhounds. "One day, Andy," he'd say, waving around that big hand of his, "I'm goin' tae own one o' my own. I'm saving as much as I can."

Andy enjoyed watching the sleek dogs run almost as much as Eddie did."When they race," Eddie said, "it makes my blood course like a river through my body."

Out of school and working at the café full time, Andy spent most of his pay on gambling. Sometimes he and Rudy still "borrowed" from the till, and if the dog won, they pocketed the winnings and replaced the money they'd taken. Andy was sure that his dad turned a blind eye, because Babbo knew every silver sixpence that was in his till at all times. He and Rudy would urge their dad to slip away from Mamma and go to the races with them, but Babbo preferred to have no trouble from Mamma.

When they hit their twenties, Eddie and Andy combined their cash and bought their own pedigreed greyhound, while Rudy became very busy with the chasing of pretty girls. Greyhounds are a loving breed, but they are trained to chase a mechanical hare and, if walked un-muzzled, will grab any small cat or dog that gets in their way. Eddie and Andy walked the dog on the Bellfield Drive where Eddie's mother lived and exercised him in a great field that was simply called the moss. That dog ran many races but won few.

All this happened before Eddie introduced Andy to Kathy,

who had no idea that her brother and new friend gambled so much. Then when Andy and Kathy fell in love, gambling took a back seat to courting.

~ ~ ~

Then the war started, and greyhound training became a thing of the past. During their internment, greyhound racing was the last thing Andy thought about. The only gambling he did during internment was to once in a while play pontoon—twenty-one—with Rudy in the evenings, for matchsticks.

~ ~ ~

Eddie stayed home from the Army because he could not carry a rifle with his deformed hand. He spent the war years breeding one dog after another, and bought and sold quite a few. Andy, of course, did not know about them.

Now the war was over, and Eddie stood in Andy's shop while Andy scooped out cones for the wee lassies.

"Andy, ye'll never believe this," said Eddie. "I've bred the best running dug ever."

"Ever?"

"Aye."

"Ye've timed him?" asked Andy.

"Aye, Maximilian's fast. Come with me over the moss and watch him go. I think he's a champion, but I need money tae get him ready for racing." Eddie spoke in broad Scots like his wife.

Andy wanted nothing more than to get back to the races; greyhounds were in his blood.

"Ye could be a bookie, Andy?"

"Now, that's an idea." Andy was suddenly thoughtful. He would make more money if he was a bookie, but would Kathy like that idea?

~ ~ ~

The Ideal Café was closed on Tuesdays so, while the girls were in school, Kathy and Andy visited Eddie and Mary.

"My God, Eddie," Andy exclaimed, looking at a stop watch. "I've never seen anything like it."

The men had taken the sleek grey and white dog called Maximilian out to a grass track while the women had their afternoon tea. Eddie had fashioned a stuffed rabbit on a wire. A homemade motor pulled the wire from the end at around thirty miles an hour. Max ran naturally and fast. Andy watched him, feeling the pull of the races pulsing through his body. The long dark days of internment fled from his veins—this dog, this Maximilian, would be fantastic at the track.

~   ~   ~

Eddie and Andy became bookies. They entered Max in the next few races around Ayrshire, and Maximilian won or placed in each one. The two men became so confident in the grey and white dog with the black ring around one eye that they believed big money was to be made. Indeed, Andy began winning. Max was an unknown at first, a long shot, so Eddie and Andy made money at the bookmaking. Andy took Friday nights off to attend the races; Kathy didn't mind because she liked the winnings he was bringing home.

It was a rag-tag bunch of men that attended the Dugs, but Eddie and Andy could handle them. Their minds dwelled on the magnificence of Max's long body; every muscle was ripped, his mouth un-muzzled, ready to snap on to the stuffed hare that spun just out of his reach. He sped out of the starting-box, and that's where the race was won.

Andy stood on a wooden box, a tall board with the odds written behind him. The working men, dirty black from the mines and the factories, would bet as much as five bob per race—some bet their whole week's pay. As the odds changed, they pushed their way towards the bookies. After fighting overseas, these men lived just for the moment: fags, dugs, and women.

Eddie shouted, "Thirteen tae one, that's yer chances on Max the nicht."

Andy collected the bets, sticking the money in a leather sack. The crowd pressed in on them; the stink of sweat, grime, and beer mingled with the cigarette smoke. Andy loved it.

When the bell rang, "They're off!" was the cheer.

~   ~   ~

Max won week after week. In April, Andy was approached by a well-dressed man who looked like he didn't belong with the riffraff. Andy recognized him right away. The man was William Kerr, a horse trainer from Stevenson. Horse racing was nothing like the illegal Dugs. Horse racing was a gentleman's sport. So why was this man at the Hurlford Dugs?

"Andy Bertellotti," he said, his gloved hand extended. "I'd like a word."

~   ~   ~

Kathy and Andy drove their old car to Eddie's place the following Tuesday while the girls were in school. They had afternoon tea in Mary's tiny upstairs flat, then the foursome went downstairs to see Max's pups. Eddie had turned an old barn into separate kennels with clean straw in each one. Max wagged his tail and looked proud, and in another kennel lay a brown bitch named Maisie, who had three pups nuzzling at her nipples.

"So ye bred him with this lovely dog," said Kathy.

"Aye," said Eddie. "Wanted tae get her bred afore the season got going, and aren't they just lovely?"

"Aye," they answered together.

"Max is the finest dug in the world," said Mary, Eddie's Glaswegian wife. "These wee pups will be as fast as Max one day."

Kathy nodded and lifted a pup to give it a cuddle. "Andy, don't ye think it's time ye told Eddie about yer visitor?"

"Max is the odds-on favourite next Tuesday, Andy," interrupted Eddie.

"I'm not surprised, he's getting better known. Listen, Eddie, I got an offer from William Kerr, the horse trainer from Stevenson. He's working for a millionaire who wants to buy our dog."

"What?" said Eddie. "Kerr is a horse man. When did he get interested in greyhounds? How much did he offer?"

"I suppose his boss must be getting into the dog business. He offered a thousand quid!"

"A thousand quid?" marveled Eddie. "That's a fortune."

"Aye," Andy answered. "And if Max wins on Tuesday, he'll pay two thousand! That would set us up for life and we would still have the pups."

"That's enough tae buy a private hoose," said Mary.

Most people in Scotland lived in Council housing owned by the town. Only the rich owned private houses. The town Council chose where most families lived.

"And we could go to Italy to see my Mamma and Babbo. What do ye say, Kathy?"

Kathy was stunned, so breathless she could hardly take a draw on her fag. "I could have my own house with a garden. We could get out of the tenements. That would be a dream come true."

"So Eddie, here's the deal. We can sell Max right now for a thousand quid, or we race him next Friday, and if he wins, we get double."

"I say double or nothing, Andy."

"Me, too. The decision's made."

37

Maximilian

On Friday evening the rain misted and thunder clouds gathered. It was a typical spring night in Ayrshire. Andy was a bit worried that Max would be racing in mud, but the trainers were strewing hay all over the tracks as Andy, Eddie, and Rudy arrived in an old van they'd converted to a dog carrier. Andy's bookie board was in back with the odds printed all down it; he marked them off as the bets came in. Eddie took Max in the trainer's entrance, while Andy and Rudy pushed their way through the throng of men.

Andy was known as Bertie with the crowd at the Dugs because his board was misspelled Bertie-Lotti. Eddie went in back to the kennels to take care of Max. Andy and Rudy set up near the rail where Andy shouted the odds for all the races. It made him feel so free after the long years of internment; if he and Rudy were Italian it was long forgotten, or at least forgiven.

The crowd smelled of grease and cigarettes; some of the men were coal miners, some were mechanics, all were drinking and having fun. Andy and Rudy were always dressed well, with shirt and jacket and an overcoat when necessary; they wanted to look like rich bookmakers. That particular night was the opportunity of a lifetime for Andy and Eddie, so Rudy was along to cheer. This time, life was going to change for the better. The noisier it got, the better Andy liked it. Men passed small bottles of whisky to each other; some drank Guinness from dark bottles.

The betting got so heavy on the big race that Max became the odds-on favourite. Andy just knew their dog was going to win; both he and Rudy bet their winnings on Max. The first two races became a blur of rainbow colour and noise—the din from the crowd, the yipes of the greyhounds in their boxes, the brrring of the bell and the announcer yelling, "They're off!" The cloud of smoke from the fags hung above like a great grey blanket.

"Between what I bet on Max and the money we'll get, we'll be in the pink, Rudy."

"He is a sure thing, all right," answered Rudy, with the crowd swaying around him.

Finally it was the last race. Andy's heart beat faster and faster and the mist changed to a spit of rain. Eddie settled the dog in the starting box. Max was whining and panting; he was ready, ready to run.

The bell rang, one, two, three times. BBBRRRIIING. *"They're off!"*

The lids flew up. The box doors opened with a clang. The greyhounds bolted—legs moving so fast they were one long rubber band, noses in a row, their sleek racing jackets wet from the panting in the box. Max shot out ahead of the others, his grey and white body a ripple of muscle, his long snout a good foot ahead of the pack.

Andy yelled, *"Go, Maximilian, go!"*

The dogs bunched up tight. The artificial rabbit was just ahead of Max's snout as he ran at a thundering speed. He was ahead of the pack by half of his body length.

"Come on, boy, come on! Go, Max, go!"

Then it happened! In an instant! Max turned his head just an inch to see the dogs behind him and then . . . disaster. He fell, and the pack of greyhounds rolled over him, yelping and howling. Max disappeared into the mass of sprawling dogs.

"*Chri-ist!*" yelled Andy.

The spectators moaned, "Ohhhh . . . No!"

Andy shoved through the crowd of men, leaving Rudy to watch the cash. The greyhounds continued rolling and floundering, whining in high pitches. Slowly they stood, one at a time shaking their dazed and dirty bodies. Max lay still on the ground, a grey and white mound. The trainers ran towards the heap of yowling dogs and the crowd quieted down. Eddie and Andy reached Max at the same time.

They bent over him and Eddie held the dog steady, running his good hand expertly all over the dog to check for injuries.

"Is he bad hurt, Eddie?"

"It's his foreleg, Andy. Look at the angle. It's broken."

"Christ Almighty, Eddie, he's done."

"We're done, Andy. We took a chance and lost," replied Eddie dazedly.

"What will I tell Kathy?" Andy's whole war experience boiled through him. He'd gotten Kathy's hopes up; he should have said nothing until the race was over. He thought of all her headaches in Darmellington and the nightmares she still had. She'd aye been skeptical about his bookmaking and gambling.

Someone brought a dog stretcher. The other greyhounds were up and wandering, but Max lay whimpering, the only one injured. The black ring around his eye seemed to stand out in pain.

"We'll get the vet, Eddie, maybe there's something?"

"Come on, Andy," answered Eddie, all hope gone from his voice. "Let's load him up."

The trio walked through the gathering fog with the drenched and injured dog on the stretcher, Rudy carrying the board. The rain soaked the men, but they I couldn't feel it. They heaved Max onto his blanket in the back of the van, and all three climbed into the cab for a minute to talk.

The race-track veterinarian came over to take a look. "I'm sorry, lads," he said. "He may have to be put down."

Andy could feel Eddie's sadness through his overcoat.

"We'll get another opinion," said Eddie, rubbing the pain out of his bad hand and glaring at the small man with the black bag. "Wrap it up for noo, and we'll see what our vet says tomorrow."

"Ye were plum out o' luck tonight," said Rudy.

"Aye, Rudy. Out o' luck is saying it mildly. Just let me know what happens, Eddie, I'll pay the bill."

Rudy sat at the driver's wheel, Andy beside him. Eddie climbed into the back of the van with the dog he loved. They were a sad lot. It would take quite a few whiskies to make them feel better.

~   ~   ~

The next day, Kathy and Andy went out to Eddie's place. Kathy had been brave and understanding the night before, even though all her hopes and dreams had flown out the window for a second time. Eddie and Mary were outside at Max's kennel. Max's foreleg was in a white cast, but he was already looking better.

"He willnae be racin' again," said Mary. "He'll be oor pet noo."

But Andy had something to tell everyone; he hadn't even told Kathy. He had had a visitor once again. "Ed, he's looking much better and I have to tell ye something. I had another visit from Kerr."

"What?" chorused Kathy, Eddie and Mary.

"Aye, he came to the shop. Kerr said he will buy the three pups. He won't pay the price that he would have for Max, but he'll give us a fair deal."

"Will it be enough for Mary and me to buy houses?" asked Kathy.

"No, we'll have to save some more, but. . . ."

"Is it enough for us to visit Italy?" Kathy's eyes were full of tears.

"Yes Kathy, it is enough to visit Italy."

"Well, now, won't that be nice. Eddie and I are quite content here for noo." Mary winked and held her man tight.

38

Haud Yer Wheesh

That night, a child might understand,
The deil had business on his hand.

Robert Burns, "Tam O' Shanter"

Winter evenings were dark and cold in Scotland. It was already November; Kerr had picked up the pups. Eddie and Andy had split the proceeds and decided to get out of the bookie business. Kathy was delighted that Andy would be in the shop on Friday nights, because the men got rowdy many a time in the dining room. Max was now a housedog in Mary's flat. No more greyhound racing for Andy and Eddie. Andy brought home a lovely wee spaniel for his girls. Aïda named her Trixie.

It was dark by four o'clock when the children got home from school. Kathy liked that time of day when the children were safely home and playing with the dog while the customers came in to buy fish suppers for dinner. By five o'clock, the factory workers crowded in with their large orders for the folks working the late shift.

"Wrap them up double, Andy. We like them hot."

"No problem," Kathy answered.

"Thanks, Mrs. Bertellotti!"

Kathy hated the Friday night nine o'clock rush. It was closing time for the pubs down the street and after several *wee halfs* of Scotch whisky and maybe a pint or two, the men would totter down Armour Street into the shop. They were always drunk and belligerent, arguing about a boxing match or the races or the war. There's nothing quite as awful as an argumentative, belligerent, stupid Scotsman. Rabbie Burns wrote many poems about the reckless drunkenness of the Scots, himself included.

The men who staggered into Andy's at half nine lived up to their reputation. They came to get sobered before going home to their wives and kids.

"What's yer name, lassie?" they'd say to Aïda if she was around. Aïda was bonnie, with black curls and olive skin, twelve already.

Kathy would chime in, "None of yer business, mister." She'd shoo both Anna and Aïda into the living room, away from the swearing and the ugly arguments.

"Why do they act so stupid, Mum?" Aïda would ask, fondling Trixie's ears.

"Well, girls, most of those men have spent the last few years overseas, fighting for their country. Now they go out drinking on a Friday night to forget about it."

Andy had begun visiting the pub for a pint or two before the nine o'clock rush. The Tam O' Shanter was just down the street, so he'd walk down and back in a half hour. The pub was a man's place; Andy enjoyed seeing his pals there.

~   ~   ~

One particular Friday he noticed that Kathy was quick to tell him what to do and quick to tell the girls off for nothing. "Are ye feeling all right, lass?" he asked.

"I'm not too good tonight. Could ye skip the pub?"

"I'll just be five minutes, Kathy. Just a wee half and I'll be right back."

By the time Andy got back, the shop was packed. The sitting

room was crammed with drunks calling for fish suppers, their tongues as usual vulgar and loud.

"I asked ye not to go, Andy," she barked at him. "I told ye I was not well."

Just then Aïda yelled, "Someone's sick!"

Kathy usually took care of these things. That night she glared at Andy and said, "I'm going to bed, Andy. Yer on yer own to clean up that man's vomit."

Andy took a pause and turned to the girls. "Aïda, Anna, go sit with Mummy and let me know what's going on." He grabbed a mop, cleaned up the floor, and served everyone else in the shop. The drunks were gone before ten.

Friday night was also Andy's card night. His pals, Andra Gillis and Archie Wallace, came through the door at ten thirty as usual. They played pontoon.

"Hello, Andy," said Archie. "Are we on the nicht?"

"I'm not sure," Andy answered. "Kathy's no well."

Just then, Anna came running from the bedroom. "Daddy, Daddy, come quick, Mummy's very sick."

The bedroom stank like eggs. Kathy had thrown up. Aïda and Anna were gagging, the dog hiding under the bed. Kathy was pale and shaking. "Andy, help me," she whimpered.

"Oh, lass, I am sorry, I was only thinking of myself."

She was sick again. Andy handed the girls the blue potty with the roses on. It was full. They ran for the back door. It opened with a bang as the wind whooshed down the entry. He yelled, "Go on, girls, go on."

"Gads, Daddy, it's awful."

Anna got the door of the lavatory open and Aïda dumped the mess in the toilet bowl.

"Daddy, Daddy," yelled Anna. "I canny see for the smell. What is that stuff?"

"Rinse the po po in the sink," said her mum. "I need it again—and get yer slippers on. It's cold out there."

The next two hours became a blur. Kathy sat on the girl's pee pot and threw up in the grown-ups'.

The two wee lassies gagged, wailed, and carried pot after pot out to the freezing cold loo, out in the entry across from the bedroom door. Andy's pals closed up the shop, turned off the hot pans, and disappeared. Andy wished he could disappear; he wasn't sure what to do.

Anna wailed, "Daddeee."

"Haud yer wheesh," he called back.

Kathy grew pale and grey. She whispered weakly, "Andy, this is not just the flu, something is wrong inside. I've been hurting for three days, but I didn't let on."

"I'll go get the doctor," he replied.

"Nooo," moaned Anna. "Don't leave us, Daddy."

"It's the only way, pet. He's not far. Just to the top of Gilmour Street and a wee bit further. Aïda, you're in charge."

"Daddy, nooo," wailed the wee one.

"Nooo," yelled her sister. "Don't leave us with all this mess."

"Shhh, girls, I have to go."

~   ~   ~

Andy ran and ran up Gilmour Street all the way to London Road where the doctor lived. He rang the bell and could hear it vibrate through the hall and up the stairs to the bedroom.

"Coming," said a loud voice. The doctor appeared at the door, glasses in one hand, a whisky in the other, slippers and dressing gown on. "What can I do for ye, sir? Why, is that yerself, Andy Bertellotti, at my door? I was in yer shop the other night."

"Doctor," he said. "Can ye come to my house? My Kathy is very ill."

"Does she have a fever?"

"She feels hot."

"Does her belly hurt?'

"Aye, could ye. . . ?"

"Mr. Bertellotti, just another question or two. Has her belly hurt for longer than a day?"

"Aye, she said it's been sore for three days."

"Is she tender more on the right than the left?"

"I don't ken."

"Does she cry out when she steps off the bed to get on the po po?"

"Why, yes, she does."

"Okay, then, I'll send for an ambulance and I'll take ye back to yer house in my car."

They were back in just a few minutes. It had seemed like hours to the children. Anna's hair stood on end, Aïda had brown stuff on her cheeks, Anna's face was red from the crying.

"The ambulance drivers are coming to take Mummy to the hospital," said their Daddy.

More wailing from Anna. The dog licked her hand.

"Haud yer wheesh," he repeated.

The ambulance arrived right at that moment.

Anna clung to Kathy's nightgown. "Mummy, Mummy," she cried.

Dr. Stewart pried Anna off Kathy's leg and sat down with her. "I listened to yer Mummy's belly, and guess what I heard?"

"What?" the girls asked together.

"I heard her appendix grumbling right through her skin."

"What did it sound like?" asked Aïda.

"It said, 'I want to come out.'"

Anna bit her lip, but she was quiet. The two young attendants loaded Kathy up onto the stretcher, and soon they were closing the doors and on their way to the hospital. The girls had followed Andy to the door.

"Do ye want me to take ye to the hospital, Mr. Bertellotti?" asked the doctor.

"The weans need me here. I wish we had a telephone."

"I wish ye did too, Mr. Bertellotti. I'll come back for ye at eight and we'll go to Kilmarnock Infirmary."

"Can we go too?" asked wee Anna.

"No, darling. I'll take ye to Aunt Jean's. Aïda can stay with Eleanor next door. Let's get this room cleaned up and get some sleep."

Anna

39

Scud Yer Bum

The dancers quick and quicker flew,
They reel'd, they set, they cross'd, they cleekit
Robert Burns, "Tam O' Shanter"

I felt bad when Mum went to the hospital. Worse when Dad said they took out her appendix. Terrible when the doctor said, "Anna, yer no allowed at the hospital."

Dad said that Mummy was very ill, but was getting better. He explained that the appendix, whatever that bad-smelling thing was, was gone in a bucket somewhere, and good riddance to it.

I was at Aunt Jean's house where my cousins, Violet and Jim, had hugged me at the door. Next day I went with Violet to school, where the kids played rounders at lunch time. I hit the ball all the way across the playground, showing them that even Bentinck School girls are good at rounders.

My cousins lived on the third floor of a red sandstone tenement on John Finnie Street. The flat had a long hall that ran all the way from the front door to the kitchen. The red carpet had white roses entwined along the long border—it was our race track. My cousins had an indoor bathroom with green and black tiles on the wall and a big green bathtub with a square edge. It was plush, not like our outdoor loo in the freezing cold entry

Jim and Violet

at Gilmour Street, where we had to get up in the middle of the night to throw appendix stuff into the toilet bowl. My cousin's bedroom had four windows facing John Finnie Street. She had a doll house that Uncle Bill had made for her, and two single beds. I slept in the left one under a satin bedspread that made me feel like I was in my Mummy's bed. Jim had a boy's room, a teeny one with a sloping ceiling and a skylight window. It was full of books. Jim loved to read and say his poetry, and I loved his smiley face and laughing Irish eyes.

Violet had very curly hair and pixy teeth that crossed in front. She looked like me, except she was a magic leprechaun and I was a wee fat Tally chip van. We dressed alike because Granny made our dresses out of the same material and pattern. The Haggertys were not in internment during the war, because Uncle Jimmy was a Catholic Irishman, and they were not enemy aliens like us. Violet was tiny like her dad, and she made her own miracles. Her eyes were the colour of wet, purple pansies, and she was my best pal except maybe for invisible Mary.

"What do ye think an appendix is, Cuz?"

"I think," Violet rubbed her chin, "I think it's another word for yer belly button."

"So, do ye think my Mummy lost her belly button?"

"Maybe they tied it back on when they were done with the operation."

"Aye," I said, taking a look at my own white stomach. "There's a knot in it, so I bet they can just tie it back on. That appendix thing sure stinks." We held our noses and laughed.

Teatime was a treat at Uncle Jimmy's—no fish and chips here. We smelled the mince and tatties cooking; mince is smashed up ground steak browned in the pan with an Oxo beef stock cube and served up with mashed potatoes. It was and is a favourite item of Scottish fare. Smother it with Bisto gravy or brown HP Sauce to freshen up your taste buds.

Violet and I played on the flat roof over Aunt Jean's wash house. We'd opened the window on the second floor staircase and crawled out on that roof. Up there, on the tar roof, we owned the world. We shared secrets, but when we smelled the yummy mince cooking, we scampered back through the window and up the stairs like the two blind mice. Jim opened the front door, and we raced him down the long hall to the kitchen.

Jim had thick black hair, slicked back from his forehead. His ears curled forward at the top in pink flaps. We called him *the Brain*. He was almost twelve and could play the piano as if he was in a concert, and he had read all of the Encyclopedia Britannica, no kidding. Jim said he'd rather be home playing games with his Mum or practicing his piano than be playing outside on the flat roof with two silly girls like us.

He announced at the table, "Come on, Annabella, good tatties and mince tonight, and after tea, we can play dominoes."

I knew I'd lose, because Jim was smarter than me, and smarter always won at dominoes.

"Hello," chirped Joey, the wee blue and yellow budgie in the gold cage that hung in the corner by the fireplace. "Wee bugger, wee bugger."

"Hello yourself, Joey," said Jim. "Wee bugger, wee bugger."

It was a cheery group around the kitchen table with its checkered cloth. There was a bit of a coal fire burning behind us, and clean white towels hanging on the pulley. Steam rose from the warm food towards the damp towels, releasing the faint smell of bleach. Uncle Jimmy doled out tatties and mince onto white plates, Aunt Jean poured creamy milk into clear glasses, and the evening sun gleamed through the window. We chattered all through the meal.

"Anna, did ye enjoy yer tea?" asked Uncle Jimmy.

"I did, thanks."

"Jim, would ye give us a couple of verses from 'Tam O' Shanter'?"

"Aye," said Jim. He was taking elocution, as many Scots children did.

"Let me explain the poem a bit," said Jim. "Anna, are ye listening? Maggie's a horse. Nannie is a witch."

I giggled.

> *"For Nannie, far before the rest,*
> *Hard upon noble Maggie prest,*
> *And flew at Tam wi' furious ettle;*

But little wist she Maggie's mettle!
Ae spring brought off her master hale, ·
But left behind her ain grey tail:
The carlin claught her by the rump,
And left poor Maggie scarce a stump.

Now, wha this tale o' truth shall read,
Ilk man and mother's son take heed:
Whene'er to Drink you are inclin'd,
Or Cutty-sarks rin in yer mind,
Think ye may buy the joys o'er dear;
Remember Tam O' Shanter's mare.

"So, Maggie got her tail torn off?"
"Aye, Anna, she did," Jim answered.
"Not very fair for the horse," I said.
"What's a Cutty-sark?" asked Violet.
"The witches' night gowns," answered her brother.
Uncle Jimmy patted Jim on the back. "Good reading, son."

~   ~   ~

That night I dreamed of witches and horses without tails, and Mum, in bed in the hospital, in her night gown, holding onto her belly-button so the doctor could not snip it off.

I left my dream to find Violet tapping my face with her fingers. "Wake up, Anna. Let's play tightrope?"

It was the middle of the night, again!

She put a finger on my lips. "Shh . . . This will be fun."

I slipped from under the covers and the two of us scampered across the hall. The street lights shone through windows and our nighties flowed behind us. The tub glowed in the moonshine, the rim white, flat, and tempting. Violet climbed up onto the flat rim of the gleaming tub, which then became a tightrope for two wee witches. We danced, pranced, and tiptoed like the witches in the poem. My cousin was magic, and the bathroom was our stage. We hopped up and flew down, lifting our legs like ballerinas, our nighties flowing like the cutty-sarks in the verses. Suddenly the door flew open. It was Uncle Jimmy, an uncle with his teeth out, an uncle in his pajamas, pajamas with a flap in the back—a flap that was not quite shut!

"What the devil?" Uncle Jimmy was furious. "I'll scud yer bums if ye don't get back in bed this instant."

We ran to our beds and jumped in before he could catch our tails.

I had never heard the word *scud* before. My Italian Daddy didn't know that word! I got my bum back in bed before my angry uncle could find his belt. Uncle Jimmy's bottom showing through that flap had made me giggle. Violet was already under the eiderdown, pretending to be asleep. I could see her covers lifting up and down, up and down.

"I'll scud yer bum," I whispered.

She giggled, her face into the pillow. Good fun could be had in the night after all.

~   ~   ~

A week later, Violet, Aunt Jean, and I walked down John Finnie Street to Portland Road, past St. Marnock's Church where we went to Brownies on Monday nights, and then round the corner to the High Street, which was busy as always. It felt good when we turned on my own Gilmour Street, even though I had had lots of fun at Violet's.

Mum was propped up in bed, looking like a pale film star and using a black cigarette holder to elegantly smoke her brown-tipped Craven "A." Aïda was sitting cross-legged on Mum's bed, reading as always. Mummy reached for me and I was in her arms. The world was right side up again.

"Can I see your appendix now, Mum?"

"Oh, lassies, the doctor threw it away."

"So, does that mean ye've lost yer belly button, Aunt Kath?' asked Violet.

"I still have my belly button," answered Mummy.

"How can a doctor take the appendix and leave yer belly button?" I asked.

"It's a mystery to me," said Mum. "Simply a mystery."

Anna

40

Whelks

"I saw thee seek the sounding shore,
Delighted with the dashing roar"

Robert Burns, "The Vision"

In April, when the pesky midgies came out and it was warm enough to go to the beach, my pals went to the seashore on Saturday, and even although Dad said the Atlantic Ocean was much colder than the Mediterranean Sea, my friends had paddled in the water, right up to their knees. I was jealous. Kids don't care if the coldness stings the legs, kids love the feel of the water lapping over each toe. They wave away the black midgies and gather whelks. My pals had picked hundreds of them, and it was quite *the thing* to have a bag of the wee snails at school to share; you ate them with a safety pin, right out of a brown paper bag.

In Scotland, we say *wulks*. Get yer tongue around it. Say it like a Scotsman does. Say the word *Wullie*. Here we go now—*wuuulks*. Try again—*wuuulks*, guid! It just runs off yer lips, see!

The wulk is a wee brown limpet that sticks to the piers and rocks at the seashore. So, on any given day, if yer daddy will drive or yer mummy will let ye ride yer bike, or let ye take the old double-decker bus, go on down to the seashore. Make sure ye take a brown paper bag or maybe yer sand bucket. When ye get to the beach, crunch on down the sand and look for a pier or

a bunch of rocks, then carefully scoop off a load of these critters. Of course ye don't eat the snails right off the rocks; yer mum has to boil them first. A wulk is not just something to snack on; it shows all yer pals that ye were at the seashore, and that makes ye a bit of a show-off.

On the way home from school Jeffrey Keast, the butcher's boy, said to me, "Would ye like one o' my wulks?" He held out a crumpled paper bag that was bulging at the sides and stained from the snails inside. Jeffrey said it had been in his pocket all day.

Imagine this bonnie boy asking me, Anna Bertellotti, if I wanted a wulk? I felt the flush in my cheeks. "Sure," I said with a bit of a gasp. I was breathless, and not just from the wind.

Jeffrey and I were in the same class and it felt good to be walking home with him. I liked his freckles and the way he walked with big fast steps. He was looking right at me, so I reached for my handy-dandy safety pin that was hidden in my pocket. I straightened out my schoolbag on my back, and reached into his paper bag.

There were lots of wulks, snuggled up nice and warm from Jeffrey's pocket. I reached in, took the brown shell between my thumb and forefinger and turned it up so the brown skin showed and then gently lifted off the skin with my safety pin. I licked it and flipped the skin into the gutter with my finger-nail. Next I reached into the round hole with the sharp pin and pulled out the kind of brown goo that was the wulk. I held it up and admired the wee thing and then popped it over my gums and chewed. I kind of liked it, and kind of not. This one was not so bad—quite salty it was; Jeffrey's mum must have put in lots of salt when she boiled them. It tasted good in the way your snot tastes kind of good, only it was a bit chewier and thicker. He asked me, "Did ye like it?"

Of course I did! Jeffrey Keast gave it to me.

"Two more please, Jeffrey. These are the best wulks I ever tasted."

I think the freckly, red-headed boy was very happy as we walked; he wore a great big smile and stopped to pull up his socks when he said goodbye. Then he coughed and covered his mouth, saying it was time he went on home. I thanked him for the wulks, and crossed over to go into my dad's shop. I waved to him from the shop door.

"Mum, Mum, have ye tasted wulks? Everybody at school eats them."

"Gads sakes, Anna! Those are awful things."

"They're not awful. They're yummy. Can we go to the sea-shore and get some?"

"Not if I have any say in it," she said, getting busy at the pans.

"Oh please, Mum, everybody eats them, even Jeffrey Keast, the butcher's boy."

"Well, we'll see," she said, in that way parents talk when they don't listen to what you say and they don't mean a word of it.

~ ~ ~

When Tuesday rolled around, Mum said we could miss school. It was a fine brisk sunshiny kind of day, and Dad wanted to take us to Barassie Beach with its fine seashore and sand dunes; they stretched for miles with their long grass, and on that lovely white sand cars were allowed to park.

Dad loaded up our black Hillman that had a nice silver emblem on the bonnet. It sat at the curb ready to start up at a moment's notice. The boot was open, and Dad stuffed two old deck chairs on board whilst we climbed in.

I had my pail and shovel, Aïda had her book; she was pretending that she was too big for the sand digging now. Mum had her fags and her fur coat for snuggling in case the wind blew hard. Trixie, our new wee spaniel puppy, jumped into the back seat where she cuddled up to me. I patted her head and pulled gently on her long ears. As we drove down the Ayr road on the way to the beach, I asked, "Mum, can I look for just a few wulks?"

"Oh, no, not that question again," she said, ignoring me.

"Just a few?"

"We'll see, won't we?" Another standard parent's answer! "I really don't want to cook snails when we get home."

"They're not snails," I said, "they're wulks, and maybe I'll find a few, I promise, only a few."

At Barassie the sun was out, but it was not really warm. There were a few folks walking on the shore. An old man and woman strolled with their wee Scotty dog on a long tartan leash.

A mum and her wee baby were hiding from the wind by sitting behind a dune.

Dad parked the car several yards away from the waves and set out the two striped deck chairs. Aïda sat on a blanket in front of Mum and Dad with her nose in her book. I ran towards the waves with Trixie, whose long spaniel ears trailed in the salt water.

"Don't get wet, Anna," called Mum.

"I won't," I said over my shoulder—although even I did not believe that statement. I threw Trixie her red ball, and she romped in and out of the waves whilst I gazed out at Paddy's Milestone, the island that is halfway to Ireland. Trixie was very smart for a puppy and fetched the ball over and over, shaking salt water on my feet and legs; it was freezing, but I didn't mind. The sun peeked out from behind the clouds, and I felt happy in my chest as I played with my pup. I took my wet socks and shoes off, but Mum made me keep my coat and hat on. She was bundled up in her fur coat in her deck chair. "The wind is chilly, lass. I don't want you in the hospital with pneumonia."

I didn't know that big word, so I kept on playing close to the water.

After a wee stroll down the beach, Dad sat down with Mummy, took out his lovely silver flask and poured himself a wee dram. "I love Tuesdays," he said with a big grin.

Mum smiled, lit her fag, and crossed her legs like the movie stars do. She blew smoke up to a silver-grey sky.

"It's almost as warm here as it is in Italy," Dad said, laughing.

"It would be nice to be there and feel the sun," she replied.

"Are we going to Italy soon, Mum?" asked Aïda.

"We'll see," said Mum.

How many standard replies could one lady have?

Aïda decided she was not too big to play in the sand after

all and helped me make a castle with scooped-up wet sand. She wanted me to make a moat, but I got bored; the sand was too cold. Trixie kept digging around Aïda's castle, so I took the silly pup away to give Aïda a chance to finish. The dog and I ran towards some big rocks. I could not believe my eyes when there, on the mossy rocks, right in front of me, were thousands, thousands of wulks.

I called over my shoulder, "I found them, I found them, Mummy."

I could see her mumbling to Daddy, then she called out, "Just a few!"

She was talking to the wind. Mr. Wind paid no attention and neither did I. I grabbed my red pail from Aïda and began collecting the wulks. I peeled each one off with a suck sound and soon the sand pail overflowed with wee critters. I carried the overflowing pail proudly back to Mum.

"Oh, Anna, ye always overdo everything," said Mummy with a grin. "Okay, ye can bring the pail home, but be careful."

I had to balance that pail in my lap all the way home in the back seat, with Trixie trying to eat the wee things. Finally the tired wee dog lay down, panting from all her running at the beach, and left me and my pail alone. Over and over, Aïda bumped my elbow in trying to spill them out.

"Leave me alone, Aïda. They will be really yummy, Mum. Ye'll see." I carefully carried the sloshy pail into the house and Mum dropped the wulks into a colander in the kitchen sink. I was surprised to see some wee jelly legs sticking out.

"Legs! I didnae know they had legs."

"The legs will disappear when I boil them," said Mum, getting out her biggest pot. She rinsed the wulks, filled the pot with water, threw them into the pot, and set the pot on the stove.

The three of us went into the bedroom, where Mum popped me into the sink to get the sand off. She scrubbed my back as if

I were really dirty and washed the sand out of all my bits with a washcloth. Dad said he'd take five minutes and walk down to the pub for a night-cap.

I got my pajamas on, and Aïda washed herself. Mum asked if we would like a story—or were we too big now?

"We're not too big, Mummy." I climbed into bed. "Could ye make up a story about a wee girl who just wanted a few wulks?"

"Oh, my God!" Mum cried out. "I forgot all about them. I left them boiling on the stove." She ran to the kitchen as fast as her high heels would go. "Anna!" she howled.

Aïda and I were in the kitchen in a Scottish minute. The pot had never come to the boil. The gas had gone off. The live wulks were on the march. They were everywhere. It was the escape of the snot balls.

"I knew I should never have. . . ."

"Mummy, I didnae. . . ."

The wulks had taken over. The stove was covered with wee snot balls sticking fast. Some were on the move, crawling on the carpet in front of the stove, scraping up the newly-painted wall. Those wulks scurried like fleas. Some had shells on, some had not. Some were naked, some were not. A few had died, others were bound to live. Trixie was barking like crazy and running around getting under our feet, trying to eat the shells.

"Gads sakes alive, girls, help me clean up this awful mess!"

Mum didn't know whether to laugh or cry. But when we laughed, she laughed. When Dad came back, he laughed. It was belly-laughing at its best. After all the laughter, after all, it was only a few wee wulks; but wulks were no longer what I ate. Jeffrey or no Jeffrey, I didn't even have a safety pin in my pocket anymore!

41

The Tonsil Factory

The wind blew as 'twad blawn its last;
The rattling showers rose on the blast; . . .
That night, a child might understand,
The deil had business on his hand.

Robert Burns, "Tam o'Shanter"

Mum said it was because I paddled in the water all the way up to my knees. All I know is I got the tonsillitis. I couldn't swallow even one sip of Currie's lemonade.

The doctor said, "Ye'll huv tae go to the Western Hospital in Glasgow."

I was not for it. Glasgow was full of tough gypsy women, gangs, and razor-slashing teddy boys. I told him I would just keep those great red and white balloons in my throat.

Mum said, "No, Anna, ye can't keep them. They have to be removed, just like my appendix, and Glasgow has bigger, better hospitals than Kilmarnock Infirmary."

I had found out from Cousin Jim that the appendix was not the belly button at all. It was a wee pink thing that lived inside Mum's belly.

Mum said, "Yer big red tonsils are telling ye that they'll hurt till they come out."

I was still not for it.

Daddy said, "I think it was the cold wind at the beach."

Aïda said, "It was those *wulks.*"

Mum said, "I told ye not to get wet." She had lost her sense of humour, and I got dragged, tartan scarf on my neck, to Glasgow on the three o'clock train. It was not fair. The Western Hospital scared me. It looked like a prison, and it smelled of bleach and dirty mops. The lights were so bright everybody looked old, even me. Dad stayed home to tend the shop. I knew he didn't like hospitals after Mum's experience. My Aunt Vi, Mum's youngest sister, came along to keep Mum company and to cheer me up. I did not want any cheering up.

~ ~ ~

"Mummy, Mummy. Where are ye? Where am I? I canny see." A stinky, plastic pillow with bits of blood and spit on it was stuck on my hair. It felt gooey. Knives were stabbing the back of my throat. "Who's there?" I smelled my aunt's perfume. She was a lavender dream. Her long shiny nails stroked my hand, caressed my skin, but I couldn't see her and my throat burned like a coal fire.

"Mummy's talking to the surgeon," she answered.

I tried to yell, "Help!" My heart said, "Help me, Aunt Vi." Not one word came from my cracked lips.

"Oh, my wee pet, my wee darling, what have they done to ye?" Aunt Vi's voice came down a dark tunnel to my brain. The operating theatre had been cold. The doctor had worn a red-rubber apron that stunk and he scrubbed his hands clear up to his elbows. I felt the big rubber mask on my mouth, a cool breeze puffing up my nose and the pong of the ether. I was in a dark cave, falling, falling.

The doctor said, "Here comes the chloroform. Count backwards from a hundred."

"Ninety-nine. . . ."

~   ~   ~

"Good morning, wee lassie, wake up." A strange Glasgow voice spoke. "Here's a wee drink o' water. Suck it up the spout."

My eyelids stuck to my cheeks, sand filled my throat; I was sinking in, sinking down, tonsils sucked out. Through my gritty eyelashes, I saw a cracked, dirty teapot. A teapot! Once it might have been bone china, but now it was worn and chipped. This crazy nurse must think I'm daft. I would never suck out of the spout of a cracked old teapot. Mummy would never make me drink from a cracked anything, never mind a teapot. Where was Mummy? Where was Mary? I was just a child and this woman was Nurse Crafty Nose from who knew where. Bile rose in my throat and I vomited. "Can I just die now, God, and go to Heaven? I'm only seven, God, but here I come. Nurse Crafty Nose doesn't care, God, not one iota, and God, the gypsy women from the other beds are snickering at me." I could hear the splatter of hail smacking the big windows above me; I wished it would rain on me.

In a while I began to see better—Aunt Violet's bonnie face was crinkled and her nose needed blowing. My hand reached to touch her pink cheek. The room spun like a top. I threw up on the plastic pillow; my head was stuck to my ear.

"Look at that silly wean, would ye," said a broad, loud Glasgow voice. It had to be a mean old woman from the Glasgow slums. I was scared. Did they have knives?

A hard-working hand took mine. I could feel the ridges on Mum's wedding ring, I grabbed on, smelling her cigarettes and her Chanel Number Five. She shushed the rude woman—"Leave my child alone."

Aunt Violet's nails held one sticky hand and Mum's rough grasp held the other. "Now, now, don't worry, pet. Mummy's here. This will be over soon. I promise." Her voice lulled me and I heard her whisper to my aunt, "Why did they put her in a ward with all these rough women? She was supposed to be in the children's ward."

I drifted away, with both hands secure and happy. Mary was with me in my dream. We were licking ice cream cones. Mummy was humming:

"Speed, bonnie boat, like a bird on the wing, over the sea tae Skye.
Carry the lad that's born tae be King, over the sea tae Skye."

I slept a deep sleep then, flying with the birds, Mary and Aïda flying with me over the ocean waves to Skye to Italy where we would make sandcastles. When I woke, the bright lights blistered my eyes. Nursing Sister Adeline Marie strode into the ward. I was hoping she was there to save me, but no, she smoothed my bed covers and said, "As fur ye, young lady, eat up that purritch; it'll sooth yer throat."

I hated porridge, and a thermometer was stuck in my armpit. I was afraid to lift my arm. I was trapped in Ward Ten with women who smelled like dirt. Mummy had left me with witches who snickered and called me names like *spoiled brat* and *Tally wop wean*. How did they know I was Italian?

In the afternoon, my four-foot-ten Mum in her high heels and sweet-smelling clothes walked in. It was visiting hour, three o'clock on the dot. She handed me an ice-cream in a cup. "Look, Anna, a Wall's strawberry ice-cream. It's yer favourite."

I smiled at the red and white cup and stuck the wooden spoon in to taste the cold ice. Soon I found out that it hurt to swallow. I was so disappointed that I bawled out loud.

"Don't cry, ye big baby," yelled one of the gypsy women.

I stuck my tongue out and immediately regretted it.

Mum took my hand. "I'm sorry that this has been so difficult, but ye never have to do it again." Another speech!

"So tonsils don't grow back?" I squeaked.

"Tonsils don't grow back," she answered.

"Can I come home soon?"

"Aye, when the Doctor says so; Daddy's ice-cream will help ye forget all about this."

"I'm not sure about that, Mum," I said.

"Well, here's something that will cheer ye up."

"What?" I squeaked.

"It's a letter from Uncle Tommy. Look, Anna—airmail. Feel this thin blue paper. Imagine; it came on an airplane."

"Open it, open it," I said.

"It says, 'I am coming back to Scotland to check on my business. It will be nice to meet Anna.'"

"Uncle Tommy is coming to see me?"

"Yes, Anna, just to see you." Mummy was smiling.

"Will he bring me a present?"

"I'm sure he will."

42

A Proposal

The war had wreaked havoc in Italy. Half a million men had died, and many more families were displaced. King Vittorio Emanuele III had been replaced by his son, Umberto II, who was coronated on the first of May and stayed in power only forty days—the people nicknamed him the May King. What an upheaval! Tommy longed to marry Lea and take her to Scotland, but he was still an interpreter for the Americans, helping with contracts and language issues. Tommy loved Italy for the perfect summer weather and was always happy to see his parents and Bruna, but he longed for Scotland: the broad accents, the wind, his café.

~ ~ ~

After six months of travel and contract interpretation, Tommy drove to Viareggio where Lea taught six-year-olds. He had visited her two months prior and had been dismayed that wherever they went her sister or mother accompanied to chaperone. Gone were the post-war days of Naples when Lea and Tommy had been alone with their thoughts and touches. As Tommy drove he could feel her silky blond hair, see her blue-green eyes and her soft laugh. He was sure she loved him—she was taking English lessons. Tommy hoped it was to help her when they moved to Scotland. First he must ask her papa for her hand.

The vineyards around the seaside town had turned burnt orange and yellow; the grapes were harvested. The Versilia Coast, which only a few months before had stained red with blood, was now the peaceful blessed place Tommy had imagined it.

Stefano, Lea's papa, stood at the door of his shop. "Come in, come in, Irmo. We have missed you," he said, "especially Lea."

Tommy kissed him on both cheeks as they did then in Italy.

"Come upstairs to my flat, we will share some vino."

Tommy followed Stefano into a small lift. Stefano closed the metal gate with a click and the lift rose two stories. When Stefano opened the door into his living room, Tommy spied the Mediterranean from his windows. "What a magnificent view," he said, glancing around a room resplendent with brocade pillows and a sumptuous couch.

"Would you like an aperitif, Irmo?" Stefano asked.

"*Grazie*, Stefano," said Tommy with a nervous laugh. He cleared his throat. "You have known me quite a while now."

"*Sì*," answered Stefano. "You seem like a nice man."

"I would like to ask permission to marry your daughter."

"Let me call in my wife." Stefano coughed, covered his mouth, choking on the bubbly wine. "You don't waste any time, do you?"

Tommy gripped the arms of the velvet chair. What did he have to offer Lea, who had come from this palace of a flat?

Lea's slender, grey-haired mamma entered the vast living room from her kitchen. She moved like her daughter; it was as if they both walked on water. She smoothed her skirt as she sat. Her husband handed her a glass of Prosecco. "So, he is asking?" She directed the question to her husband.

"*Sì*," Stefano answered, with a shrug. All of this conversation was in Italian. The couple regarded each other intently, their look translated into "I told you so."

Stefano turned back to Tommy. "I don't suppose you want to learn the shoe business? I could teach you to be a fine shoemaker."

"No, sir," Tommy answered, shaking his head.

"And you will, undoubtedly, want to take our daughter to Scotland where your business is."

Tommy realized that the couple had already talked about this possibility. "If she'll go, I will definitely take her there."

"Ah," he said, shaking his head. "You know that Lea loves the teaching of the youngsters—you would take her away from all that, *sì*?"

Tommy hung his head.

"Stefano, at least Irmo has come to us first. He loves Lea."

Tommy could have kissed Lea's mamma.

"I do," he said quickly. "I love her with all of my heart. You see, Stefano, I can make a living in Scotland. I make good money in the fish and chip business. I do not want to go back there without her." Again he looked around the opulent room. Could he give Lea what her parents had?

"Well, here's what I say, Irmo," replied Stefano. "We want the best for our daughter. You will rip her away from her sister and all she knows—you will take her away from us. But she is sad when you are not here. She misses you. If she loves you enough to say yes, we will support her decision."

Tommy stood, overwhelmed but pleased; his left hand twirled a diamond ring that snuggled in his pocket. It was a small, antique ring that he had found in Veneto. He extended his right hand to Lea's papa.

"Go now, Irmo." Stefano said as he shook Tommy's hand. "Go with our blessing. No more chaperone. Respect, please, her answer."

~ ~ ~

Lea and Tommy dined in a small bistro on the Viareggio wharf, entertained by an amusing waiter who could balance many water glasses at a time and twirl the tray round on the tips of his fingers. When the long rays of the sun reached across the sky and the sunset filled the void above the Mediterranean, Tommy asked Lea to take a walk. They crossed over the promenade to the sand below and slipped off their shoes.

"It is so nice to be alone, Irmo. How did you manage that?" asked Lea.

"I have my ways with your Papa," Tommy answered, smiling warmly at the woman he adored. They strolled, Tommy with his pants rolled up to his knees, Lea with her skirt blowing in the breeze. She picked up sea shells as they walked and wandered into the surf, running back when the water came too high. As the sun's rays died the sea turned red and gold. "Let's sit here, Lea," said Tommy.

Two deck chairs sat on the beach facing the sea—he had arranged with the waiter to bring them to that very spot. A striped umbrella tipped backwards, covering them.

"What if these chairs belong to someone else?"

"No worries, my darling. I had them brought over."

"You are amazing," she said. "*Cosa belle sedie.*"

"*Prego,*" he replied, kissing her gently as he helped her sit.

Her face was soft like the dew. They held hands, watching the clouds stretch and the sky darken slowly from pale pink to light grey as the evening came to an end. The clouds broadened as if to welcome in the gulls and seals for a nighttime sleep. The sea was calm, the waves lipped the sand, and the sandpipers scurried, curved beaks raising and lowering for their last meal of the evening.

Tommy was suddenly very nervous and instead of the masterful speech he had practiced, he blurted out, "*Lea, si sposare meh?* Will you marry me?" He was on his knees, looking up into her Tuscan eyes.

"Oh, Irmo," she whispered, touching his face and lips. "You know how much I love you, but I can't."

Tommy felt as if his heart might stop.

She put a finger on his lips and he inhaled the smell of her as she leaned down to kiss him. "You will ask me to leave *Italia*, yes?" It was a whispered question.

He nodded and slowly sat back in the deck chair. "Lea, we have discussed that before."

"Irmo, you have talked about it. I have listened."

"But, Lea," he protested.

"Shh, Irmo. I love you, but I also adore *mia familia* and *il bambini e scuola*. They are only six years old and they need me. Many of these children have lost their papas in the war. Please go back to Scotland by yourself, give me time to help these bambini. Find out if you still have a business. *Le comuncazioni sono molto difficili.* You know how bad the communication is between our countries. Are your brothers alive and well?"

As she spoke, Tommy knew she was right. He was asking her to make a commitment when he hardly knew what he was asking her to commit to. One telegram was all he had received and it was already ten months after war's end. He'd heard only that Andy and Kathy had another child. Tears ran down his face. He saw the waiter coming towards them with a bottle of *Prosecco* in his hands. He had been so sure Lea would say yes that he had asked him to bring it with two glasses. He waved the waiter away, but the man kept coming.

The waiter poured two glasses with a flourish. "*Salute,*" he said, bowing.

"*Grazie,*" said Tommy and gave him a tip.

The waiter departed looking puzzled. The couple had been sad, not celebratory.

"Irmo," said Lea, holding up her glass, "I am not saying no. I'm just not saying yes."

Evening became night, and the couple sat in the dark with a few stars twinkling overhead. She whispered, "Irmo, the war has taught me that some things have to wait until the right time

and our decision cannot be made lightly. Let's walk some more."
The lights from the promenade had long since been turned off.
"When we fled to the Pietrasanta hills, my Irmo, *mia familia* had
to care for each other, even keep each other warm in the night.
When the massacre occurred in the valley below, we knew that
our lives were a precious gift from God."

"I know this, Lea. I watched good men die." Tommy replied.
"This war changed all of us. I never dreamed when I left Scotland
in 1939 that I would be here today, still in the American Army,
with you by my side. I will go home for a while and then come
back for you, because I mean to have you in my arms forever."
The ring was burning a hole in his pocket. "Would you wear my
ring as a promise?"

She turned towards him, tears flowing unstopped.

Tommy handed her his handkerchief.

"I will wear your ring with pride, Irmo, but if you go to
Scotland and decide that I am not the woman for you, I will give
it back."

"Lea, *mia amore,* you are the woman I want for always and always. I will go to Scotland and make preparations for our home,
then I will come back for you."

"I will wait here, anxious to know what is happening."

He slipped the diamond ring on the finger of her right hand
and held her close. "Whatever lies in front of us can only be
good."

They kissed then, a deep satisfying kiss that was different
from all the others.

43

The Queen's Café

A Man's a Man for a' that.
      Robert Burns, "A Man's a Man for a' That"

1948

"I can't believe yer back," said Rudy.

"I can't believe my shop looks like this." Tommy and Rudy stood outside the Queen's Café on Portland Street. It had been years since the doors were open. Graffiti on the walls said *Good Riddance Tally* and *Nae Wops*, and the windows were boarded up.

"What am I going to do, Rudy?" Tommy asked, dismayed at the sight. Lea had been right. What if he had brought her here, to this? "This fucking war is still haunting me."

"Let's go to the Wheat Sheaf for a drink," said Rudy. "We have a lot to catch up on."

He tried to pull Tommy away, but Tommy couldn't take his eyes off the premises that had once been his café.

Tommy was disgusted. "Christ, Rudy, this was not the hands of the enemy, but our own Kilmarnock Town Council closed me down and boarded up my shop."

"Tommy, it was our own government that took Andy and Kathy, me and the weans away to Darmellington and threw away the key."

"Oh, I'm sorry, Rudy. I was only thinking of myself. We

really need to talk this out. I want to come home and I still can't
get it through my head that ye all were interned."

"Come on, Tommy, there's no solutions here." He pulled on
Tommy's arm, sure that solutions lay inside the whisky bottle.

"I'm coming, Rudy." Tommy was already speaking with a
Scots accent; it was as if it was carried in the chilly fresh air that
was Kilmarnock. They walked down Portland Street.

The Cross had not changed. The roundabout was blooming
with early tulips and azaleas. The magnificent Bank of Scotland
building stood tall, the centerpiece, with Scarlet's the florist on
one side and Rankin and Borland's the chemist on the other. The
two brothers walked up Bank Street to Rudy's café, the Ritz.
Bank Street was narrow and had many wee shops where women
shopped, dressed smartly with handbags over their arms, high
heels and nylons. Dogs ran loose and working men strolled with
fags burning in their lips. Tommy wondered if all of them had
forgotten what the war had done, then two soldiers bumped into
them, one with his arm in a sling, the other on crutches, bandage around his head.

"See, Tommy, we are still lucky. We were interned; all our
scars are inside but we have our hands and legs and our brains."

"Yer absolutely right, Rudy. Babbo would tell me to just start
over like he did. My goodness, but yer shop is bonnie." He was
angry with himself that envy came up like bile when he saw the
blue Naugahyde booths lining the back wall. The counter was
tall, and sitting there on a high stool was a young cashier. The
place was busy, and most of the patrons had ice cream in glass
dishes with a small wafer on top. "It sure looks nice in here,
Rudy."

"Aye, thanks to Peggy," Rudy replied, his voice grim. "She
kept the businesses going while we were interned. I really miss
her."

"She left ye while ye were interned?"

"No, she stayed and kept my shop open. When we came home, I got jealous and mean so she left after the war ended. I'll tell ye the rest over a pint." He pulled Tommy's arm and led him up the lane to the Wheat Sheaf. The two wounded soldiers were already there, seated at the bar.

"Look who's back," Rudy shouted to the assembled men. "This is my brother, Tommy."

Tommy did not recognize anyone, but then he had never been a pub goer. The men gave Rudy inconsequential nods.

"We'll have two Black Labels and a Guinness," said Rudy to the publican. "Pour those soldiers a whisky."

The publican poured two large halfs for the young men.

"Tommy," he began, "we were interned five long years."

"My God, Rudy, in Italy we had no idea. Was Kathy interned too?"

"Aye, wee Anna was born in internment."

"Jesus, Rudy."

"Och, we were safe enough. We lived in a condemned tenement and were not allowed to leave, except for work. Andy hid in the freight train just to be with Kathy when wee Anna was born. Sit down, man, I'll tell ye everything,"

"And I'll tell ye where I've been." Tommy had a feeling that Rudy would be jealous when he told of his exploits with the Yanks.

He was.

~ ~ ~

It took Tommy a fortnight to get an appointment with the secretary at the Kilmarnock Town Council. The secretary was an elderly overweight sad-looking woman who said, "Sorry, we leased yer property to a wool shop."

"A wool shop," Tommy blurted out. "What am I supposed to do?"

"Aye," said the woman with the glasses perched on the

bridge of her nose. "We didnae think ye'd be back and here ye are, another Tally wantin' another shop. I dinna ken and I dinna care."

"Can I lease another place?"

"I can put ye oan a list."

"How long will that take?"

She rubbed her hands together as if to warm them. "Could tak' a long time."

"I don't have a long time."

She took his passport and glanced at it. "Whose side were ye on during the war?"

"Scotland's side, of course." Tommy felt his anger well inside, but he reached into his pocket. "Will this get me further up the list?" He put three five-pound notes on the counter.

Her eyebrows rose in surprise. "Well, Mr. Bertellotti, that looks like a bribe." She reached out and slid the money into an envelope. "It might move ye up the list a wee bit, but I'm not supposed tae show favouritism."

He placed three more five-pound notes on the table. "That's thirty quid of favouritism."

That was quite a bit of money in 1947.

"Well, now." A greedy glint glowed in her eyes. "Ye've moved up quite a bit closer." She slid open a drawer and placed the envelope inside. "I might be able tae find ye something."

"Here," Tommy growled. He had fifteen more pounds in his wallet—most of a month's pay. "Hope this moves me right tae the top." He spoke with as broad an accent as he could.

"Aye, noo," she nodded, lifting the glasses off her face and smiling with skinny lips that could have used a bit of lipstick. "I might have a tiny place on Queen Street."

Tommy thought *Thank God for American dollars* and reached once more into the inside pocket of his jacket. "Will this get the bigger shop next door to the wee one?"

"Here's the key," she said, looking at the two twenty-pound notes. "It's number 5 on the corner. Ye'll like it. It's really big."

"Is there a flat above the shop?"

"Aye, if ye can find some more cash."

"I'll bring more tomorrow."

~   ~   ~

"What a location, Tommy," said Andy. "I can't believe how spacious it is. How'd ye manage to lease it so quickly?"

"I have my ways, brother."

"Shows ye what a bit of cash does, right, Tommy?" Andy said, with a grin. "And it's close to Gilmour Street."

"I'm glad of that, since we'll be living upstairs."

"That's yerself and Lea, right?"

"Right," he said. "Let's go see Kathy and the girls."

Aïda and Anna were coming home from the Bentinck School with schoolbags on their backs. They ran into the shop, and when they saw their uncle, they screamed, "Uncle Tommy, Uncle Tommy!"

"What bonny weans, Andy," he said, hugging the older girl. "You must be Aïda?"

"I am," she said.

"And I'm Anna. Ye've not met me before," said Anna with a cheeky grin.

"Nice to meet ye, Anna." She hugged him before he had the chance to bend over.

"Aïda, ye've grown tall. I remember when ye were just a toddler. How old are ye now?"

"I'm almost eleven."

"And I'm seven," Anna said. "My teacher says I'm clever and I've had my tonsils out. Mum says they're in a jar somewhere along with her appendix."

"Anna, I am happy to meet ye."

"Me, too, Uncle Tommy; are ye a hero?"

"So, Tommy, are ye home for good?" interrupted Kathy.

"Mummy, Mummy," Anna chirped in. "Did Uncle Tommy bring us a present?"

"That's rude, Anna."

"Oh, Kathy, no bother. Of course I did." He brought out two very small packages, which the girls opened in a second; they loved the small animal figures Tommy had chosen for them in Veneto.

"Thanks, Uncle Tommy. These are lovely," said Aïda.

"Glad ye like the wee animals. Venetian glass is so fine."

"Can I call this lovely wee dog Mary, after my invisible friend?"

"Of course ye can, Anna."

"See, Uncle Tommy, when ye hold him up to the light, he disappears too."

"Ye'll have to keep them on your wee shelf," said Kathy.

"I am not here to stay, Kathy," Tommy finally answered her first question. "I'm going to get my business started and make a home for Lea, and then I'll go back to Italy and marry her."

"That's quite the plan, Tommy," said Andy, finally getting a word in.

"Will ye be in my wedding?"

The two girls answered, "Yes!"

"I was asking yer Daddy."

Andy nodded his head. "Aye, Tommy. We'll all be there."

~ ~ ~

It took Tommy almost a year to get his shop ready for Lea and the rooms above in order. The business was leased, as all the businesses were in Kilmarnock at that time.

The three brothers were not in competition; they complemented each other. Rudy entertained shoppers and diners from the east side. Andy served delicious fish and chips to the factories. Tommy had the big shop and dining area where teenagers

44

The Handkerchief

Our parents always had something to talk about even though they had worked together all day through to the evening. The shop was open late, with customers coming in as late as half past ten for chips or a piece of fish. Dad had the habit of running out to the pub or his club for a wee drink at nine, and he'd bring back a wee bottle so he and Mum could have a nightcap before bed. That's when they talked, Dad's voice deep—louder if he'd been to the pub—Mum's raspy, yet comforting. Aïda and I were not so far away in our beds in the alcove and we could hear them even as we slept.

"Are ye up to the journey, Kathy?"

"I'll be fine, Andy. I feel strong and it will be wonderful to see Bruna again, and we get a wedding, too."

I was so happy to have overheard and know that for sure we were going to Italy. In the morning I asked Mummy, when?

"We'll go from June till the end of August," she answered.

Three whole months in Italy! The kids in my class were jealous when I told them, especially Jeffrey Keast, the butcher's boy, who said he'd like to be in my suitcase. When I told him I'd rather take my cousin Violet, I hurt his feelings. Perhaps I needed a new boyfriend.

Each evening, Mummy, Daddy, Aïda, and I had our tea at the small dining table in the back shop. We'd have a piece of

lovely fish with Dad's yummy chips and then we'd have a cup of tea with a chocolate biscuit, a Blue Riband maybe, or a piece of Granny's shortbread. We ate after the busy time at exactly seven fifteen when *The Archers* were on the wireless.

We left the door open to the shop so Dad could see if Big Nancy, his assistant, was busy. Big Nancy was my pal. She was young and plump and had a boyfriend around the corner. I would talk to her when Mummy was too busy to listen, which was almost every day.

As we ate, *The Archers* blared away on the wireless—the story was about a farm family. I longed to live on a farm where I could have a cow and a pig. Mummy said Babbo had geese and chickens, a cat to chase the mice, and lots of grapes. I could hardly wait.

~   ~   ~

Finally it was time to pack. I had no idea what to put in my suitcase. Mum laughed when I packed my wooly mittens.

"You won't need those where we're going, Anna."

"Are ye sure, Mum?"

"I'm sure, Anna."

~ ~ ~

The huge steam engine clanked along so quickly that I had to glue my face to the window to see the sheep on the Scottish hillsides. As we flew past Hurlford I waved to Granny's wee house; I thought I saw her wave back from her front window. My nose was stuck on the window watching green fields fly by until the smell of mashed potatoes wafted into the carriage. That good smell drew us into the dining car for lunch. We sat at a table with a white linen tablecloth and so many silver knives and forks I couldn't help but touch all of them.

"Sit up straight and mind yer manners, girls," said Mum.

The waiter said, with an English accent, "My name is Tom." His nose was a banana snout. He called Aïda and me *little ladies*, and he bowed when he spoke.

"Steak and kidney pie, please, sir. Could we have it without the kidneys because that's how our Mummy makes it; we like the steak but not the kidney." I tucked the white napkin into the neck of my dress.

Tom coughed, "Steak and kidney pie, minus the kidney. Let's see what I can do for you, my *little ladies*." He saluted Mum with his first finger and took her order of cold salmon. Dad ordered a steak and a beer and stuck his head in the horse racing form; he liked the horse races now that he was no longer a bookie for the dugs.

In a few minutes, the polite waiter carried in our plates, steaming with crunchy pie crust and little bits of steak—no kidneys. He placed those hot plates in front of us as if we were princesses.

Daddy looked up from his paper, sipped his whisky and said, "He deserves a big tip, that lad."

The train thundered on through the countryside. Mum said, "Hurry up, Italy."

~ ~ ~

It took all day and night to get to Dover. Aïda and I slept in tiny bunks listening to the clickety-clack of the wheels. Mum complained that Daddy's snores were ear-splitting and she did not get one wink. Aïda and I must have winked because we got up early to look at the white cliffs, but all we saw was fog.

Mum complained, "Dover has white cliffs, but ye canny see yer ain hand this foggy morn."

"Hurry up, Mum," I said. "I can hardly wait to be on the boat. It will be lovely."

The fog followed us out into the Channel and the waves were so big that they splashed over us, even on the upper deck. My tummy began to dance the rumba and so did Daddy's; Mummy made us go outside on deck. The boat was rolling around like an out of control swing. Daddy and I leaned over the rail, vomiting loudly. Mum took care of both of us; first she'd pat Dad's back, and then she'd hold my forehead. Aïda just counted seagulls, I suppose. Mary of course was fine.

I was glad when we finally reached Calais. My legs enjoyed the hard ground and it was just a hop, skip, and jump from the boat pier into the train station. There we went through customs. Dad had his red Italian passport and Mum her green British passport. I knew that both were stamped *enemy alien*; Aïda and I had looked at them many times. Dad said that's why the French customs officer went through every bit of luggage twice; he messed up Daddy's socks and I heard Dad say a swear word under his breath.

Mum said, "Do ye have to go through everything? It's just our clothes."

The man pretended not to speak English.

I stood behind Mummy with Bruna doll in my arms and my legs feeling like Jell-o. Aïda pretended to read and Mum and Dad smoked two cigarettes.

Afterwards, Dad remarked, "He never looked once at our

Anna's Bruna doll. That's where I would have smuggled the diamonds—as if we had any."

~ ~ ~

The French train was packed with every kind of person. Tall men in uniform, fat ladies with cats, children with jam on their lips, raggedy farmers with hay sticking out of their hats, and black men whose skin shone like marble. There were canaries and dogs and hamsters in cages, even a parrot that squawked all the time. The seats were in rows, not in carriages like the British trains, and there was no fancy dining car.

A burly French porter with a thin curl of a moustache was selling tiny sandwiches displayed on a tray. *"Parlez vous Français?"* he asked.

"No," said Dad. *"Italiano."*

The porter shrugged and stuck out the tray. *"Pour vous?"*

Dad held up four fingers.

The porter sneered and placed the sandwiches on the table in front of us. He walked away, taking Dad's ten-shilling note. Dad shook his head. "That man does not deserve a tip, but I bet he got one."

The sandwiches were triangles without crusts wrapped in damp paper; they smelled fishy. My tummy jumped but I was hungry. Mum didn't think much of the French porter or his food and nibbled just a bit. She lay back with her head on the red seat; it was her turn to feel queasy. The lines around her eyes deepened into black circles, and her cheeks needed rouge. She lit a fag.

"Parlez vous Français yerself, Mister," I joked, trying to figure out what was in the weird sandwich.

Dad laughed.

The lady sitting across from us had her dog at her side.

"What kind of dog is that, Dad?" I asked.

"It's a French poodle."

I noticed a smear of bright red lipstick on the woman's front teeth, and I got the giggles. The poodle lady's hair was done up in a puff on the top of her head and tied with a blue ribbon just like her dog's was. Both dog and mistress wore matching navy-blue jackets with red trim. She spoke to anyone who would listen in to her French lah-de-dah. She saw me giggle and smiled broadly, showing lipstick on more teeth. "*Ma cherie, le chien s'appelle Ruperto.*"

Ruperto licked me obligingly, whilst the poodle lady chatted about who knew what. I petted Ruperto and sneaked the rest of my horrible sandwich into his eager lips.

Mum said, "I don't feel so good, maybe it was the sandwich."

Dad took a sip from his silver flask and wiped his moustache. "Och, it wasn't so bad, Kathy. Ye just like to complain."

Mum let out a great sigh and relaxed down into the seat.

Aïda and I played hangman and dot-to-dot while the train clacked along the tracks.

~   ~   ~

We whizzed all the way to Switzerland, stopping at a small station nestled in the lap of a huge mountain that had a smear of snow on the tippy-top.

"Look, Daddy, snow."

"Let's get a breath of mountain air, Kathy." Dad gave Mum his hand and helped her to the door, but Mum looked wobbly and, as she stepped down, she slid, landing on the platform in a faint with her legs and arms sprawled out uselessly.

"Mummy, Mummy!" I panicked. No one listened. Was my Mummy dead?

"Help me, please! Help me!" was Dad's plea.

Aïda knelt down beside Mum.

A crowd of well-meaning people collected around them, pushing me aside. I felt like a rag-doll. I couldn't even find Mary.

It took a porter with smelling salts and the English words

"Move aside, move over, please" to help Mummy. Aïda and Daddy were busy with Mummy. I stood alone.

The poodle lady came over to me, smelling like fruit and flowers. She offered a nice soft pink hanky for my tears. I took it and wiped my face, inhaling her sweet perfume. Dad and Aïda were helping Mum find her legs. They walked her back and forth. The crowd of people began to part. My mummy wasn't dead after all. That sandwich had upset where she used to have an appendix. My throat hurt watching her. She began to smile. I wanted a hug, but she didn't see me. Dad led her up the stairs into the train—he didn't turn around. He had forgotten me. My tonsil holes really hurt.

The poodle lady came over to guide me safely back onto the train. She spoke softly in French. "*Ma cherie, ma cherie,*" she said over and over. She held my hand when I climbed up the tall steps into the big smoke-blowing monster. I turned to give back her handkerchief but she had disappeared into the crowd.

"There ye are, Anna. We almost forgot ye."

Didn't I know that? As the train pulled out, I waved through the window with the hanky; Aïda said it smelled like Evening in Paris. The poodle lady was still there, hoorah. She waved back. I think even Ruperto waved. They hadn't forgotten me.

~   ~   ~

It was dark when the grimy train pulled into Pisa. Aïda and I had been sleeping on top of each other; we didn't have nice bunks on this train. Dad woke us up to tell us we were in Tuscany and would be in Pisa soon. We had been journeying three whole days. Mum could hardly walk, and Dad had his worried face on.

Uncle Rudy was at the station with a car. "Well, hello," he said with a stagger and a grin.

"Have ye been drinking, Rudy?" asked Daddy. "Bloody hell, man, we're exhausted."

"I had to wait hours and hours. What else was I to do?" He hiccupped and Aïda laughed.

"It's not funny, Aïda," said Daddy. "I suppose I can drive, Rudy. Can ye stay awake enough to direct me to Mamma's?"

~ ~ ~

I sat on my uncle's lap all the way from Pisa to Pietrasanta. He stank like whisky and he sang off key. My Uncle Rudy was a very bad singer. Soon I fell fast asleep with my doll Bruna at his feet.

45

Pietrasanta

"Anna, wake up, wake up."

"Where are we?" I wiped my sleep drops and stuck my hand under a soft, white pillow, relieved to find the pink hanky.

The sun peeked through thick white netting that wrapped the bed. Aïda was awake. She gave me a smile, pushed the net away and tied it to a hook on the wall. We lay still, very still, listening to the noises of the strange house and the birds chirping.

"We're here, Anna, in Pietrasanta, in Nonna's house."

"Why was that big net on us?"

"I think it's to stop the mosquitoes."

It was so bright and white in the bedroom that it hurt my eyes, which were used to awakening in a dark wall-papered room behind Daddy's shop.

Mum snored gently in the corner, on a blue sofa, where she had collapsed. Daddy had covered her with a soft blanket. The room was shades of morning, with large windows that held the promise of sunshine. Mum slept on her side without a net, so I wondered if the mosquitoes had bitten her.

Aïda and I slid onto the coolness of a white marble floor, our toes welcoming the touch. My toes did not remember arriving at the house the night before, and I wasn't sure if Mary had made it to Italy. Daddy must have carried us upstairs, into the house, and laid us in the big white bed.

My heart hammered inside my chest as Aïda and I padded up the cool hallway towards the kitchen to a Nonna that we had never met. I had only seen a picture of her when she was younger and she was holding Aunt Bruna as a baby. We tiptoed past Mum, daylight streaking down on us from a high round window to show us the way to the kitchen.

Our Italian grandma sat squarely on a wooden chair. I stared at her broad face with its big blue eyes. It was a nice face, like Daddy's, only fluffier. She put her arms out towards us for a hug, and suddenly I felt shy.

"Come-a to me," she invited us.

Aïda and I were glued together, and together we gave our grandmother a squeeze. I wrapped my arm around her waist, to find a body that was very soft and smelled sweet like apples. I didn't feel so shy any more.

Nonna said, "*Bella bambini*," then she held us out to take a good look.

We wiggled away and pushed ourselves up onto the wooden chairs. I placed my forearms on the smooth surface of the table and looked around at the white-washed kitchen. It smelled as if Nonna had scrubbed every surface with disinfectant. There were all kinds of old tools on the wall, brown hammers, black chisels, old weird farm things.

I pointed at them and asked Nonna, "What are these for?"

Nonna seemed to be puzzled. I thought she spoke Scottish; she had lived in Ayrshire a long time. She nodded but had no answer.

The sink was chipped and deep with a strange, bent-over, metal faucet and directly above it was a huge picture of our grandparents. It must have been taken when they got married because they looked so young. There were photos on a sideboard: one of Daddy and Uncle Rudy when they were boys, one of Bruna in a kilt and one of Uncle Tommy as a baby. I breathed in the smell of the coffee brewing and warm rolls cooking. I decided I liked this big, strange, white house with an indoor bathtub! Maybe I could dance on the rim.

Nonna wiped her hands on her clean, white, frilly apron and said, "*Buongiorno, bambini.*" She smiled and sat two tiny cups that looked like doll's china on the big plank, then she reached for the coffee pot and poured each of us a cup of thick brown coffee. Aïda and I reached out for the sugar bowl and ladled in three big spoons of brown sugar.

"It's really strong, Nonna," said Aïda.

"*Caffè* make-a *tu* feel warm inside. *Parla Italiano*, Aïda?"

"*Piccolo*, Nonna Fiorina."

"Ah, lazy Daddy."

"*Mio Daddy ha dimenticato il suo italiano*," Aïda replied. "He only remembers a little, Nonna, and we understand a few words."

We drank our bittersweet coffee, changed our clothes, and went out to explore the garden. As we bounced down the seven steps to the patio below, Nonna watched from the veranda.

"Babbo is-a waiting in the vegetables, *a piu tardi*," she called out.

I was surprised to hear a bit of Scottish in her tongue. Aïda and I trailed our fingers in the fountain at the bottom of the steps, where several goldfish swam.

"Oh, Anna, look," Aïda said. "They're all different colours."

We stuck our faces right down into the water until our noses touched the surface and made rings. We were in make-believe land; nothing could ever be this perfect. The sun was already warm; it was never like that in Scotland. I looked out at the hills around us—there were no tenements here in Pietrasanta, no dustbins, no coal houses, just sweet-smelling flowers, marigolds, daisies, and, under a shady trellis, green vines laden with green grapes that hung just out of the reach of our greedy

Babbo

fingers. There were plum and peach trees with green fruit on their branches. The garden smelled like Hogmanay wine and apple pie.

Aïda said, "I think this is Alice's Wonderland."

Just then, a big grey cat came by and rubbed against me. "Look, Aïda, a cat." The kitty leapt up on the fountain to look at the goldfish.

"No," said Aïda, chasing her away. I think she still missed Trixie, who had died.

The kitty ran towards the flower garden, so we chased her. I beat Aïda to the garden where I found an old man wearing a wide-brimmed hat. He was kneeling on the soft dirt to prune a rose. "*Buongiorno, bambini,*" he said.

"Oh, Nonno, *buongiorno, fiori fantastico*," said Aïda, trying to impress him.

The old man was delighted. "Call-a me Babbo, I like-a better."

I liked that he spoke like a Scotsman. I touched a rose and the thorn pricked me, so I sucked off the tiny bit of red blood. A strong, dirty hand reached for me and wiped my finger clean.

"Is this the garden from *Alice in Wonderland*, Babbo?" asked my big sister.

"If-a you want it be," he smiled. "*Buongiorno*, my wee lassies, welcome to my Pietrasanta."

I remembered one of Dad's stories. I remembered the part where Aïda and I had repeated *Mediterranean, Mediterranean*. "Can we see the sea from here, Babbo?"

"Not from-a here. We take a walk up into the hills." He knelt on one knee. "How are my silly wee monkeys?" He laid down his squishy hat, wiped a sweaty brow, and held out two welcoming arms. "I am *contento* you be here with-a me and Nonna. Maybe you stay in Italia?"

"Maybe, Nonno," said the silly wee monkeys. "But we like Scotland a lot."

"Ah, Scotland; I love-a her too. I make the money in the fish and chips. But I come back to *paradisio* to live—then the war came and took my dream. But you no understand. Now, *mi bambini*, is *paradisio* once more." He stood up and took our hands, leading us down a pathway that smelled of honeysuckle and wild bay. "Look." Babbo pointed to a bird feeder swarmed by a zillion tiny yellow finches. "This is why Mariah follows us."

"So that's the cat's name."

"*Sì*, Anna. Mariah is getting old but she still chases the birds and-a helps uncles hide when they need to."

A mother goose waddled towards us with her big wings flapping. The big goose honked, scaring me.

"What's wrong with her, Babbo?" Both Aïda and I did not wait to find out.

Babbo caught us and laughed, "Manya no-a bite," he assured us. "She has-a babies, I show you." He took us by the hand, speaking in his broken English, shooing Manya and Mariah away. In her coop were ten fluffy goslings who ran around frantically as if they were playing hide and seek. He placed a baby gosling in each of our hands. The babies looked up at us with their beaks open, making tiny squawks. Manya marched around us, not sure what we were up to.

"This is a farm, Babbo. This is fun," I said, holding the gosling so tight it squawked.

The three of us climbed up a steep path where a lion's head was carved into a stone and sunk into the hillside. Water dripped out of the lion's mouth.

"Babbo, what is this?" asked Aïda.

"*Nectara*," he said, laughing. "*Bella aqua*, water of life, drink up." He cupped his hands under the lion's mouth to catch the pure spring water that came from the hills behind the house.

We cupped our hands like Nonno and drank the sparkling water. It tasted wonderful after that strong coffee.

"*Le ragazze si possono mangiare le pesche e le pere, ma non le uve.* My children, you may eat the peaches, the pears, but no grapes. In August we stomp in the big vat." He made the stomping movement. "We make-a chianti and store in the wine cellar."

All of a sudden a young woman dressed in tartan pajamas appeared. "*Prego*, I'm yer Auntie Bruna," she said half in Italian, half in a broad Ayrshire accent. "*Buongiorno*, Daddy," she said, hugging Babbo.

Bruna was not much taller than Aïda, but her face shone like the sun. Her arms opened wide to get hugs from us. "Ya wee scunners, here at last in Italia, my Anna and my Aïda. Do ye remember me, Aïda? Ye were just a baby." The dancing and hugging began. "*Bella bambini*, yer so pretty!" She held us out for inspection. "I have a college class this morning; *vacanza* is not yet for me."

"Ye still go to school, auntie?" asked Aïda.

"Just call me Bruna, I'm too young to be an auntie, I'm just a few years older than ye, Aïda. This is my last year in college. I'll be twenty soon. Anna, yer a lovely wee thing, what age are ye? Come on, let's get everyone else up."

I was so surprised at how broad her Scots accent was. Bruna did not wait for an answer, she was already bounding up the steps. "I'm eight and Aïda is twelve."

Babbo took my hand. "Bruna, she born in Scotland. She speak-a like a Scots girl. She call-a me Daddy and her Mamma, Mummy, like ye do in Scotland. Go with her."

Bruna shattered the household awake. Uncle Rudy and Daddy were snoring soundly under their mosquito nets. "Wake up, brothers, it's morning and ye're still in bed. Did ye have too much vino last night?" Bruna's energy filled the villa. Everyone was awake. She kissed Daddy with such fierceness, I thought he would pop. "I missed ye, Armando, Andy Bertellotti. I missed all of ye so much and the girls, oh, *mamma mia*, they are so *bella bella*."

Mum and Dad dressed quickly and came out to the veranda with their coffee. Dad had found his Italian language inside his head and was chatting to Babbo, telling him in Italian how smart he was to have bought this property. I wondered where this italian voice had been hiding all this time. Mum sat quietly smoking, the familiar grey cloud swirling above her head, and she was pale from the fainting on the platform.

Uncle Rudy was handsome with his shirt sleeves rolled up and his hair a mess from sleeping. We loved him, even if he did drink a little too much, even if he had lost Peggy because of it. Peggy had gone away to a place called Canada. After our uncle was done with being heart-broken, he had found a new girlfriend called Bessie. Uncle Rudy was still our pal, someone we could always talk to when Mum and Dad didn't want to listen.

"Come and sit with me, girls," said Mummy. "Try this Italian bread."

Nonna smiled at us. I sat on the wooden chair beside Mum, anxious to taste it, but the hard roll was sour and tasteless and was tough to chew. I glanced over at Nonna. She was watching, so I chewed it up anyway. I didn't want to hurt her feelings; after all, it smelled divine while it baked. Mum spread some fresh peach jam on it and then it was better.

"I will see all of ye later," said Bruna. "Today is my last day of college, so please come to our final exercise. From tomorrow on, I'll be on holiday and we can go to the beach every day. We'll make sand castles, Anna. Just wait till ye see how I make them."

"She make a *bel castello di sabbia*," said Babbo. He swallowed hard. "Bruna is a good-a girl. She keep us going when we did not-a think we could walk any further. She keep us alive with her strong spirit and her love for Italia."

"What do ye mean by that, Nonno?" I said.

"I talk about the time we had to leave home, *bambina*, and go hide in the hills."

There was so much I didn't know.

46

Bruna's Italian Secrets

I had never seen so many stars. I tried to count them, but it was impossible. In Scotland it was light till late at night so we only saw stars in the winter and then the clouds whisked them away. On Nonna's veranda, the moon shone down on us like a wise old man saying his prayers. I could see his lips moving. It seemed that we would spend lots of time on Nonna's wide deck with its cozy chairs. There was plenty of homemade Chianti for the grown-ups and scrumptious lemonade for us. Nonna had made a special *pasta ashciutta* with a lovely sauce on top. Mum said that Nonna could cook pastaciutta noodles in a million ways and that we would get used to eating late like this. We sat at a green metal table covered with a red and white checkered table-cloth decorated with candles burning in wine bottles—the wax had run down the bottles, making them look like ice-cream cones. I sat and watched the flames and Bruna held my hand.

Italian and Scottish words buzzed like bees in my ears. Daddy, Uncle Rudy, and Babbo talked with their hands flying in every direction; Uncle Rudy was explaining to his parents why Peggy had left and how he'd met a woman from Glasgow. I felt sad—Peggy was my idol. Mary agreed.

Nonna shook her head and clicked with her tongue, "*Ti, ti, ti.*"

Mum whispered, "Nonna would like Uncle Rudy to marry a nice Italian girl."

Daddy, Uncle Rudy, Aïda, me, Bruna.

The night closed in, the frogs and crickets chirped their songs, Daddy and Uncle Rudy whispered in Italian with their heads bobbing up and down. I felt scared. I heard words like *Fascisti* and *Partigiani*. I didn't know these words.

Daddy cursed. "Damn Mussolini."

"Why is Daddy swearing, Mum?"

"Oh, darling," she said, "sometimes grown-ups don't know any other words. Shh, Andy."

I wasn't going to get any information from Mum. She walked towards the railing with her back to me, her fag glowing in the night. Mummy seemed worn out. Maybe she had one of her headaches.

"What are they talking about, Bruna?" I asked my aunt.

"The war, my wee lassie," she said. "Always, always, Italians talk about the secrets of war."

"Can you tell us?" asked Aïda.

"Och, I'm not supposed to," she answered, sounding very Scottish—not Italian at all.

"Please, please, we won't tell anyone," I begged.

"Maybe tomorrow."

Maybe she'd had lessons from Mummy in the standard adult answer.

We washed dishes while Mummy went to bed. Dad, Uncle Rudy, and Babbo were still outside talking with their hands. Nonna sat listening. I think Nonna was the referee.

The next day was to be our first day at the beach. Aïda and I were finally going to see the *Mediterranean*. Bruna tucked us in, tickling us until we closed our eyes, then she went back to the veranda. But Aïda and I were too wound up to sleep—the voices blended until both languages were one. Five minutes later, we crept out to sit by the open window and eavesdrop.

Bruna's voice was the clearest. She loved speaking the Scottish language she was born with. I listened with my child's ears. Aïda had her hush finger on her lips.

"What was it like in internment?" I heard Bruna ask.

There was a cough and then Uncle Rudy's gruff tone. "Did ye know that Andy had to sneak away on a freight train on the night Anna was born?"

"How did ye manage that, Andy?"

I couldn't hear Daddy's answer, his voice had dropped to a whisper, but I knew the story anyway.

Mum called out to the veranda group. She had gone to bed. "Shh, shh, the children need their rest."

We giggled softly and stayed on our perch near the open window.

"Bruna, tell-a you brothers what happened on the mountain." Nonna spoke in plain English.

I was surprised to find out that she spoke it quite well. I touched Aïda's arm. She gave me the nod. She'd heard also. We sat up straining to hear.

"Go on, Bruna," Nonna said again. "*Per favore,* tell-a you brothers."

Aïda whispered, "Why does Nonna pretend she can't speak Scottish?"

I shrugged. "Maybe she likes secrets."

"Oh, Mamma," said Bruna. "Do I have to? It was all so sad, Andy. *Awful.* Mamma, Babbo, and I had to evacuate this house with only a wobbly wheeled cart to carry our food and clothes. We walked with Lena and her mamma, Adela. It took us two days to reach a safe place to rest. Mamma was so tired that her knees gave out."

"Did ye go as far as Farnocchia?" asked Rudy.

"Almost," she said.

"Tell your brothers about Sant' Anna," said Babbo.

Did he say my name? Now I was wide awake.

Bruna started to cry, her words a mixture of Scottish and Italian. She was not talking about me. Not at all. It was a jumble of words: "Nazi . . . SS . . . gunshots . . . run . . . beard on fire . . . *il ragazzo . . . i morti . . . mio Dio!*"

"What is Bruna talking about, Aïda?" I whispered.

"Shh."

"I'm scared."

Nonna spoke up loudly. "Babbo save a boy. Go on, Bruna. Tell you brothers."

"What boy?" Now I was really awake, but the voices lowered and we got cold and went back to bed and then it was morning. It was bright and warm, and there was no time to ask questions.

Aunt Bruna was already up and dressed in a lovely yellow sundress. She called out, "Are ye ready yet, girls?"

"Come in here, Aunt Bruna," said Aïda, pulling on her swimsuit. "We heard the talking last night."

"I thought ye were in bed."

"We sneaked to the window to listen."

"Were ye scared in the mountains?" Aïda asked in her wise voice.

"Whose beard was on fire?" I asked.

Bruna looked from one of us to the other.

"Did Babbo save a boy?"

"Oh, my, wee lassies—Ye should have been sleeping. Those were bad days. The boy's name is Marco, and yes, Babbo saved him. He's a nice, very nice boy. Let's get dressed and go to the beach."

"Did the Nazi place have the same name as me, Aunt Bruna?"

"*Sì*. Oh, Anna, not a Nazi place—a church. They call it Sant' Anna. The Nazis shot the people in the courtyard."

"All of them."

"*Sì*, it was *terribile*. Your mamma does not want me to talk to ye about it. The Nazis were bad, very, very bad. Okay, enough now, let's get ready for the beach and no more questions. Could we keep this between us, please?"

"Okay, Auntie." Aïda and I were glad to be a part of a secret, even though it was *terribile*.

If Mary ever came back I would tell her.

47

Sandcastles

That day, the next day, and the day after were all about the seashore. I forgot about secrets. My head buzzed with thoughts of sand and sunshine.

Bruna filled red and blue grocery bags with sandwiches every day, and we'd run to the rickety green bus that took us to Fiumetto. I wore rubber sand shoes and waved at people passing by.

Italian boys, wearing wooden shoes with no backs, rode their bikes alongside the bus. Bruna called their sandals *soccolli*. The boys with no shirts dragged their feet on the ground instead of putting on the brakes. They called out to us, especially Bruna, as they rode by.

I wanted a pair of *soccolli*, and asked Mummy, "Please, please, can I have a pair?"

Mum said, "Maybe," but none appeared.

Babbo and Nonna had a beach house on the promenade at Fiumetto. It had a wide painted porch and big square windows that looked out to the sea. I loved it. The Mediterranean was a miracle of rainbows. Grey, blue, soft yellow, and white waves broke on the sand, and the sea went so far out I could not see where it ended. Seagulls cawed and swooped around us, and sand pipers with white rings around their scrawny necks ran in

Bruna

little armies back and forth along the water's edge. Every day we
carried the striped deck chairs from the porch over to the sand.
Dad carried the huge red umbrella that shaded us from the hot
sun.

Mum and Dad sat close, holding hands under the umbrella.
I could see that Mummy had roses in her cheeks. She said it was
the smell of the sea and the touch of the sun that had cured her
blues.

"I'm so glad, Mummy." I hoped she would not faint on the
way back home but I had my lucky poodle-lady hanky under my
pillow, just in case.

Every minute at the beach was special. Aïda and I swam in
the shallow sudsy foam. When we were braver, we dog-paddled
in the warm gentle surf and floated in on waves that crashed

us flat on our stomachs. There was no chance of me catching a sore throat at this warm beach; besides, my tonsils were in a jar in Glasgow alongside Mummy's appendix, and good riddance to all of them. The seashore was long and wide with white sand everywhere. There were no dunes like the Scottish beaches and no whelks either. Bruna would row us out over the waves on a wooden boat; we'd bob on the waves for hours and watch the parachute jellyfish that swam underneath us.

Bruna's best friend, Lena, came to Fiumetto often. Sometimes the two big girls would walk far along the sea front to talk to boys. They always waited till Babbo and Nonna were taking siesta. Those two girls liked secrets.

All of us lived in our bathing suits, even Dad. He'd never worn swim trunks in Scotland. I had a tan already and was almost as dark as the Italian children. Bruna taught us how to make sandcastles by dripping the sand through our fingers. We'd make the sand wet, but not too wet, roll it between our thumb and fingers and drip it, drop by drop. We made turret walls, rounded windows, and moats with bridges.

"Watch me, Anna, watch my fingers, be careful or the castle will crumble." Bruna knelt beside us in her bright blue dotted swim suit; she liked polka dots, and her castles were fantastico, just like her.

After a while I'd get bored and run in the waves. By the time I got back, Aïda and Bruna would have moulded a magnificent *Castello di Bertellotti*.

"Can I jump on it?"

"Ye cheeky wee thing, Anna. I'll chase ye all the way back down the beach," Bruna would reply. "This is an Italian castle. It is meant to last forever."

"But the waves will smash it."

"We'll just let the waves be bad. Okay, Anna?"

"Okay."

It felt as if summer would last forever. Aïda and I were beach urchins who ate Italian rolls in the morning and licked ices in the afternoon; we only took siesta when Nonna made us.

Mum and Dad began to hold hands at the water's edge. The sea made Mummy nervous because she had never learned to swim, but when Dad stood close to her she seemed to forget.

Soon Mummy was paddling up to her waist in the warm surf, and she even went out on the boats with Daddy. Sometimes, when they thought we weren't watching, they kissed. Mum looked younger, like Maureen O'Hara, and she never ever had a headache.

One afternoon, under the shade, when the sun was warm but not too hot, I said, "Mummy, I saw ye kissing Daddy by the water's edge. Did ye kiss him a lot when ye were young?"

"Aye," she said, giving me a big grin. "We kissed every night when Daddy walked me home from the dancing."

"Was it a long walk?"

"It was, Anna, about three miles. I thought nothing of it, high heels and all."

"How'd ye fall in love?"

"At first, I was not even interested in yer Daddy," she said, lighting a fag. "I had lots of boyfriends who asked me out. But Eddie, my brother, wanted me to meet his pal, so I did. One especially starry night, yer father and I fell into a deep conversation. As the weeks passed, we found we had more and more to talk about. When we danced there was electricity between us."

"Was that electricity I saw when you and Dad were kissing by the sea?"

"Yes," she replied, smiling brightly.

"When did he ask ye to marry him?" I added.

"It was a summer evening in his wee shop on Gilmour Street."

"Did ye say yes right away?"

"Aye," she said, laughing. "But it was not easily accepted for Daddy and me to get married in Scotland."

"Was it because of Nonna?"

She nodded yes. "Granny Brice didn't think much of me marrying a Catholic."

"What's wrong with being a Catholic?"

"Well, nothing," she said. "But in Scotland we try to not mix religions."

I didn't know what she meant by all this, but now Mummy and I had a secret. I liked this kind of secret. I rubbed my Mum's thin silver wedding ring with its six sides as if it were a genie's lamp. It seemed that the sunshine and the relaxing had magically made my parents' love strong like it had been in the beginning. This white beach in Fiumetto had cured Mum, and my throat didn't hurt at all. Nonna seemed to have forgiven our Scottish mummy for marrying her Italian son. I did not want to go back to Scotland where they stuck kids in internment and Catholics couldn't marry Protestants. I wanted that summer in Italy to last forever. Furthermore, there was a wedding coming up!

The very next afternoon Uncle Tommy arrived. He was as handsome as I thought he would be. He was wearing his beige Yankee uniform, and he had a lady with him. Lea knelt down under the beach umbrella to hug me, her long blonde hair brushing my cheek. It felt like silk. I loved her instantly.

Nonna made a big fuss of Lea, patting her hand, admiring her dress. She asked Babbo to get a deck chair for her and then asked Lea, in Italian, if she wanted a gelato. We smiled because Nonna was not usually so jolly.

Bruna was delighted to see Tommy. "This is the man who read the Declaration of Liberation at the end of the war, girls."

It made me feel shy, but I liked my uncle's smile and the big dimples that arrived on his cheeks.

"I heard you like the *soccolli* that the children wear here in Italy," Lea said to Aïda and me.

"We do," I said first. "Who told ye?"

"*Il tuo Bruna Zia.* Here you are, Anna, a pair for you, and a pair for you also, Aïda. My papa, he is a shoemaker, he made them just for you. Your mamma told me you liked them."

I gave Mummy a kiss. "Thank you, thank you, Lea," we said together, and "*Grazie, grazie.*" The shoes had a beige strap and thick wooden soles. I liked the ones she brought for Aïda, but mine were better. Mine had red tassels and made a bigger click-clack on the cobblestones.

"*Prego,*" she replied. Then they all spoke Italian.

"Did ye tell Lea about the shop and the flat upstairs, Tommy?" asked Uncle Rudy.

"I did, Rudy, and many thanks to both ye and Andy," replied Uncle Tommy in English.

"He's made it perfect, Lea," said Daddy. It was funny to hear both languages at once.

She smiled. "I never doubted him. Now it's only a week till the wedding. I am so excited."

Tommy reached for her. "Oh, Lea, it will be fabulous, and I am so glad that my brothers are here to share it."

"We'll be right beside ye," said Uncle Rudy with a great big smile, then he sighed. "It must be nice to be getting married."

I felt sorry for Uncle Rudy, but what I said was, "I can hardly wait for my new dress, Aunt Lea."

"Me, too," smiled Aïda.

Lea bent down towards us to talk in our ears. "It will be nice to be your auntie, Anna, and you too, Aïda. On Monday we will all go shopping at Lucia's in Viareggio."

I was surprised that Lea's English was so good, it didn't sound Scottish. She must have practiced.

"Can I get a red dress, Aunt Lea?"

"Any colour you and Mummy decide on," she answered in her almost-perfect English.

48

Lucia's

First we went shopping! What a time we had in Lucia's, a large department store on the Viareggio esplanade. The mannequins in the huge windows were dressed in bright-coloured party dresses with ribbons and pearls; I loved their huge hats with the ostrich feathers.

Aunt Bruna said, "Ye know, only the rich people shop here."

Mum replied, "This is a special occasion."

"We have to look nice for the wedding, hah, Mum?"

"That's right. No homemade clothes today."

"High fashion, that's us girls," chimed Aunt Bruna.

Lucia's smelled like gingerbread pudding and had big plush red chairs for wee rests. Aïda and I pretended we were rich. My invisible friend, Mary, stayed with me to touch the silky materials.

"Watch yer sticky fingers, Anna," said Mum. "My, these assistants are treating us like royalty."

Aïda said, "Mum, the only Scottish Royalty I know about is Mary, Queen of Scots, and she got her head chopped off."

I gave the chop motion whilst the assistant dressed me, talking fast Italian. She got on her knees to pin up a pink dress that was too long on me and I could see a black lady moustache on her upper lip. I started to laugh and Mum said, "Anna, behave."

I tried on dress after dress. I kept that moustache lady busy for hours. Finally I chose a deep pink taffeta dress with bows on the shoulders and a ruffly neck. Aïda picked a blue and black striped satin dress with an enormous great bow in the back. Mine was much prettier! Bruna said we both were lovely, but I know she liked mine best.

Mum tried on dresses and suits of every colour and style, parading around like a model, but she settled on a black dress, which she said she could wear more often than a flowery one. I was disappointed—Mummy always chose a sensible outfit. She had only three suits and six blouses, yet she always looked like she belonged in a fancy magazine.

After all this clothes on and off, we were very thirsty. Lea took us to Nardini's and ordered us ice-creams with bananas, whipped cream and strawberries. I had never seen such a treat. Mummy called it a Knickerbocker glory, I called it *delicioso*.

Viareggio was a big seaside town with a long promenade and a sea wall that separated the pavement from the sand. We all began to walk along the prom. Bruna and Lea chatted while Mum strode out taking in the sea breeze. I had begun to believe I could understand Italian because the words were becoming familiar. I laughed when the adults laughed and I skipped all the time because I was so happy.

~   ~   ~

Now it was only six days until the wedding; Lea was glowing. She explained that the ceremony would be in the morning, at *del Duomo di Pietrasanta* and later, in the afternoon, there would be dancing and feasting in the street.

"Will there be a band, Aunt Lea?" I asked, practicing to call her Auntie.

"There may be more than one," she said. "The local people love weddings and your Uncle Tommy is their hero. They call him by his Italian name, Irmo." She really was good at English.

49

Wedding Day

Babbo borrowed his friend's car, a big black one. It was a short ride to the Cathedral; I kept smoothing my dress so as not to get it wrinkled. Nonna had given Aïda and me squares of white net to wear on our heads. "You must-a cover hair in Chapello," she told us, pinning the squares to our hair with bobby pins.

The bells of the Cattedrale began to peal. I looked for the bride's car. I was hoping it would have white streamers on the hood like the ones in Scotland. It had not arrived, but some of Aunt Lea's family were milling outside the church dressed in their Sunday best. The men wore hats with flat tops. We walked up the steps to the huge arched door with Nonna leading the way. Uncle Tommy, Daddy, and Uncle Rudy were already inside.

"Don't they look handsome?" said Mummy.

"Especially Daddy," I replied, admiring his tanned face and trimmed moustache. His round cheeks were happy and his eyes glittered with pride. He blew me a kiss.

When Nonna saw her three sons walking towards her, she began to cry, "*Miei figli*, how I have a prayed for this day. I thought the war would rob me of this."

Nonna went on, "Every day I pray on my rosary while we hide in hills. *Per favore, Dio mio*, let me see *miei figli* together again, amen."

Babbo came up behind her. "I pray this also."

Babbo kissed Daddy, Uncle Rudy, and Uncle Tommy on each cheek. The trio kissed Nonna on the top of her head, she was so much shorter.

She took Aïda and me by the hand. "Come-a me."

The others walked behind us; it was a parade past huge pillars with carved arches. We stepped on flagstones with names written on them.

"Are these graves, Nonna?"

Nonna whispered, "*Sì*, Anna."

Mum nodded yes.

This church was very different from St. Andrew's Parish church in Kilmarnock. It was immense and had statues in every alcove; in one stood a man with a long beard holding a white dove.

Mum whispered, "That's God and the dove symbolizes the Holy Spirit."

"What's symbolize?" I asked Aïda.

Nonna kissed her rosary and bowed in front of each statue as she passed by. I bowed also wishing I had a rosary. I saw a bright coloured window where the sun streamed through green fields filled with sheep and donkeys.

"I think this one is Heaven," I said to no one in particular.

Nonna led us into a smaller chapel; she called it *la Chapello*. Above the altar was a large cross where Jesus hung. He had blood on his hands and feet and looked so sad hanging there. I felt like crying, but Mum squeezed my hand and said, "He died for us."

I still thought he looked very sad.

Somewhere in the Cathedral, an organ played softly.

Aïda murmured, "That song is *Santa Lucia*."

She always knew things that I didn't, but I could hear Aïda's wooden *soccolli* clip-clopping and was glad I had worn my quiet sandals to match my pink dress.

On the left side of the small chapel, in a golden corner, was a lovely lady with white veils around her face and a yellow halo over her head.

Mummy whispered, "That's Mary, mother of Jesus." Mary looked kind—her blue eyes looked like Nonna's when she said her rosary.

Finally, we reached the rail in front. Everyone waited for Nonna to kneel—Babbo helped her down. She motioned for us to kneel beside her. Daddy was behind me, I glanced back, Dad nodded. Nonna moved her hand slowly over her heart. Then she took Aïda's hand and helped her make a cross. When she turned towards me I held out my hand and she moved it for me. Uncle Tommy, Daddy, and Uncle Rudy knelt on the other side. This was the first time I saw Daddy in church. I watched as he crossed his heart. Babbo knelt quickly, crossed his heart, and then stood up with his hand on each of their shoulders. I felt like I was a Catholic in my heart. Mum was already sitting in a pew so we joined her.

Nonna and Babbo sat in front of us and again they knelt, this time on both knees to pray quietly. Nonna had her red rosary beads draped around her fingers; she counted slowly, moving her lips very carefully. I wanted some rosary beads of my own.

Daddy and Uncle Rudy went back to help other people find

the chapel and Uncle Tommy stood on the right side of the altar rail looking like a Yankee film star in his dress uniform. Mum smiled; Aïda and I moved closer.

A boy not much older than me entered through a side door. He wore a white gown and lit the candles on the altar with a long taper. "Would I be allowed to do that if I was Catholic, Mum?"

"No, only boys get to do it."

"Not fair," I replied.

Aunt Lea's family filed in, each person kneeling and crossing their hearts. I tried to remember how to do it, so I practiced. Was it up, down, side to side or was it side to side then up and down, maybe it was down, up. Mum put her hand on mine to stop me. Aïda snickered.

A young couple came down the aisle looking from side to side. Uncle Tommy beamed and came forward to greet them. "I can't believe yer here," he said loudly, guiding then towards us. "Kathy, girls, this is Giuseppe and Sophia, and who is this?" he asked the wee girl standing beside them.

"I am Isabella," she smiled.

"We married right away after the war ended, Irmo," Giuseppe said in Italian. "Isabella was a lovely surprise."

"Come sit with us," said Mum. "Perhaps you can tell us how you know Tommy."

I was happy to have a pal with a green dress on. She was younger than me.

The music boomed and a lovely lady, wearing a large pink hat with a feather that reached up to the golden ceiling, walked slowly down the aisle, holding Daddy's arm.

"That's Lea's mother," whispered Mum.

"Her dress matches mine," I whispered back.

"Shh," said Mum.

The organ music got faster and a priest walked out from a side room. He wore beige robes with a purple scarf that hung to his knees. The scarf was embroidered in gold circles that entwined with a cross in the middle. A large gold cross hung around his neck.

Daddy and Uncle Rudy had seated all the guests, so they moved up front to join the groom. That was when a handsome black man slipped into the pew behind us.

Babbo turned his head and said, "*Mio Dio*, Henry, what a great surprise!"

Henry winked at me and smiled. When I saw his dimples I pointed to them. "Yer dimples are just like Uncle Tommy's."

Uncle Tommy was watching. He smiled from ear to ear. That's when the bridesmaids came down the long aisle. Lea's sister wore a bright blue dress and carried a small bouquet of white roses. Mum explained that she was the maid-of-honor. Bruna came second wearing a golden dress that I loved. I had never seen anything so beautiful.

Bruna was walking slowly, a huge smile on her face, and then she saw Henry. When she got to his pew, she grabbed his arm and took him with her to Uncle Tommy. The two men hugged at the altar. Daddy and Uncle Rudy moved forward so that there was room for the very tall black man to stand with them. It looked so funny to me to see a black man and white men stand together.

"Henry was a brother to my Irmo," said Nonna, quite clearly and loudly in English so all of us could hear.

The organ music changed. Mum called the song the Italian Wedding March. Two people stopped just inside the Chapel entrance. It was Lea and her Papa, a tall thin man with a kind face and a black suit. Lea was an angel's dream in a long white satin dress that flowed around her body. Mummy whispered, "She looks like the mist on the Mediterranean when it moves off the waves early in the morning." This was one of Mum's better speeches.

The bride and her papa moved slowly down the aisle. Lea smiled straight from her heart. I peeked at Uncle Tommy. His dimples filled his cheeks and tears streamed from his soft eyes. Lea's father guided his daughter towards Tommy, and the couple knelt in front of the rail.

The priest blessed the couple with that same sign.

My mother cried. The priest spoke in Latin and Italian so I could not understand his words, but somehow I knew what he was saying. He talked a long time and the people said a lot of "amens." Finally, the Father opened the small gate in the rail for Tommy and Lea to pass through. Again they knelt. I wondered if their knees got tired. It was all taking a long time, but I really didn't mind. The priest drank from a cup, and placed a wafer in each of their mouths.

"Can I have one, Mummy?"

"Shh."

Uncle Tommy lifted Lea's veil, and they kissed just like in the fairy-tales. Next the people in the congregation left their seats and lined up. The priest gave them all a wafer. Mum, Aïda, and I sat still. I was pouting.

As we were leaving the church, I asked Mummy to show me the cross sign.

"Ye don't make a cross when ye are a Protestant, Anna."

"Well, that's a shame," I replied. "I think I like it."

Mary showed up for just a moment to give me the thumbs-up.

~ ~ ~

When the doors opened, a great cheer went up; it seemed that everybody in Pietrasanta had come to see the bride and groom. Mummy said that Uncle Tommy was a local hero because of his big speech and the villagers loved him. The bride and groom waved and ran through a cloud of confetti towards the big car that stood at the curb. I was delighted to see white streamers on the bonnet and got busy grabbing handfuls of confetti while Daddy threw coins into the crowd in the way of the Scottish scramble. The little Italian kids went wild. Daddy threw more and more coins for them to grab, so Aïda and I ran into the crowd to help.

The bride had changed into a blue dress with white lace at the neck, and Uncle Tommy wore a fancy, light-grey suit for the reception. The dancing started. Aunt Lea was right; there were lots of men with accordions, fiddles, and mandolins. They began to play *Funiculì, Funiculà* at the same time; the music was fast and funny.

The villagers began dancing immediately to the *la la la, la la la, la, la la, la la, lah,* singing as they danced. The crowd clapped and cheered, "*Bravo, bravissimo.*"

It seemed everyone knew Henry. The girls stood in a row to dance with him. Daddy told me he was Uncle Tommy's best friend from the American Army and that he and the Buffalo Soldiers had painted Babbo's house. I imagined lots of buffalos roaming around and I laughed.

There were rows and rows of long tables with checkered tablecloths, bowls of steaming pasta on every one. Mammas had babies wrapped in blankets around their middles. They stepped onto the cobblestones, swaying with the music. Everyone danced, old and young, fit and fat. They lifted their skirts, showed their legs, and kicked their heels up.

I wanted to dance with Henry so I got in line, and when it was my turn I stood on his shoes like I did with my Daddy.

The babies cooed and Daddy played a mandolin.

Babbo poured his good red vino and men, hats in hand, lined up for a taste. Glasses clinked and Daddy made a toast—a short one in Italian. Dad wasn't the toast maker that Mummy was. He mostly said, "*Salute a tute.*"

When Henry spoke, he said, "Y'all love this man and this woman because they are the salt of the earth. Tommy, I mean

Irmo, and I met during the war, I was his driver but we became friends. I am *deelighted* to see him wed to this lovely gal."

Aunt Bruna clapped and kissed Henry on the cheek. I thought I saw Henry kiss her back.

Daddy took Nonna onto the cobbled dance floor. I was surprised at how lightly Nonna moved.

Aïda and I found lots of boys and girls to play with and were sad when Isabella left with her parents. Her Daddy said they had a long drive to make. As the evening wore on, the mandolins played softer. Mummy and Daddy danced closer. Aïda and I giggled as they floated by with not one care.

The wedding day had flown by. It was time for Lea and Tommy to say *"Arrividerci,"* and leave for their honeymoon with cans tied to the bumper of their little Fiat. The guests cheered. The mandolin played.

I had danced on my father's feet.

It was a perfect day!

50

A Trip to Pisa

Summer flew by under a striped umbrella.

"I have the best tan." Aïda showed me the white strip her bathing suit had left on her shoulder.

Of course she did—Aïda was always brown. "Look at this," I replied, proudly showing her my golden legs.

"The children at school will be jealous," said Mum. She placed her forearm alongside mine. "Even I have a tan. This holiday has been good for all of us."

"We're glad ye feel so much better, Mum."

"Yer all lovely," said Uncle Rudy. "I'm off to bonny Scotland tomorrow. It's time I took care of business. Girls, are ye looking forward to the Tower of Pisa tomorrow? I'm jealous that I won't be with you."

"Does it lean as much as in the postcard that Nonna has?'

"It does, Anna. Ye know ye'll be standing sideways when ye're up top."

"I will?"

"Ye will. Ye'll have to hold on tight."

"Aren't there any handles?"

"No handles." He laughed.

"Yer scaring her," said Mum.

"No, he's not, Mummy. I'm brave."

"Well, we'll see," she said with one of her all-knowing looks.

We took the train in the morning when the mist was still on the olive trees. There were not enough seats for all of us, so Aïda, Bruna, and I stood while Nonna, Babbo, Mum, and Dad sat. The compartment smelled like sweat and animal dung. There were a few Yankee soldiers on the train. They were smoking and talking in their movie-land voices. Babbo said they were stationed close by to help with war clean-up. Every one smiled and asked if we were having fun. I decided that I liked American soldiers.

Mum said, "I thought the French trains were busy, but this takes the cake."

That was the first time I heard that one. Mum was good with the speeches.

There were farmers with boxes of chickens; one had a pig on a leash. There were fat women with cats in boxes; maybe they were visiting from France. There were lots of school-kids in their uniforms, talking non-stop in all different languages, and holiday-goers talking all at once. It was a commotion of people. "Hey, Aïda, ye can tell which ones are English, they have suits and ties on."

"Yer right, Anna."

Mum said, "Ye can sure tell the war is over, everyone is so cheerful."

I was especially happy. I was going to the top of the Tower of Pisa.

Pisa was packed. There were people everywhere.

Mum said, "The post-war boom has brought so many to Italy."

I wondered what went boom!

On the platform, the Italian men wore soft open-necked shirts in blues and whites. The ladies wore bright cotton dresses that were polka-dotted or striped; children clacked around in wooden *soccolli* and the boys were in white shirts. Aïda and I were dressed alike in yellow sundresses. Mum was, of course, wearing a grey straight skirt with a see-through, organdy white blouse. She always dressed nicely, but that day she was stunning. Daddy had rubbed her back all morning.

Bruna told us that we were obliged to stop and visit Nonna's *cugina*, Isabella. When the large woman gave me an Italian hug, I almost disappeared in her soft folds. Isabella Peri looked a lot like Nonna but was even fluffier. The old people hugged; they had not seen each other since the war started; I saw tears run down each of their cheeks. They laughed and cried; Italians laughed and cried much more often than the Scots did.

Isabella had baked marzipan tea-cakes and made lemonade. Aïda and I licked the icing off while the grown-ups talked; this lemonade was weak—it tasted as if the lemon had been dunked for only one minute. It seemed that everyone in Italy needed to take lemonade lessons from Nonna. Mary agreed.

Bruna had an exercise book tucked under her arm. She took it into the kitchen. The talk became serious, and she wrote something on a page. I heard the words *Sant' Anna* again and watched as Bruna wrote something down. She had carbon paper; she must have been copying. Were they talking about the sad time that Bruna had told us about? Isabella's round face had turned into a bowl of soup—wet tears mixed with hot sobs. Nonna said she would spend the day with Isabella while we went to see the sights; I hoped Nonna would make her *cugina* feel better.

I was so eager to see the Leaning Tower that I forgot about Isabella.

Babbo called the square with the Church and the Tower *Piazza del Duomo*, Bruna called it *Piazza dei Miracoli*, and Daddy called it the *Square of Miracles*.

But there were no miracles for me that day.

Aïda climbed clear to the top of the Tower with Dad and Bruna. I waited and waited for Mummy. She was slow, one step at a time, her knuckles white from holding the side-rail so tight. "I can't handle this, pet. It's too steep. There are too many people. I can't breathe."

"But, Mummy . . ." I remembered that train platform and the fainting. We were half-way up.

"Come on back down, Anna. Come on now. We're going down. My heels are too high. Yer too little. We're turning back."

"But, Mummy, I'm nine now; let me go up the rest of way on my own."

"No, you won't! Yer coming back down with me! That's an order!"

"But, Mummy!"

"No buts."

"But Daddy's at the top. I want to go up there."

~   ~   ~

Mummy made me go all the way back down with her! I was bawling like a baby. I craned my neck to see the others. Aïda and Bruna leaned over the rail on the side that looked like it could fall. They were boasting, "Look at us. Look at us, Anna. We're leaning sideways."

I looked up and who else should be there but Mary. I was afraid that this would be the last time I would ever see her. I had to be satisfied with buying a tiny white marble statue of the Leaning Tower from a wooden stall in the courtyard. Mum said I could give it to my teacher, Miss Wilson, when we got back to Scotland. As if that's what I wanted to do!

Bruna said, "Don't worry, Anna, ye'll come back another time and climb to the top."

"Were ye really leaning sideways?" I asked Aïda.

"What do ye think?" she answered with a triumphant look.

Mum said, "Don't act so smug, Aïda. It's not nice."

But even when we went inside the cathedral, Aïda had on a cheeky grin that stretched from one ear to the other.

"God won't like that look, Aïda," I said, pointing up to the angels on the golden ceiling of the Duomo.

Babbo knelt at the front rail like he did at the wedding. I did the sign of the rosary with him. After Babbo crossed his heart, he joined the priest in the corner by a very tall statue of a woman in a royal blue gown that covered her shoulders and reached the ground.

"That's Mary," said Daddy.

Mary looked peaceful with her hands in prayer. She wore a tiara of gold and yellow that glowed like the morning sun. Babbo talked with his hands to the priest. They kissed each other on each cheek, then Babbo showed him the paper that Bruna had *cugina* Isabella sign. I wanted Daddy to go up front to the rail so that I could practice crossing my heart but he shook his head no.

Bruna took me by the hand and walked me over to a kneeling statue. "This is Saint Joseph."

"Ye know, Aunt Bruna, there is not one statue in the St. Andrew's Parish Church in Kilmarnock, and only one big candle up in the front."

Beneath Saint Joseph were rows and rows of red glass candle holders on a black metal holder. Aïda followed behind me, her wooden shoes clomping.

Bruna whispered, "Anna, Aïda, kneel here with me. We'll light candles for those who were killed in the war." We knelt then, and Bruna prayed. When she crossed her heart, Aïda and I copied—it felt good. Bruna's prayer was in Italian, but again I heard her say, "*Sant' Anna di Stazzema.*" It lingered softly on her lips like a butterfly landing on one of Babbo's flowers. Auntie turned, reached into her pocket, gave us a few lire to slide into the box, and then showed us how to light the small candles with a long white taper. The red glass shone when the wick lit, and each candle made swirls of smoke.

Bruna said each flame represented the souls of those killed by the Nazis.

"Tell me about that Anna place," I whispered.

"Later," she said. "Later, *bambina*." She put her fingertips to her lips. "Later. I promise."

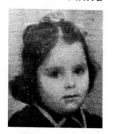

51

Secrets Revealed

"I'd like to give Kathy a second honeymoon in Florence," Daddy said to Aunt Bruna.

"I'd like to shop on the *Ponti Del Vecchio*."

"Ye want to go without us, Mummy? Will ye bring us back presents?"

"We'll see," answered my mother. She really did deserve a prize for her grown-up answers.

"I'll watch Anna and Aïda for ye, Andy," said Bruna. "My friends, Marco and Riana, are coming from Farnocchia."

"Is Marco the boy who got shot?" said Aïda.

"*Sì, bambina*, the very one. He was much younger when he was injured; he is a big boy now, almost a man."

"Did it hurt?" I asked.

"Ye'll have to ask him that yerself."

~ ~ ~

Next morning, a dusty red mountain bus pulled up in a cloud of black diesel smoke that made me sneeze. Off stepped an all-legs boy, who had so many freckles I could hardly see his blue eyes. His smile covered his whole face, and he was taller than I had imagined. In his hands was a book with a thick maroon cover. He carried it as if it was gold for the baby Jesus.

Riana, his sister, hopped off the bus; she was shorter and

wore a white scarf holding wild black hair that wanted desperately to escape. Bruna had told us that Riana was nineteen.

Last came Lena, who bounced down, picked me up, and gave me a hug. "My wee Scotland lassies, is good my English, yes?" Her perfume matched my Evening in Paris hanky.

"Girls," said Bruna, "these are my very best friends."

"Pleased to meet ye," Aïda and I said politely.

"*Vieni a casa mia*," said Bruna. "Nonna has made a special pasta." She said that in English and Italian and we all laughed; Nonna, who was famous for her *special* pasta, was waiting for us on the veranda, grinning like Alice's cat. We ran up the steps and Marco hugged Nonna so hard she almost fell over. "*Accoglienza*, welcome, Marco," she breathed, pointing to the pitcher on the table. "*Limonato, sì?*"

"*Sì*," he replied.

Nonna's lemonade was the best, not bitter like the kind we had in Pisa. I drank it down in a minute; then, before I could help myself, I blurted out, "Marco, can I see where ye got shot?"

Aunt Bruna's face was dismayed. "Anna, that's a rude question."

Marco's face turned beetroot red; his freckles disappeared in the heat.

"*Sì, va bene*, Bruna," he said, lifting his shirt. There was an angry slash that looked like Mum's appendix scar. I wanted to ask if it had hurt as much as my tonsils had but I didn't want to embarrass him more.

Babbo came out to the veranda to see what the noise was all about. He said firmly, "You girls leave Marco alone." Babbo patted the tall boy on the back and Marco covered that slash.

~ ~ ~

We sat at Nonna's green metal table eating noodles with green basil sauce. The teenagers talked so fast that it made me laugh. While Nonna cleared the plates, Marco brought the large book over to the table. Bruna, Lena, and Riana turned the pages.

I couldn't see what they were looking at. "Are we ever going to know what's in this book?" I asked.

Babbo leaned over Aïda and me. "*Miei bambini,* come-a with me to the garden. I will explain. *Scus*a, Bruna." He reached over and picked up the volume. The teenagers sat back, looking puzzled.

~ ~ ~

We sat on a bench by the fountain, Aïda beside the old man, I on his knee.

"You know, *la mia bambina,*" he said, rubbing the lines on his cheek, "Bruna, Nonna, and I stayed many days high up in the hills, *sì?*" He pointed into the sky above the olive trees. "Italy had given up hope that the Germans would ever leave our country. It was August of 1944."

"We were still in internment then, Babbo."

"*Sì,* Aïda, I know. Nonna and me, we did not know then."

I saw tears in his eyes.

"The Americans had landed in Sicily, so the Germans were retreating. You know of course that *Zio* Irmo was part of that army. The SS Italia had become cruel, very cruel to the Jewish people, and also to Italians who had already surrendered to the Allies." He took a big breath. "Never mind that, I ramble on. Mamma, Bruna, and I were hiding far away from the SS, the evil German *soldati.* We were very scared."

A lump formed in the back of my tongue where my tonsils used to be.

"Lena and her mamma, Adela, came with us; her papa was already dead at the hands of the Germans. We hid in old farm house that was only a shell, no roof, no doors. It was near Farnocchia, the small village where I was born." He sighed so deep I could feel it in his chest so I patted him. "Next morning, very early, I send Bruna and Lena to ask my *cugino* for help. I tell them,

'Be careful. No go far.' These girls no listen to their Babbo. They wander down a very steep path towards the church we call Sant' Anna di Stazzema."

"Is that the place that Bruna lit candles for?"

I had crept even closer, smelling his good sweat through his shirt.

"*Sì*, Aïda. In Stazzema many people gathered at the church of Sant' Anna. Listen-a me carefully. I sorry-a tell you. The German soldiers, bad Nazi SS, shoot rifles. They kill everyone in square. The rifles bang, bang, bang. Mamma and me can hear even from a long distance away. You Nonna cover her ears. Adela, Lena's mamma, only go whiter and whiter. Where were our girls? Where were they?"

"Where were they?" I repeated in his shirt.

"They had gone close to *chiesa,* the church, too close. They hear the screams of the people.The rifles go bang, bang over and over. The girls witnesses to this massacre. If they had gone inside the courtyard. . . ." He crossed himself. "They would not be here this day."

My face was buried in his strong neck. Aïda had her arms around his waist.

"Bruna and Lena would have died. Instead, they watch the *gli innocenti* die. Then, they run."

My tears fell, even though I understood only a little.

"Did the German soldiers kill everybody?" asked Aïda, a choking noise coming from her throat.

"Almost, child. It was called *un maddacro*, a massacre. Your mamma asked me not to tell you, but I wanted you to know about Marco."

I brought my face out from his hug. "Marco was shot, right?"

"*Sì, bambina.*"

"How did he escape, Babbo?" asked Aïda.

"He was searching for his papa. He was not in the court-yard, but on a big bay tree with sturdy branches just outside. His papa had gone to pray for Marco's sick mamma. Marco followed his papa and his *sorella*, his sister, followed him. A stray bullet knocked Marco to ground. It burn bad in his inside. Marco got up and ran fast, like a fox."

My throat ached where my tonsils had been.

"Where was Riana?" asked Aïda.

"Dearest Aïda, she was hiding under the tree, guarding her wee brother. Their papa had told them stay home but they dis-obeyed; Marco naughty boy like Bruna and Lena—too curious. Not good to be so curious. Always do as you mamma and daddy tell you. Riana chased Marco and both screamed past Bruna and Lena."

Aïda and I were silent. Her eyes were as big as brown puddles.

Babbo went on, "Lena and Bruna see a man die. He perish at their feet from his burns. Bruna has bad dreams."

I sobbed.

Aïda covered her face with her hands.

"*Oh, mei bambine,* I know this is sad, but I go on. Bruna and Lena kept running, and they find Marco and Riana. Marco was your age, Anna. He was wounded, suffering, lying in the dirt. Riana was calling for help. I hear her voice and believe it is my Bruna. I run-a very fast. Then I hear Bruna shout, 'Babbo, Babbo! Over here!' I see the wound in Marco's side—much-a blood. I must-a fix. I bandage and we carry him to our hiding place like I did for many soldiers in first war, I take-a care him. Not just-a me, all of us, we take care of Marco all night long."

"Did he cry, Babbo?"

"*Sì,* we all cry, *la mia* Anna."

"Is this why Bruna has bad dreams, Babbo?" asked Aïda.

"*Sì.*"

The three of us stayed glued to the bench for a long time, then Aïda asked, "So, what's in the book, Babbo?"

"Let me think my English. Let me finish story. We go live in Farnocchia for a time and Marco, he get well in about six-a weeks. The four children, Bruna, Lena, Marco, and Riana, they get idea. They go-a visit the people in the hills. They ask, 'You know anyone die at Sant' Anna?' The people would sob and say *sì*."

"Wasn't it dangerous for them to be in the woods?"

"Not so much then, Aïda. The SS had gone away back to the towns of Tuscany. The fighting was many miles away. Bruna, Lena, Riana, and Marco go from place to place, tents, hide-outs, farm-houses, and Marco *registrato* the names in book."

"What did they ask the people?"

"Aïda, you have good questions, is *importante* to ask good questions. They say to the people, 'Did you lose a son or a daughter at Sant' Anna?' Sometimes people say, 'My mamma die.' Sometimes say, 'My brother or my sister.' Marco write carefully the name and when they born. The people are very, very grateful. They glad their loved ones not forgotten."

Aïda was very quiet then.

"It took many, many months. Bruna, Lena, Marco, Riana go all over, even after war's end, to Viareggio and Pisa." He opened the book to the page marked P. "See."

Aïda and I saw the name *Arturo Peri*.

Babbo pointed and said, "This man was Nonna's *cugino* from Pisa, Isabella's husband. He die at Stazzema."

"So this is why you talked to the priest in Pisa," I said.

"*Sì*, look now." He turned another page, pointing. "This is Piero Bertellotti, *zio mio*, my uncle, from Lucca. Many families in Tuscano lose a loved one. *Dio mio*, I am tired." Babbo set the book down, took in a big breath, and bowed his head.

I reached up to kiss him. "It's all right now, Babbo."

Aïda held his hand. "*Grazie*, Babbo. Now we know."

Marco had come down the stairs quietly and was sitting beside us.

Aïda spoke up once more. "Marco, what are ye going to do with the book?"

Bruna stood behind Marco, translating for us. She said, "That's why Marco and Riana are here today. Babbo told the padre in Pisa about us. Padre Paulo asked Babbo to bring the book to him when he could. He said he would take our book to the Vatican in Rome. He told Babbo that the Pope would say a special mass for the blessing of this book. That is why we are so excited."

"Bruna, what is the Vatican?" I asked.

"How many names did Marco write down, Aunt Bruna?" asked Aïda.

"Almost five hundred," she answered, the number catching in her throat. "We know there are more. We will spend the rest of the summer collecting more names. The Vatican is where the Pope lives, Anna."

"Do Mummy and Daddy know about how brave you all were?"

"*Sì*, I will show them the book when they come back from Florence," she said.

"I'm glad the Pope will keep the names safe in his Vatican," I said.

"I am too, Anna," said Bruna.

Daddy, Mummy, Aïda, and I left Italy in late August. The foursome collected many more names as they travelled the countryside that summer. The book made it safely to Rome, and Mary said goodbye to me because I did not need her any more, I was all grown up.

~   ~   ~

The sun shone on the White Cliffs as the boat pulled in, and Dad and I had not been sick on the Channel crossing.

Mum said, "I am so proud of Bruna and all her friends. At first I was afraid for you to hear their story, but their story should never be forgotten."

That had to be her best speech ever.

When the train pulled into the Kilmarnock Station, my cousins Violet and Jim were waiting.

With a big smile I said, "Look at my tan, Violet."

"It's great," she replied. "I'm jealous."

My best pal and I talked for hours or maybe days; in fact, we talked for years. Ah, but that's another tale.

52

Prayers

It was a long time before I returned to Italy.

~   ~   ~

One rare sunny day in 1961, my cousin Violet and I lay sunning ourselves on her flat roof over the wash-house. We were twenty years old and boy-crazy. We believed we were worldly and ready to spread our wings. We both worked at hospitals, she an R.N., I an x-ray technologist.

"Anna," she said, "they need nurses in California."

"California!" I answered. "I'm going to Italy."

"The sun shines just as much in California, and yer granny will not be chaperoning ye everywhere ye go."

She showed me a *Life* magazine with photographs of Fisherman's Wharf. It seemed that's all it took for us to get immigration papers and jobs in California.

In late April 1962 we boarded a Pan American prop plane bound for New York and on to the west coast of America. The next day we landed in San Francisco. That afternoon I met Ron Hess. He was standing smiling, leaning on a counter in the x-ray department in Sequoia Hospital in Redwood City. I was exhausted and confused, but there was nothing wrong with my eyes. He was the handsomest boy I had ever seen, and he said hello to me.

Ron and I were married in 1964. Once again, that is another

story. In 2014, we had been married fifty wonderful years and have traveled to many countries, including Italy.

We visited Aunt Bruna, Aunt Lea, and Uncle Tommy in 1986. As we sat at the table discussing that dreadful massacre at Sant' Anna di Stazzema, perhaps that is when the seed was planted for me to write this book. We visited again in 2004, which was the year of the tribunal in La Spezia; it had taken sixty years for the perpetrators of that horrible misconduct to be taken to trial. The military court in La Spezia found ten former Waffen-SS members guilty of participation in the Massacre at Sant' Anna di Stazzema. The brutal order that sealed the fate of so many was issued by Hitler during the retreat of the German troops up the Italian Peninsula towards the conclusion of World War II. It was part of Hitler's *Burn the Earth* policy, code-named the *Achse*. The SS officers were sentenced, in absentia, to life imprisonment for their participation in the "event" that took place on August 14th, 1944. However, by this time those SS officers were old men still living in Germany. They had not appeared in court and not one served jail time.

~ ~ ~

Ron and I stood, hand in hand, high on the hill above Stazzema where the mist surrounded the tall memorial. He had his arm around me as I prayed. The memorial commemorates that day in infamy when, in the courtyard of Sant' Anna di Stazzema, 560 men, women, and children were massacred in one hour. The Nazi SS officers then piled the dead bodies in a haphazard manner and set fire to them and their church. Inscribed on that tall memorial are the names of those who were slaughtered.

~ ~ ~

To this day there are unanswered questions:

Italian authorities have been accused of losing vital documents. Many were accidentally discovered in a *Cupboard of Shame* in Rome in 1994.

Was Marco's book among those papers found?

No, because *Born in Internment* is fiction grounded in truth. Marco is a made-up character representing the survivors of the massacre.

The world will never know all the details, but be glad that somehow the names of the victims were saved for all time. My hope in writing the Bertellotti story was to show how my Scottish/Italian family survived the war with dignity and tenaciousness.

I am thankful that my family's confinement in Darmellington ended in peace, and I pray for those who lost their lives in internment camps the world over. In war, everyone gets wounded; victims of violence, injustice, circumstance.

The Bertellotti family story says this: *From the ashes of war arise survivors, brave souls, and loving hearts.*

Now I am sounding like my mother!

Amen.